"WHERE IS MY CHILD?"

Alek's question slammed into Elspeth. There was no way he could know....

"Our child. Where is it? What is it, a boy or a girl? And again, *where is our child?*"

Elspeth straightened her shoulders, fighting for a smooth, level tone of voice. "I've just put tea on to steep. If left too long it might——"

"Dismissing me, Elspeth? Just tell me what I want to know, and then I'll leave. How old is it—he... she—now, four? I want to see my child. Now."

Elspeth slowly lifted her eyes to his, remembering that night five years ago, with the huge silver moon. She'd never spoken the secret buried in her heart. And now he left her no choice....

CAIT LONDON

TALLCHIEF FOR KEEPS

Silhouette Books

Published by Silhouette Books

America's Publisher of Contemporary Romance

SILHOUETTE BOOKS

TALLCHIEF FOR KEEPS

Copyright © 1997 by Lois Kleinsasser

ISBN 0-373-48337-6

This edition published by arrangement with Harlequin Books S.A.

® and TM are trademarks of Harlequin Books S.A., used under
license. Trademarks indicated with ® are registered in the United States
Patent and Trademark Office, the Canadian Trade Marks Office and in
other countries.

Printed in U.S.A.

To my Valentines at Silhouette—
Melissa Senate, Isabel, Lucia and Tara

You're wonderful!

Tallchief and Una Fearghus

(A Sioux Chieftain captures a Scots bondwoman who tames him.) 5 children.

Liam and Elizabeth Tallchief

(As a virgin, the English lady would inherit an empire;
to save her sister from torture, she takes an unwilling staked-out half-breed.
Out for revenge, he finds love.) 3 children.

Jake and LaBelle Tallchief

(This lady jewel thief and matador wants no part of the dirt-poor,
hardened rancher with adopted, untamed sons. He turns up at her
fancy soiree and blackmails her into marriage.) 2 children.

Matthew and Pauline Tallchief

(Amen Flats has never been big enough for them since they were
children. As bodyguard to the threatened lady judge, tough tracker
Matthew stakes his bridal claim with Greek mythology.) 5 children.

Duncan m. Sybil	Calum m. Talia	Birk	Elspeth	Fiona
Emily	Kira			
Megan				

Legends of the Tallchiefs

Duncan—The woman who brings the cradle to a man of Fearghus blood will fill it
with his babies.

Calum—When a man of Fearghus blood places the ring upon the right woman's
finger, he'll capture his true love forever.

Elspeth—When the Marrying Moon is high, a scarred warrior will rise from the mists
to claim his lady huntress. He will wrap her in the shawl and carry her to the
Bridal Tepee and his heart. Their song will last longer than the stars.

*Legend of Una's Paisley Shawl
When the Marrying Moon is high,
a scarred warrior will rise from the
mists to claim his lady huntress.
He will wrap her in the shawl and
carry her to the Bridal Tepee and
his heart. Their song will last
longer than the stars.*

Prologue

In the kitchen's early-morning shadows, fourteen-year-old Elspeth Tallchief wrapped her mother's hand-stitched quilt around her. Pieces of the five Tallchief children's lives colored the quilt: outgrown clothing neatly arranged, each telling a vivid story. There was a square of her mother's apron and her father's lucky red shirt, woven by her mother and torn by a ram at shearing time.

Elspeth gripped her mother's favorite cookbook tightly against her. In the large, airy room beyond the kitchen, her mother's giant loom stood waiting for her shuttle. Her quilt rack hung close to the ceiling, ready to be lowered. But Pauline Tallchief would be not weaving or stitching quilts again.

Tears burned Elspeth's lids and she fought the tightness in her chest, dabbing at the tears with the quilt of memories.

Four days ago, the aroma of her mother's famed apple pie had filled the farm kitchen; her jars of fruit and jam lined the pantry. In the silence of the house, Elspeth could almost hear the echo of her mother's gentle laughter.

Elspeth recognized the wild rage running through her, the high fury that was said to have come down from her great-great-grandmother, Una. Elspeth noted distantly that she'd never been so angry, so torn by emotions, not even when tormented by her brothers. Perhaps it was the pride of her Sioux great-great-grandfather that prevented her from throwing dishes or raging at her parents' death.

The old quilt and her mother's cookbook were Elspeth's armor, because her brothers and sister were depending on her. She glanced at the old loom, supposedly her great-great-grandmother's. It would comfort her in the dark and frightening hours, because she was just as strong as her brothers and they were already preparing for the hardships ahead.

Outside, the cold October winds stalked Tallchief Mountain, rustling the dried aspen leaves over two new graves in the family cemetery. In the fields sloping up the mountainside, Tallchief cattle and sheep huddled together against the wind.

Down in the valley, the small town of Amen Flats, Wyoming, lay sleeping. All was the same and yet different, because in Amen Flats's jail was a—*life-taker*. Elspeth supplied the bitter tag for a man who had changed the Tallchiefs' lives.

Elspeth turned to the sound of stocking feet padding across the old house's floorboards. Her three brothers loomed in the shadows.

Only hours before, the five orphaned Tallchiefs had gathered at Tallchief Lake. Amid the winds and under a round, silvery moon, Duncan—the eldest at eighteen—had vowed to keep them safe and together. They had all pledged to find their heritage, their great-great-grandmother's lost dowry that was steeped in legends.

Elspeth clasped the old cookbook closer, the one with her mother's beautiful handwriting and favorite recipes of each Tallchief child.

Her brothers moved closer to her, their gray eyes as light and fierce as Una Fearghus's, their Scottish great-great-grandmother. Jutting cheekbones, slashing brows and gleaming black hair were gifts from Tallchief, their Sioux great-great-grandfather. Long-legged Westerners, they knew how to deal with cattle and killers, but a woman's tears of mourning would send them fleeing for safety.

"Fiona is sleeping upstairs with her cat." Duncan's soft voice curled around Elspeth.

"Ten years old or not, she'll have to be up in the morning and on the school bus." At seventeen, Calum had always been practical, but now his voice had a new note of steel.

"It's three o'clock in the morning, but we'll all go to school tomorrow." Birk touched Elspeth's hair to comfort her, but she shook him off.

Wrapped in the old quilt, Elspeth stood in the center of the kitchen and faced them, her head high, her own gray eyes flashing like steel. Her strength was forged from the same fierce blood and pride. "I don't know why that man had to kill Mom and Dad when they stopped for pizza at the convenience store. I don't know why *only* my brothers had to be the ones to track their killer down...why all of you thought you were the only ones Dad taught how to track by moonlight. The sheriff knew you were the best trackers, let you go after him, and you brought him back—walking behind your horses and only a bit bruised after what he'd done. I should have been there. I should have gone. I can ride just as well as any of you…better.''

"You had a job to do—"

She dismissed Calum's practical statement, noted Duncan's helpless expression and glanced at Birk. His boyish grin was gone, his jaw set and grim—the picture of a boy who had become a man overnight. Her temper rose, consuming her fury and the helplessness at their parents' murder days before. Her control shattered, cracked like ice. She shivered, shook free of what they knew her to be and stepped into the fire of her rage. "So you took off, hunting the killer. Elspeth the elegant was ordered to tend Fiona the fiery. She needed me, and so I did, though I wanted to throw a knife right through that murderer's black heart—I can, you know—I can throw a knife or shoot a bow or a gun as well as any of you. It's just that I prefer…never mind what I prefer.''

She preferred her mother, alive and well, and dancing in her father's arms, kissing him. Elspeth dashed a tear from the old cookbook, clutching it tighter. It was hers now, just as her brothers and Fiona were. She'd tend her family, but right now she would have her say.

With the flat of her hand, she pushed the broad chest of each of her brothers, one by one, and stepped back to face them, her long nightgown swirling at her ankles. "Poor, dainty Elspeth. Elspeth the elegant…isn't that what I'm called?" she asked, referring to names they called each other in play. "Isn't that true, Duncan the defender…Calum the cool…and Birk the rogue?"

"Aye." The word rumbled slowly from her brothers' throats, and Elspeth lifted her head, determined to hold on to her pride.

She lifted the tiny scar on her thumb before their noses. "Aren't I one of you, a nick in my thumb to prove it? Didn't I raise my thumb to the storm just two hours ago and pledge with you to do my part?"

"Aye!"

Elspeth shed the quilt. She wouldn't let her brothers see her weak. "You'll pick up your shorts and socks, and I'll set a schedule. Mother would have no one visiting a dirty house, and neither will I."

"Aye." The rumbling male voices came stronger, more fierce. It was said that Tallchiefs had backbones of steel, and now they would be tested, each ready to do his or her part. There would be no Tallchief Ranch on the county auction block or brothers and sisters torn apart. At eighteen, Duncan would try for legal guardianship, and Calum's methodical business brain would plow away at the family and ranch accounts. With his brothers, Birk would take his new share of hard ranch work. Fiona also would try something new—minding her p's and q's at school, taming her wild side until she got home.

Elspeth recalled the plan that Duncan had plucked from the fierce night wind and clouds; she held it before her brothers like a sword raised in a challenge. She paced before them, faced them like a general facing his troops. "Tonight, beside the lake, Duncan held Fiona close, promised to keep her safe and all of us together. As he says, we're wrapping our heritage around us to keep us safe and together. I will continue as Mother and me were doing, reading Una's journals. We'll each search out and bring back to the Tallchiefs some beloved piece of her dowry that was sold to keep Tallchief Mountain."

She ran a fingertip over a place mat her mother had woven, and an icy sword cut through her. She'd learned to weave on her mother's lap.... Elspeth's bottom lip trembled before she firmed it and faced her brothers, hovering uncertainly around her, wanting to protect her. She wouldn't let them. She wouldn't crumble and show her fear because she had no less pride than they did.

She gripped the place mat, crushing it to her with the cookbook. "Stand and fight, Tallchiefs. Isn't that what we've always said in hard times? Tonight we tossed an 'Aye' into the storm to guarantee our safety. Duncan says we should have family meetings and report on progress of finding Una's dowry. Each piece has a legend, though Mom and I couldn't translate the shawl's. I'll find Una's shawl, the one she brought from Scotland, and I pledge to bring it back to the Tallchiefs."

She searched her brothers' taut faces, mourned for their boyhood that had been murdered days ago and flung herself into their arms.

"Stand and fight...." She allowed the tears to flow, dampening the shoulders of her brothers, wrapping them in her arms and keeping their strength around her. "We'll be safe. I promise you. I'll keep us safe and so will you. There will be no one finding fault with how we're dressed or what we eat or if we do our homework. We're staying together."

"Aye!" The four Tallchiefs pledged at once, and for a moment, Elspeth thought she felt the caress of her mother's hand upon her cheek.

"Aye," she whispered to her mother's kitchen. "We'll be safe. Sleep well."

One

The month of March came to taunt Elspeth with a birthday that never came and yet would never go away. Elspeth came to Tallchief Mountain to mourn the loss of a baby that had never been born.

Bound by blood and love, the Tallchiefs had left her alone on their mountain to face her demons—when winter protested its death and the scent of spring lurked nearby. As she listened to the wind outside the tepee her brothers had fashioned for her, Elspeth sat upon her pallet and loosened her single braid. She'd combed her sleek black hair around the beaded shift that once was her English great-grandmother's and Elspeth touched the elegant beadwork, its points forming the Tallchief Mountain symbol.

Every year at this time, she came to Tallchief Mountain to mourn, and her brothers had wanted to ensure her safety during her retreat. When she arrived

today, she'd found the tepee ready for her, fresh wood
cut and stacked nearby. Fish waited in the lake's weir
for her dinner. Inside the tepee she'd found a bag of
Tallchief wool to hand card, the routine and rhythm
giving her peace at the evening fire. There were bundles of her favorite herbs neatly hung from a cross
pole, a blackened teakettle, a china pot with a matching cup and saucer—all the necessities Elspeth would
need. Another cross pole held the branch waiting for
her free-style weaving. She had in mind a wall hanging, the first of an exclusive contract with a Denver
art dealer. She'd needed only a backpack filled with
her clothing, her Navajo spindle and her Tallchief tartan shawl.

She gathered the soft length of green-and-blue wool
to her, holding it tightly. Elspeth closed her eyes; she
needed this respite from her family, though she loved
them more than herself.

Duncan's second marriage brought him joy, and
Calum's new wife would have his baby. Engaged
twice before, Birk was circling Chelsey Lang, a gentle
heart and a good friend. Always a rebel, Elspeth's sister, Fiona, fought her current war against "predators
of the environment" in Wisconsin.

Una's journals spoke of the loss of her dowry, sold
to protect Tallchief Mountain. To each item was attached a legend, and two of the legends in Una's
dowry had come true—Duncan and Calum had
claimed their true loves.

As a girl, Elspeth had dreamed of Una's paisley
shawl and the legend attached to it. She'd pledged to
find the shawl and bring it safely to the Tallchiefs, but
the relevant journal entry had been smeared, perhaps
by tears, and the legend had escaped Elspeth.

As a woman, one night in Scotland had her wanting to forget the legend entirely.

When she had returned home from Scotland, she'd ripped the page from Una's journal and torn it in pieces. Regretting that her temper had ruled her and that she'd destroyed part of her inheritance, Elspeth had then placed the pieces in an envelope for safe-keeping. There would be no true love legend for Elspeth now; she no longer believed in a love for herself. She wanted the paisley shawl now for the beauty of the merino wool, the fiery golds and reds blending in a paisley design. More, the shawl was hers by right of an inheritance, and she wanted it wrapped around her like her family.

Elspeth traced the bold vermilion streak she had added to the Fearghus tartan on her lap. The red stood for the Native American Tallchief blood, and its addition to the tartan indicated that the two fierce clans had been woven together. She was restless; perhaps it was the seer blood passed down to her through her Scottish great-great-grandmother, added to the shaman inheritance from Tallchief. A woman bred from warrior chieftains would be restless on a day like this, when the wind tossed the black waves of Tallchief Lake and the mountain jutted into the mist. The untamed tempest and the isolation of this special place quieted the stormy darkness within her.

Una, a bondwoman captured by an arrogant Sioux chieftain, had reveled in the tempest. But Elspeth wanted no more storms in her life; she'd had enough pain to last her two lifetimes. She wanted the rest of her life to be as smooth as the doeskin shift she wore, or the silk thermal sweater and pants beneath it. She'd put order into her life, wrapped the safety around her like the blue-and-green tartan, and so it would stay.

In the center of her tepee, smoke curled upward, soon caught by the fierce wind.

Alek Petrovna had been her fierce wind, taking her innocence upon an ancient Scottish stone and giving her a child. Elspeth the elegant was taken by a laughing gypsy of a man after a few traditional dances around the bonfire.

"As good as I've had," he'd said as though comparing dinner fare, rather than making love. "Is this enough money?"

Bit by bit, she'd pasted herself together, warmed herself with the joys of her family, and now, at thirty-three, she'd finally found a measure of peace. She wanted quiet now, and Calum's marriage to Talia Petrovna, Alek's sister, could destroy that.

Elspeth held very still, drawing the sounds into her—winter wind whipping the snow-laden trees, branches snapping beneath the weight. Mist shrouded the mountain, and somehow that comforted her, a reminder of the fierce elements that had always been there since the beginning of time.

She studied the tepee slowly, considering the neat contents and the branch-rack waiting for her new wall hanging. Her unique designs had drawn attention at the last weaver's fair, and with pride Elspeth had signed a generous contract for her work. She had constructed her life as tightly as her weaving, carefully planning the threads of it. Only in March did the fabric of her life weaken, and she came to Tallchief Mountain to strengthen herself in an age-old tradition.

Talia Petrovna's marriage to Calum would draw

Alek to the Tallchiefs. Elspeth wanted to be strong when next they met—and she knew that day would be soon.

Alek Petrovna cursed as he ducked a pine branch laden with snow and ice, only to have another hit his scarred cheek.

Alek impatiently snapped the branch and tossed it aside. He had scars earned from years of reporting on wars. Not one of them compared to the pain caused by the black-haired witch he sought, Elspeth Tallchief.

As a journalist specializing in war zones, he'd seen too many orphaned children. He'd ached for years for a child of his own, only to discover that Elspeth Tallchief had hidden his...what? A boy...a girl?

Alek's research had been thorough. Not even her family knew of his child...and Elspeth's. She'd hidden his child away so neatly that not even the Tallchiefs knew her secret. He'd get it out of her. One way or another, he would make Elspeth dance to his tune.

So she would camp on a mountaintop by herself, would she, when March caught the Rocky Mountains in a wintry shroud? "Damn fool idea, setting up a tepee in zero-degree weather. Her brothers shouldn't have—"

Years of covering stories in frozen war zones had prepared him for the elusive, dangerous trail that wound upward to Tallchief Lake. The mountain soared, bleak and ominous, against the gray sky. Mist layered the top, obscuring it and a fierce wind threw the pine branches at Alek, like blows to a warrior running a gauntlet.

Elspeth traced her bloodline to Sioux, but Alek's

tracking ability had come from his Apache ancestor…as perhaps had his need for revenge.

He thrust aside another punishing branch. He'd find Elspeth Tallchief, dig her out of her safe hole and make her pay for what he'd missed, that precious time a father spends with his child.

Alek fought the tight pain in his chest, the cold that invaded his flesh, though he was dressed in layers of clothing and a heavy Arctic parka. His Russian blood reveled in the freezing temperature, heated by the passion of anger that had churned within him for months.

He leapt over a broken limb, his boots sinking into a mound of snow. He'd only just discovered Elspeth's little secret when he'd had to go on assignment. He'd made a promise to a dying friend that he would complete the project. Now Alek had missed an additional four months of his child's life by covering a senseless war and trying to stay alive through it.

Talia's wedding photos had arrived last December in the middle of a storm, the sound of thunder matching the battery of gunfire and the rockets. Tucked neatly into his sister's wedding party was, unmistakably, one Elspeth Fearghus. *Tallchief,* he corrected bitterly.

He wiped away the snow that clung to his beard, tossed it away just like Elspeth had done his child. He'd set his traps for her, one by one, and she'd have a fine time escaping him.

Alek stepped into a clearing, searching the shadows enfolding the lake. Outlined against the fierce, wind-tossed lake was Elspeth.

Her long black hair flew up and away in the wind. In the dying light, her face was blurred, a pale oval turned to the mist high on the mountain. She leaned into the wind as though it were her lover, as though something wild and fierce within her matched the icy blast. Her fringed leather shift offered little protection against the cold. Her legs were encased in leather with thongs laced around them to keep them tight.

She walked slowly by the black fury of the lake, blending with the elements rather than fighting them. The wind bowed and battered the cattail reeds bordering the lake; it pasted the shawl and her shift against her, the dim light revealing the trim, lithe outline of her body.

Alek controlled his need to rage at her; control ran contrary to his impulsive, passionate Petrovna blood. So she thought she was safe here, did she, a lady strolling through a winter storm? A private retreat away from her brothers and family where nothing could harm her?

Family wouldn't keep her safe against him, not this time. Alek stripped away his gloves and fished for a small box from a safely buttoned inner pocket designed to hold camera film. The earring, a fragile affair of dangling beads that ended in a silver feather, seemed to leap into his hand and nestled there, taunting him—as it had hundreds of times before—with the memory of that night.

He smoothed his thumb over the earring. He'd come through hell to face this woman and to claim his child.

"Alek." The name cut through the emotion that tightened her throat.

He stood in the shadows of the pines bordering her clearing. There was no mistaking the set of his shoulders beneath the battered parka or the arrogant stance of his long legs clad in camouflage print.

He shoved back his parka hood, and that same black stare locked on her, this time without the laughter. His hair curled wildly, tossed by the wind, and there was nothing gentle in his set jaw darkened by stubble.

One look at Alek Petrovna, and Elspeth fought a wild rage she hadn't known since her parents' death.

One look at Alek Petrovna, and she knew he'd come for her, like a black wolf facing his prey.

The first time she'd seen him, almost five years ago, she knew that fire stirred between them—like flint striking sparks on flint. They'd come together, full circle, and with the look in his eye and the emotions unravelling her, they would surely lift swords—

Elspeth inhaled and held her breath, steadying her impulse to run from him. Alek wouldn't raise her emotions, not this time. She'd worked through her pain, and now it was ashes.

Elspeth straightened and watched him walk to her, that swaggering, loose walk of an athletic big man, focused and sure of his purpose.

Alek didn't stand near her; he loomed over her, his black eyes locking with hers. "Say something."

Just like that. A demand drawled in the deep tones of a Texan, skipping the pleasantries. He was nothing like his fair-skinned, light-hearted sister Talia.

"Hello, Alek."

She noted the scarring on his left cheek and throat; she remembered as though it were yesterday, instead of almost five years ago, the burned-smooth texture beneath her fingertips when they made love. A new scar ripped through a black eyebrow, and another ran from his bottom lip into his chin.

"Hello, fair Elspeth. Or should I say sister-in-law? We're related, aren't we?" He pushed the fact at her like a spear. "Too bad I missed the wedding. I was trapped by the siege for two weeks." He caught the wild spray of her hair in one big hand, taming it. "But I'm here now."

In the next heartbeat, Alek lightly jerked her head back, lifting it for his inspection. "Older," he murmured, not sparing her in his appraisal.

"Wiser." She eased her hair away from his grasp, and wondered if anyone escaped Alek Petrovna unless he granted permission. But she would, because she'd already paid the price.

"Where's my child?"

His question slammed into her, shattering the layers of protection she'd pasted around her. There was no way he could know—Elspeth fought for the smooth level of her tone. "Please explain."

The line between his brows deepened. He spaced the words precisely, a predator more than a journalist marshaling facts. "Our child. I know the how of it. Where is it? *What* is it, a boy or a girl? And again, *where is our child?*"

She refused to let him tear open her private wound. She wouldn't let him push her back into her pain. Elspeth straightened her shoulders, meeting his searing stare with her calm one. "I've just put tea on to steep. If left too long—"

"Dismissing me? Just tell me what I want to know, and then I'll leave. I want to see my child."

She would not allow him to pounce in and out of her life so easily. "But you'll come back because you're angry. More than angry. You want to hurt me."

"Damn right I do. And I will," he shot at her in a low, passionate voice. His lips tightened. "You should have told me. I'm easy enough to find."

Elspeth glanced at Alek's powerful six feet four-inch body, then lifted her chin. She had given him more than what was safe, and now she owed him nothing.

"I know your strength, fair Elspeth, and your passion. You can clasp a man dry...wring a child from him, then— Is the child mine or—?"

She gripped the Tallchief tartan shawl to keep her hand from flying at his face. She refused to enter a verbal duel with Alek, now or ever again.

The doctor had thought her baby had been a boy....

She lifted her face to the wind, letting its bite cool her heating temper. "You'd better leave. More snow is coming." Then she turned and walked toward her tepee.

No sooner was the tepee flap closed behind her than Alek ripped it open and stepped inside in a blast of wind and snow. She let him loom, his head angled from the slanting, insulated canvas of the tepee. Elspeth ignored him; she kneeled to toss wood on the fire. She watched the flames lick and grow, and then settled to pour tea into a china cup. She folded the tartan and glanced up, only to find him glowering down at her. His anger vibrated in the small space.

She resented his harsh presence in the soothing tepee, draped with bundles of herbs. The disquieting scent of an enraged man swirled through the small space.

He opened his fist, broad palm up. Her mother's silver-feather-and-obsidian-bead earring gleamed against his dark skin. Elspeth's grandmother had given it to Pauline Tallchief as an engagement gift. The earring looked fragile in Alek's scarred palm. "You lost this that night. A village woman, a midwife, gave it to me last fall. She said that by the look of you, you were 'breeding' when you left Seonag two weeks after we met at the festival.''

Elspeth sat upon her pallet and clasped her arms around her bent legs, resting her chin on her knees. She studied the fire and wished Alek Petrovna back into the past.

He threw his gloves down and ripped open his insulated jacket. ''Well? Where is my child? How old is it—he…she—now, four?''

Elspeth slowly lifted her head to face him. She wouldn't give in to the temper that flickered at his taunts. She'd dealt with a houseful of wild Tallchiefs, every one of them difficult and arrogant, and nothing could be gained by facing Alek on this primitive plane.

For a moment he held her eyes, then ripped off his coat and tossed it into a corner. While Elspeth forgot to breathe calmly, he ripped the dangling beads and silver feather from the stud and slowly pushed it through his right earlobe. Blood ran freely from the wound, dripping onto his thick sweater.

''Alek!'' She leapt to her feet, grabbed a towel and lifted it—

His fingers circled her wrist, staying her. ''I'll wear your mark, you bloodless witch, until I'm damn well ready to remove it.''

He took the towel and sent her sprawling upon the neat pallet. As he placed the cloth to his wound, his black eyes slowly, insolently studied her body.

She knew he was taunting her, driving her to the edge, making her remember that night with the huge silver moon when he'd spread her beneath him, anxious for her first taste of this laughing, passionate lover. ''Alek…there is no child!''

Heartbeats later, as he stared coldly at her, her words echoed in the tepee. She'd never spoken the secret buried in her heart, and now it tore her apart once more.

Alek slowly removed the towel, ignoring the steady flow of blood. "No? Another lie, like the name you used when we met? Fearghus. Yes, that was it...Fearghus, not Tallchief."

She hated giving him anything. "Fearghus was my great-great-grandmother's name. I used it to make connections, to make my studies easier—"

"Ah, yes. The American weaver woman, they said, come to Scotland to study the Paisley shawl at its Scottish roots and to dig out some legend about the one you inherited. Now tell me about my child."

"Alek..." Elspeth swallowed the pain that had never dimmed. From his sister Talia, Elspeth knew how deeply the Petrovnas cherished their children. Perhaps he needed peace just as she did, and then he would leave. "There was a baby. I miscarried—"

In that instant, Alek paled, his eyes closing as the knuckles on his fists turned white. A vein pulsed in his muscled throat, standing out in relief, and his nostrils flared, dragging air deep in his lungs. Then the next heartbeat, he crouched before her, his brilliant eyes damp and cutting at her from beneath fierce brows.

"Damn you! If it's true, not another lie, you must have taken something...did something. You discarded my baby like dirty laundry without the slightest care about...the father. Then you ran back here where you'd be safe, tucked away in this nest of Tallchiefs. Oh, yes, I've researched the entire family and I'm good at what I do. They won't be able to help you....

Well, nothing can protect you now, Elspeth. Not from me. You've given me no choice—''

Elspeth leapt to her feet; she couldn't—wouldn't—stop the anger welling up and bursting from her. Alek had stepped into her life, wrenched her pain from the past and spread it before her. If he believed she had deliberately lost their baby... She hit his chest with the palms of her hands with enough strength to send him sprawling backward.

Elspeth slashed a dark look at him as she stalked back and forth over the small area near the fire. She stooped to toss the bloody towel into the fire, wishing Alek were as easy to remove from her life. The towel ignited, and so did her temper. ''Your baby. Your choice... Pushing earrings through your ear—''

''Earring. One ear. Singular.''

''Oh, yes. You're a journalist, aren't you? Five years ago, you were off for a little romantic holiday before you returned to the wars. What was that you said when you were done and ready to be on your way—'As good as I've had. Thanks for the good time'? I burned that wad of money you tossed at me, Alek. Thanks, but no thanks.''

Because he looked so shocked, she saw no reason to spare him. She doubted that anyone had cut Alek down to size, but he'd forced her into a corner. ''I've never told anyone, Alek. You want the clinical details? Fine. I'll send you the doctor's name and the hospital in London. I was studying with a talented weaver, a distant relative, when—''

She dashed away the tears flowing down her cheeks and folded her arms protectively across her body. ''Damn you, Alek.''

She closed her eyes, waves of pain crashing over

her again. Elspeth felt herself sink to her knees, heard her trembling whisper above the cold mountain wind. "He was only three months into term, Alek. According to the doctor, it was for the best.... For the best..." she said, repeating the phrase that had echoed through her heart for years.

She hated the sobs tearing out of her, and pressed the tartan to her face to muffle them. She was naked now, stripped of control by Alek Petrovna, and she hated him for that.

Two

Elspeth's cries tore into Alek; he hadn't prepared for this...*twist,* he decided was the right word. A story twist that didn't make sense for him. He'd planned a methodical revenge, not the softening within him.

Well, hell, Alek thought, suddenly drained of all his revenge, his motivation for bringing Elspeth to her knees. He'd planned his revenge, devising a plot that would tether Elspeth to him. He'd intended to take his revenge methodically, slowly. He'd hated her for hiding his child, for leaving him with an ache too deep to bear.

There was no child to hold in his arms....

The ache grew within him, even as his hatred for Elspeth eased. The miscarriage had torn her apart, her sobs proof of her mourning. Elspeth had wanted that child as desperately as he—Alek read that knowledge in the aching curl of Elspeth's body, her fingers gripping her tartan length. She'd always mourn the baby—

Alek carefully placed the china cup upon its saucer when he wanted to smash it. He rose slowly, a healed broken bone or two aching now. He stood very still, his fists clenched at his sides, bracing himself against losing a child he'd never known.

Elspeth lay curled upon the woven blankets. The sobs came raw, straight from her soul.

He swallowed, moistening a throat clogged with emotion.

Alek closed his eyes, listened to the wind howl beyond the canvas and saw Elspeth as she was back then—dancing passionately around the Scottish bonfire. He saw her lie upon the ancient rock, her face flushed with desire, her lips swollen from his kisses. Half-drunk on native brew and whiskey, he'd thought of her as a moonlit goddess with slender curves and dark, mysterious places. He'd teased her, enchanted with the chase…loved her—took her virgin body for his own. She'd tasted of life, a drink he'd needed to remember his attachment to the human race.

He'd wanted that child desperately, because he wanted his life to go on, a damn Petrovna trait. Then, too, the selfish gene within him needed more, a healing only the gift of a child could offer.

"Elspeth…" He crouched by her side and placed his hand on that sleek hair, lightly, tentatively, afraid that she would push him away. "Elspeth, don't cry."

She dashed his hand away.

He hated the sound of crying. He'd heard enough for a lifetime. He wiped his hand across his face, steadying his shifting emotions. Alek gently placed his hand on her head again. When she did not push him away, he stroked her hair lightly down to her shoulder.

The silent sobs racking her body shot up his arm, straight to his heart.

There was nothing he could do but lie beside her.

Alek held very still, allowing his tears to flow down his cheeks. When she didn't draw away, Alek stroked her hair, drew the tartan plaid around her and whispered her name. He laid his arm gently across her back, so as not to frighten her. He wanted her close to comfort her, and yet for his own need, as well. They'd created a baby between them, and he wanted to linger in the thought before burying it. "Elspeth...shh."

She turned her face to him, a blur of black eyebrows and lashes and shimmering eyes. "You're crying."

The tip of her nose almost touched his. Her breath swept across his lips. "You'd better go. The snow has begun."

He fell into gray eyes shimmering with tears and cursed himself as he whispered, "How do you know?"

"Listen to the wind...." she whispered unevenly, and instead he heard his heart beating slowly, cautiously.

"I'm not going anywhere." Alek's lips touched hers once, lightly. "I'm sorry for that night." Was he? That night had given him hope that the world was still pure.

Tears shimmered in her eyes, and her look was disbelieving. He kissed her again to soften the past, a kiss much like those he gave his sisters when they ran to him with scraped knees. Then Alek forgot everything but the taste of Elspeth's lips. He licked a tear from them and she stiffened, drawing away.

"How dare you!"

Alek traced the black hair crossing her damp cheek with his fingertip.

He watched a single swallow move down her elegant throat. He kissed her again, softly. "The child would have been my first."

Her lids closed, but he wouldn't allow the dismissal. He slowly brushed his lips across hers, finding one corner of her mouth and then passing to the other. He remembered the clean smell of her, the scent of wind brushing through the heather and then, when she lay trembling and warm, the intimate scent of a lover. He remembered how sweetly she had given herself to him, as though she would not touch another lover in her lifetime.

Alek damned his tears and the emotion welling up in him. Without a care for his plans to make Elspeth pay, Alek buried his face in her throat and clung to her.

Elspeth held very still in his arms and then, with a sob, she wrapped her arms around him, holding tightly. She began crying again, and this time he rocked her against him. She cried until exhaustion allowed no more and the fire burned low. Alek tucked his chin over her head and drew the shawl over her carefully. Tonight they mourned a child.

Alek watched Elspeth sleep, drained by her emotions. While the firelight flickered on her too pale face and gleamed upon her black hair, Alek's mind moved through his discovery that there was no child.

For months, he'd built his life around a plan for revenge, to hurt Elspeth and to claim his child.

He could not claim the child, but he wasn't ready to leave Elspeth alone—not just yet. Not until he'd untangled the twists and examined them, and sorted through his emotions, laying them to rest. He knew he would not rest until his feelings were resolved, like digging out ends and pieces and shaping them into a composite story...making sense of the whole and how he felt.

He wondered if he could ever rest...Elspeth had tormented him since that night in Scotland.

The stick he'd been holding snapped in his fist. Unsettled after his wife's death, he'd taken Elspeth's virginity and placed his child within her womb.

He'd hurt her that night, walking away from her. But he wanted no more emotions then, to haunt his mind, his heart.

Elspeth had faced pregnancy alone—she should have found him...it wasn't his fault that he didn't know.

Still, he wasn't without sympathy for her—for any woman stranded by a man who gave her a child and walked away. Young and alone, Elspeth had suffered the brutal loss alone. Alek fought the guilt riding him. He'd never thought of himself as one of those irresponsible men, denying their actions.

Elspeth sighed and shifted restlessly on her pallet and Alek held his breath, waiting for her to settle. Then his mind began to move into the puzzle, trying to stabilize the whys and the hows and make sense of them to his satisfaction. He needed a measure of peace and Elspeth's torment had left him none.

He'd changed her life. According to the townspeople and to Talia, Elspeth had changed dramatically after her visit to Scotland.

After her loss of a child....
After her loss of innocence....

Alek shifted restlessly, uneasy with his thoughts. He'd run on the steam of revenge for weeks, months, and now he felt empty and guilty and aching.

His story with Elspeth was unfinished and he wanted it resolved, needing the last line and the last period in place. This time he couldn't walk away too soon.

Alek remembered Elspeth that night, all fire and excitement and glowing with happiness.

He saw the woman upon the pallet, sleeping, drained by tears, a shadow of Elspeth-the-girl. She intrigued him still; he knew and disliked the thought. There was fire in her, temper and rage, all locked inside her until he'd arrived. Alek doubted that few people had seen what he'd just experienced, those locked thoughts of Elspeth, now freed. He wondered what else lurked beneath her cool surface.

For the moment, he had her and he'd keep her close until he unraveled whatever ran between them...until he solved the mystery of whatever nagged his heart and mind about Elspeth Tallchief. She wouldn't dislodge him easily—not until he was ready....

What was that she'd said that night? The Marrying Moon? What did it mean to her?

After one last glance at Elspeth, Alek settled down to sleep and prayed that he didn't dream.

Elspeth awoke when Alek moved to toss wood into the fire. He crouched by the flames, looking like a Gypsy with his wild black ringlets and the earring pushed into his earlobe catching the light. The barbaric act surprised Elspeth again, at odds with the expert way he poured tea from her china pot into a cup. He refilled her teakettle and placed its handle on the iron bar over the fire. Taking care, his hands too large for the task, Alek placed the china cup and saucer nearby, and the scent of mint tea swirled up to her. "Drink your tea."

She sat up quickly and wrapped the tartan around her. She ached, drained by crying, and wondered if she had aged a hundred years. She stared unseeing at the fire, pitch shooting sparks, and resented Alek, a marauding invader in her quiet sanctuary.

The line of his jaw was unforgiving, and his eyes shadowed as he studied her. "What's to eat?"

The intimate tone of his voice shocked her. Elspeth scrambled to her feet and found that he'd removed her moccasins. She sat quickly and jerked them on, binding the leggings with leather thongs to her knees. When she pushed back her long hair, Alek looked amused.

"It isn't as if it was the first time I removed your clothing."

She fought a sharp retort and smoothed her shift. She realized that Alek's scent clung to her, just as it had that night.

The sounds beyond the tepee told her that it would be foolish for Alek to leave. He knew it, too. "I'm staying the night, and we've got to eat. You can either tell me what you have in your pantry, or I'll dig it out," he murmured, watching her as she wrapped her tartan around her and prepared to leave. Alek's hand caught her wrist. "Where are you going?"

Away from him…to the silence she needed to restore her balance. He'd seen into the wounded heart of her; she'd give him no more. "There are fish in the weir. The baked potatoes under the coals should be done now. There's butter in a tin near my loom.''

"Good.'' He grinned, that charming, careless, boyish grin that had won her heart. She steeled herself against a man who could cry for a lost child and who could sweep away a girl's heart with eyes that promised laughter.

Elspeth stepped away from him and into the welcome bite of the freezing night air. She took her time retrieving two trout from the weir, listening to the coyotes and the night, to the sounds of branches snapping under the weight of snow…to the sound of her heart. She'd known for months that her life would change; the restlessness within her would not deny it. She'd known that Alek would come to see his sister, Talia, newly married to Elspeth's brother.

Beyond a smooth, moonlit span of snow, Alek loomed in the trees, a huge bear of a man, watching her as though he thought she would escape him. Elspeth refused to give him any pleasure and ignored him as she returned to the tepee—until he stepped into her path. ''What was that you said, about the Marrying Moon on that night?''

"I can't remember, Alek. Please step aside.''

How could she forget? When she was growing up, she'd plucked the legend's words from various references in Una's journals. Before Scotland, Elspeth had believed and clung to their hope, dreamed about them, certain that the shawl and the legend would bring her true love. Though she didn't know the entire legend, those words had brought her peace in hard times.

"Uh-huh. Sure, you can't remember.'' He took the fish from her, hefted them appreciatively, then looked down at her. "I'll find out. Facts, Elspeth. I'm good at digging them out."

She let that challenge pass and entered the tepee. Alek stepped inside moments later with the cleaned fish, invading her privacy and taking far too much room. Accustomed to fending with soldiers in the wild, he took the sticks by the fire, skewered the fish and propped the ends of the sticks against the cooking rocks. "Handy, aren't I?" he asked as the fish began to sizzle and cook, fat dripping into the fire.

Elspeth decided to ignore whatever Alek threw at her. She folded her tartan neatly, arranged the pallet and tried to dismiss the alien scent of a man amid her familiar ones. A contrast of vivid passions, Alek was an uncertain commodity, one she couldn't afford in her neatly structured life.

"Everything neat and in its place, right? Elspeth the elegant, isn't that what they call you? There's Duncan the defender, Calum the cool—although my sister seems to have him heating nicely—Birk the rogue and Fiona the fiery. Then there's Elspeth the elegant, the secret keeper." Alek reached across a mound of her clothing and the bag of uncarded wool. He picked up Una's wool cards and rubbed them together, testing them and Elspeth. "Tallchief Cattle is managed by Duncan, who holds most of the shares, and the land is in all your names. Calum manages family investments."

She braided her hair into two sections, tying off the ends with leather thongs, aware that Alek watched her. She wouldn't give him a drop of insight into her. Elspeth resented his digging at her life—and his touch upon her possessions, upon her. No doubt he'd interrogated Talia quite thoroughly. Elspeth ignored Alek's

probes, scraped aside the coals, found the baked potatoes and placed them on a cooking stone to keep
warm.

Alek pushed on, nudging the silence Elspeth had
drawn around her. "Talia told me about a Tallchief
custom, that of the Bridal Tepee...where newly mar-
rieds share their first days." He studied her tepee and
settled upon the empty branch waiting for her work.
"Mmm. Let's see. You've never been married, or at
least none of the Tallchiefs know of it, and you don't
date. You go to weavers' fairs, take custom orders at
a good price and, so far as I can tell, your role now
is that of a maiden aunt, a mentor for the family—but
then, you can't be a maiden, can you? You've raised
them and now you're happy living on the fringes of
their lives—rather like an old maid...the friendly
aunt...your niece Megan's baby-sitter and the reliable
mentor for a new Tallchief bride. Talia speaks highly
of you."

She resented the dark flash of temper he drew from
her, slashing like a sword across the fire at him. Alek's
eyes narrowed, meeting her challenge. "The Marrying
Moon, Elspeth. What is it?"

She ignored him and lifted the teakettle aside;
Alek's hand shot out to cover hers. She fought to remain impassive; his fingers were dark and long and
blunt and covered with scars. The scars had been fresh
when he'd first touched her.

He leaned close to her, and there was nothing gentle
in his expression. "I'll find out. Your great-great-
grandmother Una Fearghus was quite the historian.
Talia thinks reclaiming the dowry is romantic. I know
of Duncan's and Calum's legends, but not yours...

could it have to do with a Marrying Moon, whatever that is?''

Elspeth inhaled slowly. Alek's keen mind could forage for details somewhere else. "Let go."

"When I'm damn ready." Alek released her hand and sat back.

They ate quietly, tension humming between them. At last he lay back with the ease of a man used to discomfort in wars, drew his coat around him and slept deeply.

Her earring caught the firelight and gleamed in his ear, taunting her. The earring had been her mother's, the mate to it safely tucked away. How dare Alek Petrovna intrude into her life again?

Elspeth shivered slightly. She'd known from the first moment she saw him laughing at her in Scotland, catching her in his arms to dance around the bonfire and dropping a teasing kiss upon her lips, that Alek Petrovna would change her life. She'd known when he first touched her that he would become a part of her life. Back then she'd believed Una's journals, that there was a Marrying Moon, that hearts bonded magically and forever beneath it.

She'd never been touched or kissed in the way that Alek had that night on that ancient Scottish stone. She'd known forever that she couldn't, wouldn't, be touched lightly and that, in her lifetime, only one man would hold her heart.

Alek didn't qualify. Not a man who used Elspeth as comfort for his dead wife, a woman he'd loved.

For years later, she was disgusted by what she'd done, making love with a married man. Months ago Talia had dropped the tidbit that Alek had been mourning his late wife on his visit to Scotland.

The past lay cold and hard behind her. Elspeth cleaned away the meal and sat to do her evening carding. Pushing the cards against each other and taking the neat roll of wool away gentled the stirred emotions in her. She'd never forgotten or forgiven him. The legend's words taunted her...*Marrying Moon, scarred warrior, shawl, mists*...she tossed a soft roll of wool from her cards into the smoldering fire, wishing she could rid her mind of those haunting words as easily.

Suddenly Alek propped himself on his elbow and stared across the fire at her. "I'm not done with you, Elspeth, not by a long shot. I had a right to know about my baby and I was easy enough to contact." He gave her a hard, promising look, then lay down again.

She managed to doze, only to be awakened by Alek's cry. "These kids need food, shelter, medical attention! He'll lose that leg.... Oh, God, look at the little girl...come here, baby.... Oh, no...she's dead.... Honey...do you know where you live? Her parents were killed—"

Elspeth ached for what he'd seen, for the children. She wrapped the tartan closely around her and steeled herself against Alek's tossing and muttering. His life was no part of hers, and she would be glad when he was on his way....

"Alek Petrovna..." Elspeth muttered as she passed the shuttle through the taut wool on Una's loom. She banged the beater down, pressing the sage green into the pattern. His name grated in the large, sunlit room, filled with a weaver's clutter—a basket of shuttles and foot-long spindles filled with wool from Tallchief sheep, dried bundles of flowers, leaves and stalks hanging from the wall and a shelf lined with jars filled with berries for color. Skeins of every color hung across one long wall, filling it from top to bottom. Her collection of Navajo drop spindles—notched at the top, with a disk near the bottom of the shank—hung on a peg.

Neatly folded throws rested in a stack, ready for shipping. Each was of natural color and had taken a solid week to lay on the warp and to weave. Clearing her work calendar to allow time for the new Denver gallery contract hadn't been easy. Perhaps that was why she'd needed her retreat more this year. Or was it because the seer and the shaman blood in her sensed that Alek would be rising out of her past?

Elspeth regretted that moment when she'd broken for the first time in her life. The one person she did not want to see her wounds was Alek Petrovna.

She gathered her dark red shawl around her, the natural color from her favorite ewe at the ranch. She stared at the sett on a smaller loom—the repeated pattern of mauve-and-cream lines passing regularly through the dark brown background. The shawl was a gift for Talia, and its gentler colors would suit her fair coloring.

Alek's statement, rich with pride and arrogance, seemed to echo in the quiet, airy room—*You can't stay up here by yourself. It's too dangerous. You're coming back with me.*

Elspeth inhaled and straightened as she remembered him challenging her. *Of course* we *can stay up here. If you won't let me stay in your tepee, I've built shelters before. We can be neighbors.*

In the end, Elspeth had been forced to trek back down to Amen Flats with Alek. Her home offered protection from him that the wilderness could not provide.

She resented the way he looked at her, as though contemplating how she would have looked carrying his child. He wouldn't get to her, not this time. The tiny, quiet town of Amen Flats would soon bore Alek; he'd go on his way and—

Elspeth glanced out her window, past her herb garden, to see Talia, striding toward her house, black Hessian boots gleaming. Olaf, a huge black dog of mixed breed, bounded at her side like a puppy.

Alek, as dark as Talia was fair, wore his parka over a navy turtleneck sweater and canvas trousers layered with pockets and tucked inside his laced hiking boots. With their arms around each other, Alek and Talia were clearly happy. Alek had shaved, and his grin flashed at Talia, and then darkened and died as he met Elspeth's gaze through the glass.

A warning prickled, then skittered up her nape and beneath her skin; with trembling fingers, she smoothed her single braid and gathered the dark red shawl closer. She didn't doubt that Alek had contrived Talia's visit this morning. *I'm not done with you, fair Elspeth....*

Talia entered Elspeth's kitchen, her arm tucked into Alek's, and swooped to kiss Elspeth's cheek. Talia was four months into her pregnancy, and her unpredictable emotions were definitely on the happy side today. She beamed at Elspeth through happy tears and hugged her. With Alek in tow on one side and Elspeth on the other, Talia looked like a child at Christmastime, blinking through her tears.

"I'm so happy. Now everything is perfect. Calum and Alek talked about everything last night—that's why Calum didn't come, since he's catching up on some work. Alek cooked a marvelous dinner last night—oh, Elspeth, he's finally settling down. We won't have to worry about him in those awful wars anymore. Mom cried when he told her he was planning to settle in Amen Flats."

Alek met Elspeth's startled look and arched his scarred brow. Elspeth forced her hand to steady as she poured herbal tea into the china cups and saucers. "How nice. I was just ready for tea. Join me?"

"Love to." Alek's Texas drawl raised the hair on the nape of Elspeth's neck. He swept away Talia's woolen wrap and tossed it to a chair. Elspeth didn't like the way he arranged his parka across the back of her kitchen chair, as if he intended to stay.

She sliced the freshly baked loaf of whole-grain bread—she'd fairly attacked the rising dough, a substitute for bashing Alek and rendering him out of her life.

"Sleep well, fair Elspeth?" he asked too softly and too innocently.

"I always sleep well." She lied. She'd had dreams of Alek as he was that night in Scotland. A huge, laughing man whose lips had lightly touched hers and with enough magic to take her soul. The curve of his mouth had enticed her, mobile and generous and so soft she could fall into him with the brush of a feather. His chest had gleamed in the firelight, his heartbeat heavy with passion. Her stomach contracted almost painfully as a memory slid by—the moment he'd given himself completely to her...

"There's Calum. I knew he couldn't stand to be away from all the fun!" Talia dashed out of the kitchen.

Through the kitchen window, Elspeth watched Talia run toward Calum, who was scowling and clearly admonishing her about the dangers of pregnant women running. She leapt upon him, and he staggered back under the onslaught of her momentum and her flurry of tiny kisses.

"The Tallchiefs are fertile…Duncan's Meggie was born before they'd been married a year, and Talia was likely pregnant when she married Calum. They're very happy…a good match," Alek murmured softly at Elspeth's side.

"Yes. She's been wonderful for Calum." While she loved her sister-in-law, Alek was another matter. He stood too close, his heat invading her clothing.

Alek trailed a dried stalk of lavender down her cheek and close to her ear as he whispered, "'When a man of Fearghus blood places the ring upon the right woman's finger, he'll capture his true love forever.'"

Elspeth pivoted instantly, only to be pushed back against the counter by the closeness of Alek's body. His hands locked to the counter at her hips as he studied her. His thumbs brushed her hips, jolting her. No one touched her casually, much less caressed her with familiarity. She sent him a look that would send another man running, but Alek leaned closer.

"Calum placed Una's garnet ring on Talia's finger, and the legend came true. What was Duncan's legend? The one about the Tallchief cradle? Ah, yes… 'The woman who brings the cradle to a man of Fearghus blood will fill it with his babies.' Sybil and Duncan had Megan, a little sister for Emily, Sybil's daughter, didn't they?"

He'd been prying at her life again, firing her resentment of him. When Elspeth frowned at him, Alek leaned closer. "I'll find out, fair lady Elspeth. I'll find out about the Marrying Moon and the legend you guard in that cold heart—"

Elspeth lifted her chin and met his black, raking stare. "I think you should make this easy for all of us and leave."

He chuckled at that. "Tell me about last night. Did you dream of me?"

"You overbearing, conceited and stone-headed oaf." Elspeth knew in that moment why Una had once dumped cold porridge over Tallchief's head. Why LaBelle, her grandmother, had tied Elspeth's grandfather Jake to a chair.

"True," Alek returned undaunted. "But from the way you kiss, I doubt you've been practicing since that night. Almost five years have passed—rather, four years and nine months—and I would have thought—"

Alek flicked a glance at the window, to Calum and Talia, wrapped in each other's arms. "Did you really expect life to turn out beautifully after that moment on the rock? Did you really think that one night—a brief sexual episode—would bind us happily ever after?"

"You...back off!" Elspeth despised her low, threatening tone, yet she hated Alek's taunts more. He'd come too close, cutting her nearly to the bone. Five years ago she'd thought just that—that she had met her mate, that they had bonded. But Alek had ruined that fairy tale by calling out his wife's name and devastating Elspeth before he went on his way.

Now he pushed on. "I've had months to forage in your life, putting the pieces together, Elspeth. A Bridal Tepee—a Tallchief tradition—the Sioux equivalent of a honeymoon palace. Hmm...and you have one alone.... Tsk-tsk, what am I to think? That you've been pining for me, your lost lover?''

Alek leaned over her, but she refused to move back. ''Is that temper darkening those gray eyes? Or is it passion, fair Elspeth? I think you still want me.'' Then he stepped away, leaving Elspeth clasping the counter for support.

Calum walked into Elspeth's kitchen carrying Talia. ''She shouldn't be running,'' he stated with a proud grin as he lowered his wife to her feet. She stood on tiptoe to kiss him, and Calum beamed down at her.

''Sit,'' Talia ordered after taking Calum's denim coat away. Calum towered over his fair wife, grinning sheepishly while she smoothed his black hair and straightened his collar. Quiet, methodical and a professional investigator for companies with problems, Calum had captured Talia, claiming her for his own, almost instantly. Talia hadn't made the chase easy, and still didn't, keeping Calum on his toes.

When he sat, Talia plopped happily into his lap and snuggled against him. ''This is nice. I'm so glad Alek is moving here. Though that was no reason to stick that earring in his ear—a commemorative moment, he said. I cleaned his ear last night, and then he rammed the earring back in again. He said it was a keepsake and won't give details.''

''It was a very private moment.'' Alek met Elspeth's searing glance.

''I hope it was properly sterilized.'' Elspeth smiled lightly and showed her teeth.

''Thank you, Elspeth,'' Alek returned too easily.

This town isn't big enough for the two of us, and I am not the one who will leave. Elspeth ran the shocking thought by and decided that if she wanted to, if

Alek pushed her far enough, she would extend her own brand of welcome.

Calum frowned and glanced from Alek to Elspeth and back again. Her brother knew her too well, despite the protective cloak she'd drawn around her.

"Elspeth, come sit."

Alek was there, pulling away her chair and waiting for her to slide into it. She refused to look at him. He slid into a chair next to her, and she edged her thigh away from the intrusion of his. Alek pushed his thigh firmly against hers and continued, "This Marrying Moon thing really interests me. That's what you went to Scotland to find out about, wasn't it? Talia said that you couldn't read the entire passage in Una's journal and wanted to find the original legend. Maybe I could help. I'm good at translating rotten handwriting and bits of phrasing—like putting together a puzzle. I'd like to read Una's journals if I may."

"No." Elspeth didn't spare him pleasantries, and for a moment, Talia's eyes widened. Calum glanced sharply from Alek to Elspeth and cuddled Talia closer.

Talia stepped into the silence. "Alek, Elspeth has just signed a marvelous contract with a Denver art gallery. It's an exclusive contract...much more money than the custom work she's been doing for her clients. Oh, she's marvelous, taking bits of people's lives and blending them with wool and textures and colors. The gallery wants her to specialize in Native American designs, and if she wants, she can blend artifacts into the hanging. She did a sky, mountain, lake and meadow hanging for Calum and me, and it was gorgeous...a living harmony of blues and browns, something quiet and forever, you know. The wool was from Tallchief sheep, and she'd gathered the natural dyes from the Tallchief mountain.''

Alek reached to rub Elspeth's dark red shawl between his finger and thumb. ''She does beautiful work. I've seen the Tallchief tartan and kilts. She must be a very patient woman.''

Elspeth fought the simmering temper threatening her; she didn't care for him discussing her as if she weren't there.

''She learned from her mother. She designed the Tallchief plaid from Una's journals.'' Like a child, bursting with excitement one minute and then sleepy the next, Talia settled closer to Calum. She took his hand and placed it over their baby. Una's garnet ring gleamed bloodred as Talia caressed his hand. ''Everything is going to be just great. Alek is shopping for a car—one he can restore. I hope it's got a comfortable back seat. He was known for his necking and hot lips while in high school, almost more than his awards in writing.''

''I agree. We're going to be just one big, happy family. You know, I've missed necking in back seats.'' Alek looked at Elspeth and showed his teeth in a bland smile.

Talia snorted delicately. ''You and Anton—Anton's our other brother, Elspeth—steamed up a few windows in your time.''

Alek flashed her a grin. ''The steam was to keep my nosy sister from seeing how bored I was.''

''Amen Flats is a typical small town. There's not much excitement here.'' Elspeth traced the woven place mat with her fingertip. She didn't want to think about Alek Petrovna's hot lips or his necking tournaments in back seats.

"I'm staying." Alek's statement came back like a shot. Her fingers trembled, and her cup clattered against its saucer.

Ah! Alek thought, Elspeth doesn't like to be pushed or teased. She prefers the comfort of her shadows. Yet what he wanted, to find the heart of the woman, to understand his fascination with her—in the turn of her lips, the fire in her smoky gray eyes—would require a bit of prodding and testing.

Alek inhaled abruptly. The need to hold Elspeth close and soothe her, comfort her, ran through him like a freight train, winding him.

He wondered if she ever laughed—she had before their night in Scotland. He wanted to see that smiling curve of her lips, the happiness in her eyes.

Alek let his lashes drift down to shield his eyes— sometimes Petrovna eyes gave too much away.

With Elspeth, he had an uneasy suspicion that he would always want more.

Three

"**D**uncan...Calum...Birk...I will not have you interfering with my life." Elspeth snatched the loaf of freshly baked bread away from Duncan's reach. She swooped to pluck the plate of farm butter from Birk's poised knife. She placed the cutting board with the bread and the butter on the counter, then seized a buttered slice just before it entered Calum's open mouth. "I am not a young girl needing my three big brothers running interference for me. It wasn't wanted when we were younger, and it definitely isn't now. All of you stop."

"Eating?" Calum looked meaningfully at his empty hand and then lifted an eyebrow at her.

"You know very well what I mean. Stop sniffing at the trail of something you think is disturbing me. With April coming this week, I'd think you'd have fields to plow and seed to sow." Elspeth resented the sharpness to her tone; her brothers meant well and loved her.

Birk and Duncan leaned back in her kitchen chairs with almost the same expression—like wolves protecting the pack's only pup. Her three brothers crossed their arms over their chests and studied her.

Duncan was the first to speak. "One week ago you came back from the mountain together. You were wearing a big Keep Back sign. Alek is wearing your earring in his ear—I'd recognize LaBelle's gift to Mother anywhere—and you're—"

"Frothing," Birk supplied. "She's beating her loom to death at warp speed—no pun intended." Birk, younger but no less protective than his brothers, watched her with shadowed gray eyes. She recognized the determined set of his jaw and the narrowing of his eyes, a reflection of a stubborn gene shared by all the Tallchiefs.

"Birk, you are almost engaged to Chelsey Lang. Why don't you pay attention to her instead of me?" she asked too quietly.

"I pay plenty of attention to Chelsey. I just may marry her, but that doesn't enter this discussion."

"Chelsey is far too sweet and too sensible to marry you." Elspeth had fought their protective instincts all her life, matching wits to keep them from suffocating her. She sipped her raspberry-leaf tea. "Let's have this out here and now. You three have been hovering around me since the day Alek arrived."

"How did Alek get the earring, Elspeth? The last I remember, you were wearing it when you took off for Scotland." A methodical thinker and well paid for it, Calum began laying out the facts.

"You're not yourself. I don't like it." Duncan's statement was blunt, demanding an answer.

Birk glanced at her studio. "You're weaving night and day, Elspeth. You've got circles under your eyes. You always weave when you're upset. You almost killed that bread dough. What's wrong?"

"I think I'll have a little talk with Alek." Duncan glanced meaningfully at his two brothers.

"I am weaving more than usual because I want to complete my orders before I start with the gallery. Duncan the defender...you will not," Elspeth tossed at him.

"Aye, I will," he returned doggedly. When a Tallchief used the word *aye,* it was a pledge.

Calum dropped a tidbit that didn't ease her stormy mood. "Alek bought the old newspaper office. He's planning to put the *Sentinel* back in business."

Birk stepped into the battle. "I'm lending him some power tools. He's just bought the old Potts place—"

"He didn't!" Elspeth held her breath. "The Potts place? Next door?"

A contractor by trade, Birk nodded. "It needs work from foundation to roof. Alek said he's got nothing but time. Says after all he's seen torn apart, he wants to rebuild something."

"He's a busy little boy, isn't he? He'll have to pick somewhere else." Elspeth regretted the bite to her tone. She glanced out the window to the old house, overgrown with trees and shrubs. She quickly poured a bracing cup of tea to settle her nerves. At the moment, she felt as if she could weave a road straight up to Tallchief summit and back down again. She took a sip, disliking the unsteady emotions caused by the mere mention of Alek Petrovna.

"You'll be neighbors," Duncan stated as though willing to set up a fortress to keep Elspeth safe.

"I'll talk to him." Calum, married to Alek's sister, was primed to investigate whatever storms Alek had created for Elspeth.

Elspeth discarded the safety of silence; her panic stayed. "Calum, spend anything from my accounts to buy him out."

"It's not worth what he paid for it, Elspeth," Calum reasoned after a glance at his brothers. "And he'll want to make a profit."

"What is it with you and Alek?" Birk studied his sister.

"I will not have that man living on my doorstep."

Duncan pulled on his leather gloves. "You're right, Birk. She's too sensitive about Alek. We'll have to find out why. If she won't tell us, he will."

Elspeth's brothers stood up, flinty eyed and powerfully built westerners ready to protect what they held dear.

Elspeth rounded on them, her hands on her waist. "Back off."

"This isn't like you, Elspeth," Calum reasoned. The three of them, all inches taller than her five foot nine inches, looked at her steadily. "Alek isn't the kind to play games, Elspeth."

"He wants you." Duncan tossed away Sybil's hours of tutoring his curt manners.

"It's more than that," Calum added. "There's something there, running between them. Talia doesn't know anything other than that Alek has been interested in Elspeth's life. My wife is hoping for a little thing between you called romance."

"Romance? With Alek?" Elspeth's fingers wanted

to grab a shuttle and let it fly through the weave, easing her emotions. Instead, she grasped at the hope Alek would disappear. "He'll get tired of Amen Flats. In a way, he's like Fiona, always searching for something, as though a piece of them was missing and needing an anchor to make them whole. There's not enough excitement here to keep him interested."

Women. Alek Petrovna needed action and a variety of women. She chewed on the thought. Alek wouldn't be satisfied until he'd pitted himself against the hardest assignment or a woman who fascinated him.

"Maybe he's found what excites him more than anything else...it can move that way between a man and a woman sometimes. In the past week, I've seen how Alek watches you—when the family is together. Sybil and Emily agree." Duncan now drew in the support of his wife and his fifteen-year-old stepdaughter.

"The earring, Elspeth. Why is Alek wearing it?" Calum prodded.

For once, Birk was too quiet, then he stated slowly, "Elspeth hasn't been the same since her studies in Scotland five years ago. She's more cautious and she's built walls, not letting anyone come too close. Lacey, who practically lived with us after Mother faced down Mrs. MacCandliss about her treatment, or lack of care of Lacey, said the same. Now that I think back, Elspeth was as much of a fighter as Mother—once her dander was up. Not as wild as Fiona, but subtle and effective. I haven't seen that since she returned from Scotland. Except for her midnight forays to Tallchief Mountain."

"Aye," Duncan and Calum stated together. The word sounded like the growl of wolves who had sniffed the danger near their pack.

"Haven't you three got something to do?" Elspeth asked more sweetly than she felt, and reached for Duncan's ear. One tug widened his eyes. One by one, she pushed them out her door.

The old Potts place sat in full view of her studio, and Elspeth gripped a shuttle tightly as she stood before the large windows lining the room. She looked past the large rack of beams that served as her wooldying shed, her gaze skimming her dead herb garden and resting on the house next door.

Alek was there, piling old boards, limbs and weeds into a huge pile. Dressed in his laced boots and worn camouflage clothing, he moved easily, powerfully, leaping over a branch before hauling it to the pile. He tossed the For Sale sign on top with the air of a man who was sinking in his roots to stay. A tall, powerful man, Alek braced a boot on a stump and surveyed the house. With his back to her, Alek was all long legs and wide shoulders.

No man should have that much black, curling hair, nor look as if he hacked at it with a knife when it got in his way. It glistened in the sun, touching his shoulders and mocking her. Her fingers itched to trim it, to cut it as she did Birk's—but with her hands near Alek's hair, she didn't trust herself not to pull hard.

Elspeth wished Alek and her brothers into another country.

She studied her new work, which was just beginning to take shape. The design waited for her, springing not from her usual paper layouts, but from something simmering inside her. Elspeth sat at the rack that had been used by her mother and grandmothers before her and chose a tan wool. Whatever beckoned to her from inside the design had waited and now wanted life—it simmered and heated beneath her fingers.

Alek hadn't expected his smoky-eyed neighbor to welcome him with a tuna casserole, freshly baked bread and a smile. And she hadn't.

In his new house, Lacey MacCandliss, a petite, curly-headed elf and adopted member of the Tallchief family, raged at Birk, who yelled back. The two contractors had taken time away from competing long enough to help Alek with the basic necessities of safe electricity and major plumbing.

He'd expected Elspeth's offer to buy and Calum's methodical dissection of why he might want to consider another home. Calum was already questioning Alek's motives and Elspeth's reaction to him.

A tall, cool blonde with cornflower blue eyes had stopped to introduce herself. She had been distracted by Birk's yell at Lacey and had listened intently to them. "I'm Chelsey Lang. Birk and I are going together. He's busy now or I'd talk with him. Tell him I came by, okay?"

Alek nudged a loosened foundation stone back into place with his boot. He'd planted himself near Elspeth's castle, near enough to spot her looking at him through the huge windows of her studio.

Alek blew her a kiss.

She reached to the side, and shades slashed down between them.

Little kept Alek from leaping over the picket fence that separated them. On a second thought, he began working the rotted old fence free from the ground and dragged it into the pile to be hauled away. He wanted no fences between Elspeth and himself, on any level. Thorns from the old rosebushes raked across his hands and arms, and when Alek could no longer avoid it, he looked at his scarred hands.

His palms were soft, and he wanted calluses from working outside in the fresh air. He wanted roots and growing plants and babies.

He wanted a woman to hold in his arms at night, to hug in the morning—Alek fought the churning, cold pit inside him. He didn't know if he could put down roots, but hell, he would try.

When Elspeth had entered his life, he'd been a desperate man, one wanting to survive. Now he wanted more than to survive. He wanted a life here in Amen Flats. He took the leather gloves from his back pocket, an inheritance from Mr. Potts, who could no longer do yard work. Alek intended to get his calluses and along the way, he'd get Elspeth's secrets.

At forty, he should have been immune to teenage sexual hormones raging in his body. But one look at Elspeth, and he wanted to examine firsthand just how long she could remain untouched.

He worked furiously, needing the late-March wind cooling him and the labor to dull the fine edge riding him. That damn soft promise of a mouth had haunted him for a week, no less enchanting than the first time he'd kissed her. She had tasted as sweet as the Scottish heather smelled in the night air; the taste of her haunted him. He swiped the sweat from his cheek and whipped a handkerchief from his pocket, tying it around his forehead. He pitted himself against the disaster of the yard with an intensity that eased his need to pull Elspeth against him and kiss her until she melted.

His conscience didn't help, especially when the townspeople chatted with him about his neighbor. Full of life and as fierce as any of the Tallchiefs, she'd laughed and gone off to Scotland. Una's shawl had come from the Paisley town mills in Scotland, where Elspeth had journeyed to seek her heritage.

According to Mr. Potts, the whole town had seen her off, and then Duncan and his brothers had brawled with any takers. The townsfolk cherished friendly brawls—a tradition in Amen Flats. Fiona and Lacey had jumped into the fray, banging heads and riding shoulders. At some point, Birk had tossed Lacey over his shoulder and carried her out into the street, instructing her to stay put and safe. She was on him instantly, landing a punch in his stomach and crawling up a ladder that wouldn't support him. Birk had yelled threats to her, watching her cross the rooftops to Maddy's Hot Spot Tavern. Then he'd stopped to accept a kiss on his cheek from an elderly woman who had changed his diapers. He helped her carry her groceries from the store into her car and accepted another kiss before he stalked back toward Maddy's.

The sheriff had ignored the brawl at Maddy's request. The lawman had turned up his radio, an Italian tenor shrieking loud enough to set off the town's dogs.

Stories about the Tallchiefs saturated Amen Flats, and sorting them out, Alek found that Elspeth's adventures had stopped after visiting Scotland. *He'd changed her life, shredded it with one night.*

Alek jerked a rotten post from the ground, tossing it onto the pile. He was responsible for the Elspeth who had returned to Amen Flats: she'd built a home for herself, was too cautious about relationships and had settled into her safe castle, weaving into the night.

Alek's shirt tore and he ripped it away, just as he wanted to rip away the past and his guilt. Yet she should have told him— He switched on the tape player, turning up the passionate Russian folk music that stirred his blood.

"*Alek.*" Elspeth's call stopped Alek as he braced his bare shoulder against a loosened post supporting the back porch.

Dressed in a loose cream blouse over a long chambray skirt and moccasins, Elspeth picked her way over the rubble. The ends of her dark red shawl, wrapped tightly around her against the biting wind, reminded him of the flying banner of a lady going off to war. From the yard, she looked up at him on the porch. Alek leaped to the ground and strolled to her; he wanted to see every expression on her face and know when he had fired her passions enough to ignite.

Alek studied her braids, wound like a coronet on top of her head. Oh, yes, he wanted to see her ignite. To lose that fine hold on her emotions. He'd seen her heart break, and to soothe his guilt, he needed the heat of her temper.

She backed up a step, pleasing him. Like it or not, Elspeth Tallchief had been affected by him. He admired the way she lifted her head; she wasn't a woman to give herself easily and yet, she had five years ago. Why?

"You can't do this, Alek. You cannot move in next door to me."

He laughed at that. He'd always gone where he wanted, and this would be his first home. "Says who?"

He enjoyed the way she struggled for control, the flash of smoke in her eyes and the flush spreading

slowly up her cheeks. The reluctant skip of her gaze
down his sweaty chest and then the control that took
it upward to meet his eyes caused his senses to leap.
Without effort, Elspeth possessed more sensuality than
any woman he'd ever known, and he resented the
lurch of his body. Alek studied the quickening pulse
along her throat and found himself lost in the clean
smell of her—the scent of wildflowers and herbs, and
Alek breathed very slowly, inhaling a light, exotic
scent. *Elspeth.*

Her sea-gray eyes darkened, stormed and locked to
his. The pulse in her throat pounded heavily, and Alek
wondered what she'd do if he placed his lips upon it.
She inhaled and he found himself wondering if she
wore lace or plain white lingerie.

Elspeth's breath came out in a hiss. "It won't
work—you living next door to me."

"I'll live where I want. You lit a flame or two before you left for Scotland, and the locals say that Tallchiefs have a backbone of steel. You've changed, Elspeth."

"I've changed for the better. If it comes to rooting
you out, I will."

He stroked a gleaming strand of hair away from her
cheek, tucking it back into the black braid flowing
down her breast. Unable to stop, Alek allowed his fingertip to slowly move downward. Elspeth stepped
back instantly, her eyes flashing with anger.

"Why don't you make it easy on yourself and tell
me about the legend? Your edges are showing, fair
Elspeth." Edges, he thought, nice little edges to explore, to fit together until the puzzle was complete.

"I wonder why." The whip in her voice took him
by surprise. She leapt to the porch and switched off

his tape player. Without thinking about the why of it, Alek leapt up to the porch and bent to brush his lips across hers.

She jerked back, flattening against the old boards, her eyes widening with surprise and then narrowing as her temper flared. He reveled in the blaze of emotions, trolling a fingertip down her flushed cheek.

Then Birk yelled at Lacey, doors slammed and Elspeth frowned up at Alek. She spoke in a controlled tone, the effort clearly costing her. "Amen Flats is a small, boring town. Other than for Talia—and she shares my beliefs about overly protective brothers—there is absolutely no reason for you to be here, Alek. Especially living next to me. I don't like noise while I'm working, or half-naked men parading in front of my studio window."

"So you've noticed me." He leered at her, pricking at her edges. What right did she have to keep all that heat bottled inside her, when the scent of her caused him to steam? "It's beautiful you know, when you weave. Your arms and hands are flowing, artistic, and there's a timelessness about your movements. But I wondered what you thought about when you wove and now I know. You ogle men from the corner of your eyes, Elspeth-mine. It's nice to know you admire me, that I am the object of your lust." Alek delivered the taunt and watched her struggle for control. For effect, he reached out a sweaty arm and flexed his muscle. He was showing off like a teenager, trying to get a girl to notice him. Alek tossed the mocking thought aside, and gave himself to studying Elspeth.

Her gaze slowly skipped to his arm; she wasn't as immune as she pretended to be. When her eyes locked to his, they were steel gray, shooting sparks at him.

"Lust doesn't come into it. What do you think you're doing, Alek?" she asked too carefully, her face very pale.

"Settling down, fair Elspeth. Making my nest. Issuing a town paper in two weeks. The middle of April is a wonderful time for a first issue. I'm shopping for a work truck and a Chevy classic in that order. Take care of business, that's Petrovna's law—finishing what I start. What do you think I'm doing?"

"I think that you are being stone headed and totally obnoxious. You thought you had a score to settle, but there is no score now. And there is no Petrovna law in Amen Flats. Leave me alone."

Alek took a step closer. "We're not done, Elspeth. Not by a long shot."

"*Back off.*"

"Stand and fight. Isn't that what the Tallchiefs say?" Alek caught her scent, clean and yet exotic, and realized that his body was taut, remembering that night.

"There will be no fight, Alek."

"No? Because *you* say so?" He knew the air had shifted between them, warmed by the past and enticed by the future. He leaned closer. "You think you can cut me out of your life? Forget that I would have been the father of our child? I can still see you, smell you, after all these years. What was that about the Marrying Moon, Elspeth? What did you mean that night?"

She gasped slightly and moved back. Alek took her wrist. Her pulse fluttered and raced beneath his fingertips as he brought her wrist to his lips. "You knew what you were doing, Elspeth. It was there in your eyes, heat and smoke burning me."

"I knew what I was doing, but not that you needed

a substitute for your wife. I didn't know you were grieving for your wife until Talia told me last October, when Calum brought her here." The words were hushed and rapid, held too long and now rushing out. "Do you know how I felt after and for years later, thinking I had given myself to a married man?"

Pain and guilt over hurting Elspeth tore at him; instincts told Alek to protect himself against her barb. "I didn't know you were a virgin until it was too late. You were twenty-eight, and ready."

"And you took."

Alek's head went back. The truth hit him like a fist. "And we made a child. I want another."

He hadn't meant to state the thought, the need to be a father, but once the words caught the wind, he knew he meant them. He saw into Elspeth Tallchief, the strength in the silence, the fire rising out of the smoke. Then the fine control leashing her emotions. He'd wanted children, ached for them, dreamed of holding them in his arms. If Elspeth would have come to him, perhaps he could have—

Yet that high pride of hers—and his own actions— kept her from notifying him.

If he'd never known about the child, perhaps the ache would have been less...but now he'd had a taste of the dream, and so the loss had deepened.

And with it came a new kind of bitterness.

They both owed each other a dream, Alek raged silently. They owed each other a child.

"This won't work, Alek. You'll get tired of whatever game you're playing and move on."

"Sometimes you have to dig beneath the surface...make things happen." He lifted an eyebrow to spear at her with his gaze. "I always finish my stories

and tie up loose ends. I happen to like puzzles, Elspeth. Get used to it.''

Sunlight skimmed along her lashes as she glanced
beyond him. Anger flashed, steely, hard and bright before she looked up at him. "You have a visitor, Alek.''

Alek stepped back and glanced at a young woman
with too-tight jeans. He recognized the hungry smile;
the casserole dish she carried caused more excitement
than her look.

To set Elspeth simmering, he turned to greet the
curvaceous blonde bearing his food.

Laden with scents of mountain pine and newly tilled
gardens, April 1 usually entered Elspeth's open windows as she wove. The sound of Alek's power saw
ripping through lumber grated; the sound of his ham-
mer caused her headache. His dented pickup needed a
muffler badly, and when he wasn't working on the
house, Alek tinkered with the truck. This drew the
Tallchief brothers and a host of teenage boys, complete with the teenage girls tagging after them—to say
nothing of the boys on bikes. The rubble stacked in
his backyard grew daily, and big new windows now
faced her house.

A meandering line of daffodils divided their prop-
erties, punctuated by the old rosebushes, which Alek
had trimmed. At least she'd have the roses this summer, some small token after he'd invaded the quiet
street.

Elspeth longed for the old Kostya place, which bordered Duncan's ranch, but it wasn't for sale. There she
could have her privacy with no irritating, half-naked,
muscle-flexing, arrogant, grinning Alek Petrovna.

Elspeth kept to herself, finishing Talia's present and

the order of woolen throws. She sketched her new wall hangings for the exclusive contract. The dealer already had several of them, and when they were first shown, the price would be outrageous.

Outrageous.

We made a child. I want another.

She wanted to free herself of Alek's statement, to stop it from tearing into her thoughts. Yet that *I want another* remained, despite her will, nagging at her. It seemed just as permanent and irritating as the man himself.

To free herself from her new neighbor, Elspeth pitted herself against the heavy loom until her body ached. Alek had women running after him, eager for a taste of the worldly bachelor who was settling down in Amen Flats.

Elspeth firmed her back. Alek could flirt with an army of women bearing casseroles, and she wouldn't notice. He could flex his muscles and—Elspeth inhaled sharply. Alek's muscles had been the object of her wandering eyes, and she regretted that. She jerked down the beater and regretted that, too, because she'd made the weave too tight.

Then she glanced out the window. Alek stood on a ladder, hammering away at the rain gutter, his body taut. The sun glistened on his muscles, which were pulsing with each blow. Elspeth found she was holding her breath and let it out in a rush. Alek did not affect her, not in the least.

Just then, Alek wiped the sweat from his forehead with one hand and caught her gaze. He blew her a kiss.

Hours later, Elspeth smiled at Sybil, Duncan's wife, and kissed her niece, Megan. "How is Marcella Portway?''

Sybil groaned dramatically at the mention of her client. ''That woman will drive me to fake her ancestry. I've never done that, but the thought appeals—just to get rid of her.'' A genealogy expert, Sybil had been hired to track Marcella's family gene pool to a Spanish nobility that didn't exist. ''By the way, Duncan has been worrying about you.''

''Are you scouting?'' Elspeth watched Megan toddle to her mother. At ten months, Megan was already a handful, ready to explore.

Sybil laughed and kissed Megan's black hair. ''Something like that. Come on, Elspeth, don't tell me that Alek isn't appealing. He's got all those rough edges that women love to smooth out. Add all that charm and the dark, Gypsy look, and any woman would be happy to have him interested. He's very romantic and absolutely enthralled with Talia's pregnancy. Now she has four men clucking over her.''

Elspeth helped Megan crawl up onto her lap and handed her a tea cookie. ''I'm certain some women would find him fascinating.''

Sybil laughed outright and grabbed Megan's fingers before she could snatch Elspeth's notebook. ''Elspeth Tallchief, you know very well that Alek is interested in you. He's flirting outrageously with you. Sharlene Davis almost fainted when he pushed your shopping cart at the grocery store and you walked off and left him. You've avoided him when possible, and he's not giving up.''

Sybil kissed Megan's soft cheek. ''Didn't Una call it the awakening? That's what it felt like when Duncan came calling. It was as if I'd been waiting for him all my life, maddening creature that he is.''

"Una said the awakening is when a man comes calling softly, when he places himself in a woman's care, needing the softness within her. Then she awakes, cherishing the gentleness he's shown only to her, wanting to heal his scars with her touch. If I have shadows under my eyes, it's because of hammers and saws. Alek is too—"

"Passionate, Elspeth—passionate, emotional, fierce and proud. He likes to laugh and play and flirt. He's everything Talia is and more—heavier, deeper, as though he's been tempered by life's hardships. I'm a survivor and I've recognized that something horrible prowls through Alek in his dark moments. From what I know of him, his wife died tragically. His scars are from trying to save her. They'd been in love since they were teenagers, and he had to give permission to unhook the life-support equipment that kept her alive."

Elspeth's fingers trembled slightly, and she held Megan tighter. She refused to think about the texture of Alek's face that night, how he had taken her exploring fingertips and kissed them.

The brisk knock on her kitchen door startled Elspeth, and she rose, holding Megan on her hip, to open it. Alek, a carpenter's pencil tucked above his ear and dressed in his usual tattered olive drab T-shirt and worn jeans, looked at her through the screen door. Megan, spoiled by the Tallchief males, squealed and leapt at him as Elspeth opened the door.

Alek reached for the toddler, cuddled her and grinned. "Now, this is a girl who knows how to greet a man. She's got good taste, too...blackberry jam. Want to share, kitten?"

Megan laughed and held up her fingers to Alek's

mouth, and he sucked them noisily, making approving noises of how she tasted.

Elspeth moved back slightly, overpowered by the way Alek stormed into her quiet home. "Come in, Alek."

He tugged her braid as he passed, reached for the platter of freshly baked cookies and handed Megan one. She giggled and offered it to him. Around the granola cookie, Alek said, "Thanks. The smell of these things has tormented me for hours.... Sybil, how's the article on genealogy coming? I need that for the first edition."

"I'm just polishing it. Emily is thrilled about the paper and the column you've opened for budding writers. Mrs. Freeman has the older circle working full-time on stories about pioneers. I understand you're just getting the newspaper in running order and then you'll step back."

"I'm working with Brad Klein. He wants to stay in the area and use his journalism degree. If things work out, he'll take over pretty quickly. It's a shame that all the equipment hasn't been in continuous use. It's like a woman left to waste when she should be loved." Then he turned slowly to Elspeth. "Hello."

She stiffened; his Texas drawl was back, intimate and sexy and curling around her. There was no mistaking the message in his eyes as they lowered to her lips. Elspeth hated the heat moving up her cheeks and the quick amusement in Alek's expression. He swept a finger down her cheek and tapped her beneath her chin, startling her with his play.

"She's shy." Alek grinned at Elspeth.

Sybil laughed. "Elspeth doesn't know how to take you. I think Megan and I need to be going along."

Megan pursed her lips at Alek, and laughing, he bent to give her a kiss. A bit of Megan's blackberry-jam feast transferred itself to Alek's cheek and stayed there.

Minutes later, with Megan and Sybil gone, Elspeth faced Alek, who leaned against her counter, long legs crossed at his ankles. She tried to keep from looking at the juicy glob of jam stuck to his unshaven cheek. "Shouldn't you be leaving?"

"Nope. I've got business here. I'd like to do a story on Una's journals. Or would you consider doing a story on weaving?" He munched on another cookie.

"My family inheritance is private, and there are other weavers. My mother taught them, the same as she taught me." Elspeth snatched the remainder of the cookie from his fingers and tossed it away. She grabbed Megan's washcloth and swiped at his cheek. "I should think you would have enough food in your house. Every woman in Amen Flats has brought you a casserole. You could have opened a restaurant."

"Every woman but Elspeth Tallchief. Bothering you, is it?" Alek's expression darkened. "If you don't know how to take me, then I'll have to make certain you figure it out, won't I?"

Elspeth refused to answer to his bait and began to move past him to the safety of her workroom. "You may leave. I have work to do."

Alek caught her wrist, smoothing the fine skin as he studied her hands, more slender and lighter in his. Then he took them and placed them on his cheeks, her left palm against his scars. Alek closed his eyes, and when they opened, Elspeth stepped back, frightened. There was too much heat in him, skimming over her,

needing something she did not want to give. Alek
would have to fight his private wars by himself.

"Please leave."

"Do you know how much I needed you close to
me that night? How much I've thought about you—?"
His voice was uneven, raw with emotion that startled
Elspeth.

"Alek—" Her thumb brushed the scar on his lip,
and Alek pressed it there. Unable to move, to look
away, Elspeth met his black eyes. She saw his pain
again, the shadows enclosing him.

Only minutes ago he had laughed at Megan; now
he was serious, lines deepening in his forehead. "I am
sorry, Elspeth. I should have handled the matter better."

"The *matter?* As in you should have worn a brown
suit in lieu of a blue one?" She fought to draw her
hand away, fought to keep her fingers from stroking
his lined brow.

"I made love with you, Elspeth. There's a difference."

"And you would know, wouldn't you?" she demanded bitterly.

Alek took her hand against her will and lifted it to
his mouth, pressing his lips to the center. Over their
hands, he looked at her. "It took some time before I
sorted out what had happened. I was riding an emotional maelstrom that night, and making love to you
confused the issue. I moved through the next weeks
like a sleepwalker—lucky to keep my life, in some
cases. But I knew that whatever happened that night
went deep with us. You were twenty-eight, Elspeth.
Most women have experience by then...you didn't.
Why hasn't there been someone to care for you?"

She trembled and fought the panic rising in her. Alek was prowling too close. "Alek, this has gone far enough."

Alek took her hands and placed them over his heart. The steady, heavy beat pushed at her palms, and Elspeth looked away, aware that her senses were racing, that after all the years, she was affected by Alek. The knowledge still startled her.

"I need answers, Elspeth. You are going to give them to me, like it or not." He bent to brush his lips across hers. The second time, he leaned closer, and Elspeth held her breath as his lips lingered over hers, brushing, warming. He was asking now, needing—

Alek inhaled quickly and straightened away from her. "That's how it is, Elspeth-mine," he murmured, and was gone.

Elspeth flattened back against the wall for support and found herself shaking.

Whatever had passed, the bond that she knew they'd forged that night remained. It shimmered and tangled between them, twisted and heated and forged like an ancient Celtic design. She'd known from the moment he'd come to her side, his eyes hot and laughing, and his hand taking hers...

Elspeth placed her shaking hands over her face and tried to control her emotions as she had since that night.

Yet her instincts told her that it was the same as when she'd first met Alek, the heat and the need to claim him for her own...to bond with him...to meet him on a plane where they both demanded and both gave— Was it true? Did she bond with Alek so deeply that even with their past, he could still affect her on a level that she did not want to revisit?

"No." Elspeth firmly reined her impulse to seek out Una's legend of the shawl, to place the pieces together and try to unravel the words. The words came to haunt her—*scarred warrior...placing the shawl...the Marrying Moon...tepee....*

Before her encounter with Alek in Scotland, she'd believed the words would unravel into a romantic truth just for her. Now she had no illusions.

"No. I will not let him interfere with my life," she promised, and forced herself to walk to her loom.

Four

"Alek Petrovna, Jr., don't ignore me." Talia, dressed in overalls and a sweater, picked her way across the rubble of Alek's new office. She tottered on an uneven board, and instantly Alek and Calum swooped upon her. Two big hands gripped each side of her overalls at the waist and lifted her over the board. She glared up at them, both with a big hand on her shoulder to steady her.

"Wouldn't want the baby to get hurt." Alek rubbed Talia's gently rounded tummy.

"The percentages say that we'll have a girl," Calum stated, and bent to kiss his wife. He caught the back of her overalls in his hand, tethering her and drawing her back to him. "You've been up all night practicing. Tell him."

She stared at her husband and stated indignantly, "I

was merely baking baklava. You didn't have to sit in the kitchen and placate me with nods and hmms."

"Sweetheart, it's darn hard to sleep with you marching in your Hessian boots and muttering in corrupted Swahili. The Russian folk music didn't help, either." Calum kissed her nose. "You were stewing, precious. I'll leave and let Junior take his medicine. Make certain you're home in time to take your nap, or I'll be hunting you."

Talia snuggled against him, contented and loved. "Well...okay. Just because I know you'll send out Duncan and Birk and probably Alek, too. But I want a kiss first."

After Calum had left, Alek noted, "That was some kiss. He'll be steaming all afternoon."

Talia grinned. "Calum is in that 'gee can I...is this good for the baby?' stage and too ready to protect me. He needs reassurance and pampering."

"I'm glad you're together." Alek glanced at Elspeth's house and tasted her mouth again. He inhaled and stuck his hands in the back pockets of his jeans.

"You're mooning over her, Junior. I never thought I'd see the day when hard-to-catch Alek had it bad." Talia slid her arm around him to soften her tease. She leaned her head on his shoulder. "You just don't know how to handle yourself around her. Elspeth can't be pushed, and you are...you've got that 'ugh, me man' look around her, just like you want to toss her over your shoulder and run off with her."

Alek snorted. The raw hunger prowling his body wasn't easily denied. The sound should have deterred Talia, but she plunged on. "I've got experience with that look. Sybil agrees. Both Duncan and Calum had quite recognizable 'ugh, me man' looks and flames in their eyes when they decided they wanted us. Both of them just swooped, and you've got that same look. Take my advice, Alek...Elspeth isn't the kind of woman who appreciates a swooper-taker."

Talia rounded on Alek, her long, straight blond hair flaring out to catch the sunlight. "Junior, you're tired and you need someone to share your life and diversify your focus. You keep pouncing on Elspeth, trying to corner her at every family gathering, and she'll take you down."

"Stop calling me Junior— Will she?" The prospect fascinated Alek; he wanted Elspeth out of her shadows. If he was right, the contract in Denver would make a distinct change in their relationship.

"She's just as tough as her brothers. They had to be, carrying more than teenagers should to survive. Pride and steel has been bred into them for generations."

Talia placed her hand on his shoulder, her blue eyes concerned. "Alek, I won't have you toying with Elspeth. She's too rare and she's been wounded, though we don't know from what. Sybil agrees. We haven't told her brothers. They're old-fashioned about a woman's honor and very protective of family. Emily at fifteen is having an awful time with the Tallchief males, but no more than Fiona and Elspeth had as girls."

Talia touched his scarred cheek, her blue eyes soft upon him. "Move carefully, Alek. Elspeth's isn't the only wounded heart around. You've been needing an anchor for years. Just to look at you makes my heart ache. Until you look at Elspeth, and then I think...I think there just might be hope, because if there's anything you like, it's a challenge. The Tallchiefs aren't an easy game, but worth every minute of it.''

"Elspeth is too quiet." He'd done that to Elspeth, put the walls up.

"She's very controlled, like Calum in a way. He doesn't share himself easily, even now with me. We're working on that. Elspeth doesn't share with anyone, not the things that are deep in her heart. I've often wondered what would happen if Elspeth decided she wanted to claim a man as her brothers have claimed loves. She just could be explosive, Alek.''

"Am I supposed to be scared?" Alek had a quick flash of Elspeth, aroused and ready to fight him. He liked the image, savored it.

"A normal man would be. Petrovna males sometimes lack...shall we say delicacy and fear of an enraged woman?''

That night, Alek stepped back from the flames soaring against the night sky. Despite his hours gearing up at the newspaper, teaching and writing articles, Alek was restless, his emotions taut. The discarded boards and rubble ignited, matching the primitive need that had grown within Alek throughout the day. The flames reminded him of his wife crying out for help, her clothes burning—that was a distant nightmare.

The firelight illuminated a tall, strong pine tree, the top swaying in the night wind. His night with Elspeth vibrated through him, the heat of their bodies, the pagan way he had claimed her, the pounding of hearts and of bodies flying through passion.

Alek inhaled sharply and rubbed Elspeth's earring. Primitive...pagan...alive...happy—that was how he'd felt that night. As though nothing could keep him from…from having his woman.

He tossed a board on the flames and scowled as it ignited.

Two hours later, the fire had burned itself down to coals. Familiar now with Elspeth's daily schedule, Alek glanced at her home. A slender, curved body passed into the night, heading toward the fields. "Well, well. Things are looking up, Elspeth-mine," Alek murmured. Edges, he thought, all those nice little interesting edges to keep things from getting boring.

On a Saturday night, Amen Flats's single street was busy. Birk's motorcycle and Lacey's truck were parked at Maddy's Hot Spot. Carefully choosing her site on the field overlooking Amen Flats, Elspeth kneeled to unroll the blanket she'd draped across her shoulder. The occupants of the grass field—a buffalo herd—grazed peacefully a safe distance away. She took out her binoculars and notebook, braced the thermos of hot jasmine tea against a fallen limb and lay, stomach down, upon the blanket. She needed to escape the sight of Alek fighting his demons, his fists bunched, his body taut as he stared at the dying fire.

Elspeth knew he thought of wars and the fire and his wife. She shook her head, tossing the past away into the fragrant April night. Elspeth applied herself to the task she enjoyed, that of protecting Amen Flats in a subtle but effective way. Angela Tremany had been stalking Alek for two weeks. But Angela was also pressuring a younger man with a wife and newborn son. Angela's past record said she could be successful, the hunt more satisfying than keeping what she had caught. Alek could take care of himself, but young

Stephen needed protection. And Angela did not want to lose her wealthy older husband.

Angela's silver sports car cruised down Amen Flats's main street, then parked in the lot behind Stephen's office. Elspeth jotted the time in her notebook and picked up her binoculars. Dressed in a bustier, a thigh-revealing skirt and huge sunglasses, Angela slid into the office door.

A branch broke near her, and before Elspeth could jump to her feet, a big hand flattened on her back, staying her.

"My, my. Look what we have here," Alek drawled as he crouched beside her. Dressed in a black shirt and black jeans, Alek looked as if he could face any street gang. His shoulder-length hair curled damply to his shoulders; the moonlight caught on his scarred lip and skimmed across his broad shoulders. He'd showered, the soap scent clinging to him, blending with the fresh spring-earth fragrances.

Elspeth allowed him to turn her; she didn't protest as he eased her knitted cap from her hair and smoothed her single braid to her chest. She wouldn't fight him on any level, and soon he'd get bored. "I thought you were roasting marshmallows."

"This is more fun. What are you doing?"

Elspeth glared up at him. "Let me up."

"Sorry. Can't. You look too good that way." His amusement threatened her control, and his hand, though firm, gently held her wrist.

"I don't want to hurt you, Alek."

"Try, why don't you...." He issued the invitation in a slow Texas drawl and blew a kiss at her.

She moved quickly, but Alek's large hand splayed between her breasts, pushing her back. She lay quietly, barely breathing as he looked slowly down to his hand on her black sweater. He frowned, smoothing the softness gently, his fingertips trembling. His tone was deep and raw and achingly uneven. "Elspeth—"

Elspeth shifted restlessly. She wanted to clasp Alek's hand against her, to take his mouth. But kissing Alek meant she'd be opening herself. "I don't want to go over this again."

"No? Your heart is racing beneath my hand." His thumb moved, sweeping across the hardened tip of her breast. She gasped, trying to shield her emotions and failing.

Alek leaned closer, his black eyes gleaming in the night. "I'll have what I want from you, Elspeth—Petrovna's law. We finish what we begin." Then he bent to pull her against him.

For a heartbeat, she let down her guard, feeling very feminine, delicate and soft—then the hair lifted on the nape of her neck. This was Alek, a man bent on revenge.

His lips moved against her ear, sending tingles down her body. "So this is what you do before you go to the theater on Saturday nights and collect your free tub of popcorn. This is why Duncan and Calum don't want their wives with you on a Saturday night— you're a troublemaker, Elspeth." He nipped her ear. "What's next? The old movies you rent at the video store? Well...sweetheart, I like old movies," he said, imitating Humphrey Bogart.

The second stroke of his thumb set her temper simmering. His grin caught the moonlight, igniting her, and Elspeth reacted instantly. She grabbed his shirt and pushed hard, intending to leap free. A lifetime of pushy brothers had taught her a thing or two.

Alek grunted, fell back and swooped out an arm to catch her, jerking her lightly toward him.

Instinctively Elspeth straddled him and pinned his wrists beside his head. His body lurched just once upward against her, and he shuddered before lying beneath her. "Elspeth, I do believe that you are not always shy."

Elspeth realized to her horror that Alek was aroused.

"Now, this is more like it," he drawled in a deeply pleased tone. His wicked expression challenged her. "Ah-ha! The dominant position. I like games, especially ones with you. So you've tossed me on my back and straddled me. I'm your prisoner, Elspeth. I yield. Now what are you going to do with me?"

They both knew that he could easily overpower her, and Alek grinned up at her. He lifted his hips playfully and bounced her upon him; the movement forced her—an experienced horsewoman—to clamp her thighs tighter against his hips.

In her lifetime, no one played with her, treated her lightly. "This is no game, and we're not teenagers. I am going to get up, and you are going to let me." She braced her hands on his chest, aware that Alek's body thrust at her through the layers of their jeans.

"I feel like a boy around you...." The admission was dark, begrudging, and the look in Alek's expression denied her freedom. Beneath her, Alek was big and solid, his heart pounding against her braced hands. "How long do you think you can run from me? From what happened?" he asked softly, easing her hand to his mouth and brushing his lips across the palm.

She braced herself awkwardly above him, her breasts too close to his face as Alek slowly looked downward.

When his teeth nipped her fingertip, she refused to be intimidated. "I am not running from you, Alek."

"No? Then let's talk about it." He sucked her finger and sent her a look that said he wanted to taste her from toes to forehead and back down the other side. A bolt of heat shot to her lower stomach, startling her. Alek watched her as he slowly licked and sucked another finger.

"Alek..." She could almost taste his mouth on hers—fierce, hungry, delighted, tormenting—but fought the softening heat of her body and tried to breathe quietly.

"I knew we were making a baby that night, your heart pounding like a wild bird against me. Why didn't you stop me?"

Elspeth closed her eyes against Alek and the memory of that night, of Alek poised to enter her fully, shocked by her body's resistance.

Alek caressed her back, kneaded muscles taut and aching from hours at the loom. He went right for the tight knots, working them. Elspeth fought to hold her body still when it wanted to arch against him.

"Do you know what it does to a man to know he's been the first and probably the last man to love a woman?" Alek's voice was husky, deep, sweeping through her.

"Let me go, Alek. You've had your fun." In another minute, she'd be arching to the motion of his hand.

"Not yet, Elspeth. Not until you stand and fight and we settle what is between us. Not until you tell me what Una's journals say about the shawl's legend."

There was no softness in him as he rose to stand over her. He pulled her to her feet, and Elspeth stared at him, her mouth open. Alek Petrovna dared to treat her as if she were a child.

He wanted to treat her like a lover, the evidence bulging against the confinement of his jeans.

"What are you going to do with that?" he asked in that slow Texas drawl, and looked down at her fist. "Go ahead. Take your best shot."

She knew where to punch to knock the air from his inflated ego...but she wouldn't. Moonlight glinted off the edges of his teeth as he grinned, daring her. She wouldn't—

Then she did, and heard the satisfying grunt and the whoosh of air.

Elspeth tried to walk away slowly, then she began to run.

In her house, she ripped away her sweater and jeans and slid into a cool, old-fashioned gown, racing for her loom. She didn't want to know what was inside her, why she ached to have Alek hold her close and safe. On another level, her body recognized her first lover and ached with stark, primitive needs she didn't want to acknowledge.

She slid through the familiar, comforting shadows of her home, passing Una's journals on the living-room floor. Next to them was a huge wooden bread bowl, filled with arrowheads she used in her wall hangings. Elspeth probed the buckskin scraps, stick men painted on them, and found the envelope containing the pieces of the shawl's legend. She closed her eyes, willing herself back to safety. Suddenly she needed to know about the legend of Una's shawl. Her hands trembled as she shook the pieces from the envelope, and they tumbled into a square of moonlight on her woven rug.

Her fingers trembled as she eased the pieces into a page. The ink had been blurred by moisture, and the lines wavered, emotions sweeping from Una to the paper. *The Marrying Moon*. The moon had been a huge disk that night, lighting Alek's fierce expression and bathing their naked bodies in silver.

Melissa! Alek's cry had echoed through the night, spearing into her, killing her dreams.

Elspeth turned on the lamp, holding the pieces of paper up to it. Her instinct told her that Una's legend and Alek seemed entwined from that night.... Both were too close and too dangerous.

"A scarred warrior"—the piece fluttered from Elspeth's fingers, and she replaced it, running her finger across the other words: "mist," "mountain," "wind." References to a shawl punctuated Una's journals, but the entire legend was only on this page. It amused Una that Tallchief found the shawl so lovely, and she had blended a legend from his ancestry with hers. On another page Una had written,

Heat lives in the shawl. When a warrior wraps his lady love in it and the Marrying Moon is right, they will know the flames. I think my coppery-skinned husband blushes when I tell him this and he remembers that night beneath the Marrying Moon. He won't say the words, but he knows that something passed between us that night that would unite our souls forever.

Elspeth squeezed her lids closed. She'd believed so deeply from reading Una's journals that if she could just find the shawl, romance would come to her.

Romance was a foolish, girlish dream waylaid by

the necessities of survival and coming upon her later than most.

Elspeth rummaged through a file she had created years ago while trying to find the shawl. The shawl had been sold with the rest of Una's dowry to protect Tallchief land, and passed through several hands and then out of the country. Elspeth wanted that shawl desperately now; it was hers, and with it in her keeping she would be safe.... She wanted all the bits of the Tallchiefs' lives tucked safely within their keeping. They'd learned early to depend only on themselves in dangerous times, and she clung to that knowledge now.

She sensed the room's shadows shifting, and Alek tossed her gear onto the sofa. "You forgot this when you ran away. You've got quite a punch for someone who is supposed to be elegant and coolheaded."

She wanted to take *cool*, wrap it around his neck and squeeze tightly. "Get out."

He glanced at the journal and the torn pieces of the page. "That tells about the shawl, doesn't it? You've pledged to return it to the family. It bothers you that you've dropped your quest."

Alek braced his western boot on the low rock hearth beside her. He leaned closer to her. "Let me tell you something about quests, Elspeth. Either seek them out with everything you've got, run them down and claim them...or forget them. But I don't think you can forget the shawl. Would you like help?"

Elspeth came smoothly to her feet, thankful for the long cotton gown, high at the neck and sweeping her toes. "Leave, Alek."

His gaze swept down her loosened hair, to her breasts, taut against the well-washed cotton. He closed his eyes, and a muscle tightened in his jaw, a vein throbbing heavily in his throat. Then his eyes cut to hers. "If you would have told me about the baby, I would have married you...taken care of you. We could have made it work."

Her body jerked in response to the passion in his expression. "Stay away from me, Alek."

"Not likely." The bitter lines around his mouth deepened, and then he was gone.

An amateur playwright, Talia Petrovna demanded a party at Maddy's Hot Spot after the success of her Saturday-night play, *Beer and Boomerangs*. With the *Sentinel* ready to hatch, Alek should have been working with Brad.

The newspaper was what he wanted, to start that beautiful old equipment running, to write about small-town USA, Amen Flats, about new babies and tomatoes the size of basketballs. But words didn't hold him now; images of Elspeth distracted him too often to hold the thread of the story.

Full circle, Alek thought. He wanted to come full circle with Elspeth and this time to play for keeps.

He almost regretted Elspeth's contract with the Denver gallery. Almost. He'd set out to force her into interacting with him, and the contract would do that. Now he wanted time alone with her, without brothers to rescue her and without convenient separate living arrangements. The gallery would provide an ideal environment to manage the elusive Elspeth.

Manipulative? Yes. Hungry for her? Yes and yes. Used to being alone, without tethers, Alek turned the idea.

He'd left it to her to tell her brothers about their

past, and she hadn't yet. All hell would break loose the moment they knew.

Alek lifted a beer, blew the foam off it and nodded to Maddy for another. The beefy bartender chewed on an unlighted, worn cigar and waved to the sheriff's patrol car on the street. Maddy plopped a pitcher of beer on the table and groaned. "The sheriff has all the dogs stirred up. He's left his mike button on again. It's bad enough the sopranos are in heat, but does he have to try to sing with them? Jeez, he sounds like nails on a blackboard—throw in a bull moose in mating season."

Birk Tallchief—without Chelsey in tow—lifted the edge of a sheet draped over a painting of a nude woman. He peered under it. "I like that tall, fully stacked look. I don't know why you're desecrating good art."

Alek's gaze slid to Elspeth at another table. The long, lean look appealed to him.

Maddy's thick neck shortened as his jowls sank into his battered black T-shirt. "Women. They're delicate. Don't want any of them offended. Did you ever watch any of those temperance movies? The women stormed bars, took hatchets and smashed them to smithereens. Scared the hell out of me."

Alek watched the lines of dancing couples. "Line dancing. Whatever happened to men holding women against them, you know the old thigh-nudging thing and dips? The way a girl snuggled to a guy and he had both hands free to roam? The old blowing-into-her-ear thing? Slow dancing had its moments."

Talia laughed and cuddled against Calum. "I think someone is in a romantic mood...you're outdated, Alek."

"Is that so?" He surveyed the room, his gaze focusing on the woman he sought. Seated at a table with Sybil, Elspeth was deep in an intense conversation. Dressed in a black turtleneck sweater, loose slacks and a shawl, Elspeth had been snatched from her house by Talia. Elspeth's black hair was twisted in a fat, gleaming knot that caused Alek to want to loosen it, to feel it sift through his fingers. Small silver disks resembling moons dangled from her ears. *The Marrying Moon*...

Alek's fingers went to his earring, a new habit he'd recognized when thinking of Elspeth. The sight of her standing in that old-fashioned gown had had him wanting to pick her up and cradle her, soothing the past and giving her new memories.

Duncan and Calum and Birk shared an expression. Birk clapped a hand on Alek's shoulder. His wry tone was understanding. "Son, you're horny."

"Could be. The urge comes upon me infrequently, but I'd say I was ripe now." Alek looked straight at Duncan, who had already tensed.

"Pick someone else." Duncan's tone was low, primitive, a man protecting his loved one.

Calum studied Alek. "It's more than that. There's something running between them. He's set Elspeth on edge."

Edges. Alek should have been satisfied that the Tallchiefs recognized the cracks showing in Elspeth's life. He wasn't. He wanted to smooth those lovely, secretive edges. The Tallchiefs knew something brewed between the eldest Tallchief sister and himself, and Alek had no doubt that he'd be called out if they knew it was a baby. From what he'd heard of Fiona, the sister causing trouble in Wisconsin, she'd raise hell if she knew.

Tonight his thoughts were drawn to necking in a back seat and the taste of hunger on Elspeth's lips..,.

Talia stood instantly, clearly prepared to smooth any tense moments between the Tallchiefs and her brother. "Come on. I've been waiting for this." She tossed a tape at Maddy. "Play that, will you?"

"Like I have a choice," Maddy grumbled, and padded off to the tape player. "Probably some stuff with fiddles that think they're violins."

The high-voltage sounds of a Russian folk song filled the room, surprising the country-music dancers. Maddy went down behind the bar, protecting himself from the barrage of plastic roses used as table decorations that came flying at him. Talia moved into the open space, placed her Hessian boots in position and lifted her arms. "Alek?"

He groaned and rose slowly to his feet. He glanced at Calum. "You should be doing this. Anton and I will give you Talia's Petrovna dances. She has no idea if they are authentic, but it was either that or eat her meals of an indefinable origin."

"Alek!" Waiting for him, Talia clapped dramatically and stamped her boots.

"Do something, Alek. My wife is pregnant. See that she doesn't hurt herself," Calum ordered in the tone of a western gunslinger.

"You'll have to learn this, Calum. No more of that Latin smooth stuff if you want to keep up with the Petrovnas." Alek glanced at Elspeth and knew he would dance for her.

Talia began dancing, moving her boots to an intricate step and weaving to the music as it grew faster.

Alek picked her up and held her as he lifted his free arm, going around and around. Talia laughed, and together they began an intricate, fast-paced dance, boots stomping. They shouted and swirled around the room with Talia laughing up at Alek. When the music was almost finished, Alek lifted her and gently twirled her into Calum's waiting arms.

Another fiery folk tune caused the western crowd to groan. Alek's heart pounded with his exertion, and with another passion. He knew what he wanted. He walked across the room to stand by Elspeth. The room quieted suddenly, and he sensed that everyone was watching; he didn't care who knew that he was coming for her. Elspeth glanced at him and flushed. Before she looked away, Alek caught the smoky anger in her eyes.

Smoke and steel, he thought. Heat. Passion. Soft mouth and gentle heart.

In the next instant, Alek caught Elspeth's hand, drawing her to her feet. He lifted her high, treasured her slender body in his hands and slowly lowered her against him. She'd been smiling as Talia and he danced, and the curve of her mouth remained, enchanting Alek. He caressed her lower lip with his thumb, brushing the soft indentations at the corners.

The magic was still there, coursing dark through her gray eyes. Was it the passionate music still playing in his mind, his body? He tossed that thought away; Elspeth had made his body pound, his heart need. Alek ran his finger beneath her chin and lifted it. Slowly, taking his time, he placed his lips on hers and waited. After a long heartbeat, her mouth lifted to his, pushing slightly, returning the brief kiss.

Alek caressed her waist, lost in the feel of her softness vibrating beneath his hands.... She began to respond slowly, magnificently.

There, Alek mused. There was the edge, the silvery gleam of passion streaking in her smoky eyes.

The hoots and wolf whistles started, then stopped when Elspeth drew herself up and stared at the crowd, which quieted immediately.

Alek stepped back and nodded. He'd thrown down another challenge, and Elspeth's cool veneer had begun to melt. He chose to leave her, let her simmer for the moment. Because if her protective walls began to crumble now, Alek didn't trust himself. He turned his back and walked away, and in every step sensed her uncertainty. He'd touched her, reached for her bruised heart, and gotten inside for a moment. However Elspeth liked to hide in her quiet shadows, in her loose clothing, she wasn't immune to him. Nor could he walk away from her unaffected; he'd wanted to carry her out into the moonlight and— His hand shook as he raised his mug to drain it. He didn't want to feel tenderness for Elspeth. Nor the need to lock himself close to her, thrust into that lean body of hers and let her satisfy his hunger.

Alek shifted restlessly. A forty-year-old man who had seen everything and done most of it shouldn't be desperate for a taste of a woman who didn't want him.

The three Tallchief brothers got slowly to their feet, and three forbidding frowns pinned him. Instantly Sybil, Lacey and Talia swooped and drew the brothers into a western two-step dance.

Alek propped his boots on an empty chair and met Elspeth's dark stare. He watched as she slowly rose and gathered her shawl about her.

Alek caught her at the door, his hand shooting past

her head to open it. Elspeth did not look at him, but swept out into the night. Elegant, he thought, pure elegance of a lady who is just about to lose her temper.

Alek caught her within ten steps, walking along with her. She slanted him a cool look. "I prefer to walk alone."

He looked at the round moon and inhaled her fragrance and kept walking beside her. "It could be dangerous."

Still keeping his gaze, she snapped her fingers and instantly, Olaf and Thorn appeared from the shadows. Talia and Duncan's huge dogs were gentle with children and dangerously protective of the Tallchiefs. The sheriff, playing a Caruso tape loudly, paused on his drive through town. Both dogs howled, lifting their heads to the moon. The sheriff turned the music down, and the dogs quieted. His spotlight hit them.

"I can tell when those dogs are around that the Tallchiefs are together. Who's that with you, Elspeth?"

"Talia's brother, Alek."

"Alek Petrovna? The guy on television? Heard he's putting out the old newspaper in another week. See if you can get his autograph, okay?" The sheriff's patrol car glided down the street to Caruso's vibrating tenor.

With his finger, Alek scribbled "Petrovna" on her back.

She jumped, glaring at him. "How dare you! Don't think you can pick me up and kiss me like that, Alek. It looked like…like a claiming…as though you were making certain that everyone knew that you wanted me…as though you were pasting a big She's Mine sign on me. Everyone saw—and then you had the nerve to—"

"Hey, the sheriff asked for my autograph, okay?"
He bent nearer, enjoying her heated expression.

"Oh!" Elspeth turned and walked a few steps with
him at her side. She rounded on him again. "Never—
repeat, never—write 'Petrovna' on me, and while I'm
at this, don't ever kiss me again, Alek."

"I like kissing you, Elspeth-mine. I'd like to catch
up on that necking, too." To reinforce his statement
and to ease his need, Alek bent to brush his lips across
hers. "Ah, you're a fierce woman, Elspeth. When you
come calling for me, I might be half-afraid to step into
all that passion. You'll have to hold my hand and woo
me."

"If I came calling for you, Alek, it would be to end
this."

"End it, but first you'll have to stand and fight me.
You'll have to clear out what's between us," he challenged, then bent to kiss her ear and blow into it.
"You're hot for me, Elspeth...sweet on me. Admit
it."

Her head went back, but before she could slash at
him, Alek jerked her into his arms and placed the tip
of his tongue exactly in the part of her mouth. He
kissed her thoroughly, fitting the slender, taut shape of
her body to him, absorbing her into his loneliness,
feeding upon the warmth stirring within her. Then Elspeth's lips moved to his, and her head slanted and
rested upon his shoulder, cupped by his palm. Something savage, haunting and painful settled within Alek
as he held her. He wrapped his arms around her waist
and lifted her against him until her eyes were at a level
with his.

"I like touching you and kissing you, Elspeth."

When he placed his face in the curve of her throat

and shoulder, her fingers hovered, then stroked his cheek. Her heart raced against his skin. She tensed, her voice a whisper. "Do you?"

"It's not necking, but it's a promising start," he admitted.

"I've never necked."

"Then you're behind, too. Care to catch up? My pickup has new upholstery."

"That rattletrap. Whatever you paid for it, it was too much."

"I've never had a chance as an adult to putter and repair, to make things right. I like it."

Her fingers splayed through his hair, played with the curls and touched the earring. "Petrovna, we both know that you can't stand here all night, holding me like this. You'll get tired eventually."

Then Elspeth bent her head and nipped his lip. She said quietly, "Thorn...Olaf...come," and the two huge dogs leapt, bracing their paws on Alek's back, waiting for Elspeth's next command. "You'd better put me down," she said quietly. "They might think you're detaining me."

She was wrong. He could hold her all night. "I'd like to. Or you could detain me, like you did that night you played detective."

"There are people who need protecting. You don't."

She'd needed protection from him that long-ago night, and he'd been too wrapped in his grief and passion to recognize it. "Who held you when you cried, Elspeth?" he asked quietly, lowering her to her feet.

The flash of emotion in her expression told him more than he wanted to know; Elspeth had never allowed anyone to comfort her since the death of her parents. She'd always been so strong for the rest of the Tallchiefs. Yet he'd held her that night in the tepee and knew how terribly fragile she was.

This time, Alek didn't try to hold her when she moved away. He shoved his hands into his back pockets to keep from reaching for her as she walked away.

The taste of Elspeth lasted long into the night. To keep his sanity, Alek began writing queries for the shawl. Clive Hardeness in London was friendly with a group of specialized antique collectors, and he would be a good place to start. Alek rubbed his earring and looked at the midnight light in Elspeth's studio. He would have what Elspeth sought and he would know why she had whispered, "The Marrying Moon."

Five

"Elspeth!" Mark Redman hurried across the gallery's office to greet her. Outside the gallery, May sunshine spread like warm butter over Denver's streets.

In Amen Flats, the *Sentinel* had become a three-week success story. Alek had worked night and day, giving her some reprieve from the noise next door to her. There was no reprieve from the jump in her heart, the tightness of her throat each time Alek looked at her. Focused, she corrected. Alek had focused upon her and was testing her, playing games that didn't interest her.

She told herself that again…that Alek's games didn't appeal. He was out to prove something, and she wouldn't have any of it. She could hold her distance, she told herself, and he'd get bored. While she was away from Amen Flats, she'd forget his taunting kisses and the way her blood heated at his torments. She'd return to Amen Flats, restored and without thoughts of Alek.

A pleasant businessman in his thirties, Mark wore a loose silk shirt and slacks, and his long hair was in a ponytail. He took in her leather vest, chambray blouse and woven belt, long skirt, soft moccasins. He grinned as his practiced fingers traveled over her woven bag. "Perfect. Just the artsy look that sells. Keep the braids, will you? Sometimes we get an artist who looks just fine, and then the night of the opening, they go off and change it."

Mark touched her vest's leather fringes, decorated with beads. She didn't mind his examination of her woven belt, the intricate, ancient designs. "Perfect. You look great in the Tallchief plaid, too. We've sent out invitations to our clients, and they'll love to meet you. You saw the brochure we did on you? I want you to be comfortable about how you're managed."

"The brochure was wonderful, and the braids are here to stay." Elspeth allowed Mark to hold her hand. She liked him, this easygoing man who had stopped by her booth one day and asked about her work. An expert on wools and textures, Mark had presented a comfortable advance on the contract to deal with his gallery exclusively for two years. She saw no problem when he'd asked her to promote her work by making appearances.

Mark studied her face. "You're tired. Probably scared about the showing and working too hard. Take the day to rest, will you? We've got to wow them tomorrow night."

"I'll be fine, Mark...if your assistants don't think my driftwood for free-form wall hangings are firewood. They're from Tallchief Lake."

"We'll take care of them. You're comfortable with the showing schedule we worked out? You're okay to travel with the exhibits after the showing? Having the artist there to explain technique will add up to sales. Did you bring me anything new?" Mark rubbed his hands together; he sounded like a child at Christmas.

She liked the friendly way he draped his arm across her shoulder. Then she moved away, unused to comfortable men. "I have new pieces. They're out in my van."

Mark pushed the intercom buzzer. "Make certain Ms. Tallchief's things are taken to the apartment, will you? Bring her work to me." He winked at Elspeth. "I can't wait. My partner says you're certain to set record sales and your price will go up. He'll be at the opening tomorrow night. He's the one who really liked your work in the first place. He's already bought several pieces."

"Really? That just shows he has good taste. I look forward to meeting him. Who is he?"

Mark chuckled. "He's the silent end of the deal. He bought in as a silent partner in December. Prefers to handle his own introductions. The guy has a big past— has traveled everywhere and has made a bundle in investments. He's a celebrity wanting to remain anonymous, and I respect his wishes. I like him, and he's been good for building a new clientele. It's kind of cute to see a big tough guy go all woozy over your work. He touches it as if he revered every thread. Once he pointed your work out to me, I recognized your talent right away."

After two and a half months of Alek invading her life, Elspeth looked forward to Mark's offer of the gallery's apartment, to traveling with the exhibit for the next two weeks...and escaping Alek Petrovna.

Mark showed her around the gallery, explaining to her about the natural light bringing out the colors of her work. Mark latched on to her weaving like a mother hen picking over her chicks.

"What's this? Not your usual," he said as an assistant brought in one of her new works.

The hanging was slender, lacking the Native American elements of her other work. The tightly woven, hand-spun wool had leaped into her fingers, pale stripes of mauve and tan. In places, she'd used a fork as a beater, keeping the weave tight and heavy. In others, the weave was looser, freer. The weft, running horizontally, was tighter in places, giving a curve that flowed throughout the piece. She'd kept the frame simple to highlight her weaving. The colors heated to gold and dark red, circling a pale cream center with one burst of brilliant vermilion, then eased to deep waves of mauve and tan.

Mark skimmed his hand down the uneven, nubby texture. "Emotion vibrates in this. The colors shouldn't work, not in that design...but they do. It's almost alive beneath my touch. What's the theme? Life? No, nothing so broad. Its message is infinite, too deep to explain—the heat and feeling in it just fly out. Is it titled? We'll have to put something really pricey and obscure sounding on it."

"I haven't decided." The colors had come to her at sunset, the dying light glistening in the wool, the texture—now smooth, now rough—presented shadows upon its surface. Elspeth didn't want to think about what she had created, or why it was different from the rest. The design and texture had sprung from her heart, unfettered by her plans and sketches.

The making of this work had cost her, wrung something from her that both hurt and gave joy. The elements in her other work sprang from her heritage, but this was new, coming from her alone.

Mark jotted a note. "Names...titles, hike up the price. Make a list. We'll pencil it in later. By the way, my partner has ordered some dresses for you...for the promotion events. They're pricey, but just the thing to present you this first time."

"Mix...mingle...talk wool. Make sales." Mark glanced down at Elspeth's cerulean blue silk gown, which was supported by two tiny straps. A shimmering fringe ran across the bodice, then the gown clung, defining her slender body until it flared from her calves to her feet. Mark eyed her hair, pulled straight back into an elegantly twined chignon. "Wow! What a babe!"

Elspeth shot him a frown. Her stomach ached, and she rubbed her palms together. "Don't grin. You know I'm nervous. You have no idea how I dislike this...packaging. The clothes in the apartment are too many, too expensive and...exotic. I feel naked enough with my work on display." She resisted telling him about the mountain of seductive lingerie, scraps of lace and satin she'd found among the clothes.

"Just part of the game...don't want a little-villager image who sells cheap." Mark flipped the blue topaz beads at her ear. He touched her bare upper arm. "You've got muscles, kid. It's exciting to know that a strong woman created your work. Just a selling point my partner thinks will work as we package you for the public.''

"I'm not the exhibit. My work..." Elspeth began. Her head throbbed, and in another minute she would return to her room. The gallery was packed, brightly lighted and everything she wanted to avoid.

The guests wanted too much, picking at the pieces of her life. One woman wanted to know if Elspeth had children, and how nice it was to pass a feminine tradition down to children.

Elspeth ignored the familiar pain and answered that her works were her children.

"I must have that," a woman told her husband, pointing to the untitled hanging. "I'm not much on that Native American–theme stuff and plastic arrowheads, but this would be great in our bedroom—it's so sensuous, so erotic.''

"Plastic arrowheads," Elspeth muttered to Mark.

"Shh.''

Mark leaned closer to Elspeth. "Do more like that...the erotic stuff. We'll pick up another clientele—''

"Not a chance—''

Mark turned, his expression lighting as he shook hands with Alek Petrovna. "Hey, guy. We've been waiting for you. This is Elspeth Tallchief, one talented weaver woman.''

Alek, dressed in a collarless black silk shirt under an expensive suit jacket and loose slacks, loomed at her side. His brows and lashes gleamed in the bold light, his cheekbones cut at angles across his face and there was nothing soft about his mouth and jaw. His scars and shoulder-length, unruly hair only added to his dangerous look, drawing women's eyes. Alek did not look away from Elspeth. One eyebrow lifted, mocking her. He took Elspeth's hand and raised it to his lips. He did not let it go at her first tug.

The shawl draped around his shoulders was fringed and elegant, fluttering as he moved. Elspeth noted the merino wool and the fiery gold-and-red design made in Paisley, Scotland.

Una's shawl.

She almost ripped it from him, but didn't only because she treasured the fine work and her heritage. The man was another matter. Alek had found a new way to enter her life. The shawl was his declaration. Aware that the crowd was focused on Alek, a tall, striking man dressed in a suit and a fiery feminine shawl, she rounded on Mark. She sheathed her fury in a whisper. "Is this your partner? Is this the man that I'm supposed to travel with, to the exhibits?"

She could feel the snarl of anger curling in her. Alek should have looked silly in the shawl; he didn't. The soft, fiery texture only enhanced his dark skin and black, amused eyes, and she hated him more for that.

Surprised by her hushed fury, Mark was alarmed. "Well, yes. Alek is my partner. He pointed me to your work. I'm glad he did. The first pieces we sold brought a hefty price, but with this showing that will go up. Elspeth, this is Alek—"

She rubbed her temples, her headache pounding. "I know who he is. Mark, you should have told me—"

"I'm her admirer. Let's not belabor details, Elspeth. Mark, don't sell that piece. It's her best work, and let's show it off." Alek reached out the flat of his hand to caress the hanging in a blatantly sexual manner that took her breath away. Then he wrapped his arm around her waist and eased her through the crowd, despite her resistance. "I knew blue would look good on you."

They were on the patio and alone. Elspeth jerked free and gripped the wooden railing. In another minute, she'd— "What do you think you're doing?"

Her earring gleamed in his ear, challenging her.

Clearly bothered by Alek's commandeering and Elspeth's unexpected temper, Mark strolled into their battlefield. He looked worriedly from Elspeth to Alek. "Is everything okay?"

"Go away, Mark," Alek murmured. "She's just a bit nervous."

"Yes, please, Mark. Go away. I'll be fine." Elspeth wanted Alek to herself. She wanted to strangle him. He'd invaded her life and now her heritage. When they were alone, she said, "I want that shawl. How much?"

"You'll have to fight me for it, love. Or you could tell me about the Marrying Moon."

Every nerve in Elspeth's body stretched taut. No one had ever dared to toy with her, to push her as Alek had done. She wasn't certain how she might react, but with Alek the prospect excited her more than weaving. "You deliberately packaged yourself in something that is mine. This could be war."

"Mmm. I'm not going anywhere. Do your damnedest." He leaned to brush a kiss on her nose, playing with her.

"You'd better take care of it. You chose this—" her hand swept down her gown "—and those bits of lace called lingerie. Alek Petrovna, you are a jerk.... Where did you get that shawl?"

"As a matter of fact, Talia picked the lingerie. I told her I wanted to give a woman friend something nice. Since I've been out of the lingerie game for a while and you were the wearee, my taste ran to bare flesh and nothing else. She has matching styles that she wears for Calum alone. The shawl is from a Paisley shawl collector. Sybil described it to me perfectly. It needs a broach, don't you think?'' Alek's hand caressed the shawl.

She couldn't let him get away with that. Elspeth caught his curls in her fist and drew his face down to her level. He didn't deserve kindness. He'd invaded her privacy; she didn't intend him to leave unmarked. Alek's kisses had been hot and hungry, leaving her without a complete thought. She intended to do the same to him and maybe more. Elspeth tossed away the red flag of caution tugging at her; Alek needed a lesson, and she intended to give it to him.

''Here's a challenge for you, Mr. Petrovna.''

She intended the kiss to be sensual, but she hadn't prepared for the instant tenderness he returned, the gentle tempo of his lips brushing hers lightly and hers following his. He tasted of everything she'd missed and everything she wanted to grasp selfishly for herself. Unaccustomed to greed, Elspeth reeled in the need to vanquish Alek, to pit herself against him. She moved closer, allowed her body to lightly touch his. Alek tensed, the movement satisfying her.

No, it didn't. Nothing could satisfy her but bringing him to his knees.

A siren wailed in the street below as Elspeth trailed a fingertip down his cheek and watched his expression harden. Because she knew she must, Elspeth stood on tiptoe and lightly kissed the scar on Alek's lip.

He jerked her to him, wrapped his arms around her waist and hauled her into the shadows of the potted bushes. Elspeth gripped the shawl with both fists. "Alek, you're over your head."

"Am I? You'll have to show me, won't you?" Alek's hands went beneath the soft shawl. He touched her breasts lightly, tracing the shape of them. Elspeth breathed quietly, uncertain now. His prowling fingertip slipped beneath the bodice and stroked her softness. She wanted to be immune to his touch, to walk away unaffected. Alek leaned close to her, placed his scarred cheek against her smooth one and stood very still, allowing her the freedom to walk away. He wasn't holding her; he breathed heavily, his fingertips smoothing her breasts, following the shape of her slowly. Then his hands cupped her breasts firmly, possessively. He bent slowly to place his face in the curve of her throat and shoulder. Her heart pounded heavily, racing.... The woman in her stirred, softened and wanted....

Elspeth closed her eyes. Alek wasn't taking; he was giving himself to her care. Nothing could have been more effective.

His lips moved, kissing her throat, and she feared to breathe, her fingers fluttering against the soft wool around his shoulders.

She wanted him against her, deep inside where heat forged them as one—where the pounding of their blood couldn't be defined as his or hers.

She'd have him frothing and then she'd walk away, leaving him to simmer in what he had started. There would be no Petrovna's law where she was concerned; Alek had tossed her a challenge she couldn't resist.

Elspeth slid her hands under his suit, caressed his chest and placed one palm over his heavily beating heart. Alek tensed, then ripped away the shawl and his jacket and caught Elspeth close again. "Touch me. Make me feel, Elspeth."

He pulled the pins from her hair, releasing it and burying his face in it. Elspeth fought the emotions rising in her; she was too susceptible to Alek's tender touch.

Alek bent and lifted her in his arms. He raised her to kiss her throat. Elspeth dug her fingers into his shoulders, shaking, fighting. She hesitated, poised at the edge of a dangerous abyss, hovering between staying in the shadows and taking what she desired.

Desire. Heat. Hunger.

Alek's heated face pressed against her throat, and he dragged aside one strap of her dress with his teeth, instantly claiming her breast with his lips. Shocked by the intimate heat, the laving of his tongue, Elspeth tensed, caught on the edge of surprise and delight. Another flick of his tongue, the edge of his teeth, and she fought the fire rising in her, stepped into heated space and gave herself to the gentle suckling until she was shaking. She pressed his head against her, running her fingers through the black curls and gave herself to the heat of his mouth, the sensations coursing through her, the need to be alive, to take, to give. When Alek lowered her, she raised her arms to capture him and gave him her mouth.

He was gentle, tempting her tongue with his.

She was on fire, wanting him closer.

This was Alek, her Alek, her lover and— He groaned unevenly, shaking in her arms, exciting her. His hands trembled when he touched her lightly, and it wasn't enough. Elspeth nipped at his throat, and Alek shuddered; his hands smoothed her hips, then locked to her and pushed her against his steely need.

His palms ran down her thighs, trembling, easing the gown higher until he touched her soft, quivering thighs. His fingers explored the lacy elastic of her stockings and then found the satin lace covering her femininity.

She moved slightly, and his fingers caressed the damp satin, sliding inside to the heat—— "Alek!"

His body supported her as the pounding, the intimate clenching, began, riveting her until she climbed the peak and then gently, slowly melted against him.

Alek shook, taut with need as he kissed her and soothed the tremors running through her. "Elspeth," he whispered hoarsely against her loosened hair.

His tone sent her tumbling into another time, when another woman's name crossed his lips.

Reality and shame came creeping softly to her. She wanted to walk away and couldn't, her legs still trembling. Alek had taken her beyond what she wanted, to prove she could take him down——

He smoothed her hair, drawing her head to rest on his chest. "Let me hold you."

Alek rocked her gently, and Elspeth gave herself to a safety she hadn't known since her parents died. She should have moved away; she couldn't. She closed her eyes and knew that she didn't want to think, to fight him...not now.

"You are not a nice man. I think I'm going to kill you," she said finally, faced with the reality of a gallery filled with clients already curious about her. She had to get away; she'd exposed her needs. She trembled and waited for Alek to speak. In another minute, she'd shatter....

He brought her hair to his lips, his eyes burning as

he looked down at her. "Blush is definitely your color."

Alek turned her and began combing her hair. She shivered, emotions streaking through her; she'd just threatened to kill him—not seriously—but she intended to nick him in a few places where it would count.

The novelty of being tended startled Elspeth; usually she was the caregiver. "You've done this before."

Of course he had; Alek Petrovna had devoured experienced women. "I had baby sisters. Anton couldn't be trusted not to tie their hair in knots."

She didn't believe him, not for a moment. Alek had touched her with experience.

Mark suddenly appeared in the lighted doorway. "Come on, Elspeth. They want to meet you. She's been nervous all day, Alek."

"She's relaxed a bit." Alek's Texas drawl was back and filled with amusement. He stared down at her, the angles of his face rigid and reflecting his desire for her. She'd done that much at least—raised his desire. A quick learner, she could have him panting and giving her the shawl....

He jerked her hair lightly, forcing her to look at him over her shoulder. "You'll have to work a bit harder to get that shawl, my fair Elspeth," he whispered huskily.

"You think I...?" She began to wonder if her hands would fit around Alek's thick neck.

Mark came closer, clearly curious about Alek combing Elspeth's hair. Alek made one long braid, then reached to neatly tear away a fringe from her bodice, which he used to tie off the braid.

Mark moved to Elspeth's back. "Good job. Gave

her a neck massage, did you? Good for tense muscles.
I should have thought of that—the Native American
look mixed with a contemporary businesswoman. You
missed a strand, Alek. Do it again.''

"Do you want to?" Alek was not amused.

"Heck, no. You won't catch me braiding a girl's
hair. Your hands are shaking. Alek, you look like you
want to strangle someone. Be cool, guy. She'll be
okay—''

"I think tomorrow I'll strangle you slowly," Alek
muttered darkly.

"Will the two of you stop?" Elspeth wanted to escape Alek's touch and her shattered emotions and the
people waiting for her.

Somehow she managed the evening, taunted by
Alek wearing Una's bright shawl around his broad
shoulders. Folded triangularly, the fiery red-and-gold
point shot off one shoulder, the fringes dancing as he
moved. He wasn't prettily handsome, his features too
rugged. The scars on his cheek and lip enhanced his
masculinity, and the soaring scar in his eyebrow
needed a woman's touch to smooth it.

Looking like a dangerous pirate, he caught the attention of a lush brunette, who snagged his arm. He
smiled down at her, and the woman issued an open
invitation by leaning closer and licking her glossy lips.
A blonde slid her hand through his other arm, and
Alek laughed outright at something she said.

The blonde pushed her breasts against him and
spoke intently. Alek leaned down to listen, the woman's red lips almost touching the earring—LaBelle's
earring—and Elspeth found her hand curled into a fist.
His hand rested on the woman's waist—

Elspeth lifted her head. He had held her only

minutes ago, his tall body rigid and trembling against hers. Now he had another body against him and another one just as willing. Alek's charm flashed across the room to Elspeth, and she tossed it back with a light "no, thank you" smile.

He said something to the women and moved purposefully through the gallery crowd toward Elspeth. She wouldn't move away from his advance; she wouldn't give him the satisfaction. When he came to her side, she leveled a cold look at him. A swaggering, arrogant, hot-for-sex pirate was exactly what she did not want in the arena of her life.

Alek placed his hand on her waist and walked her across the gallery. As they stood in front of "Untitled," his hand dropped an inch lower to rest on her hip, fingers splayed possessively. Pushing, she thought. Always pushing.

"'Untitled' is very erotic. What about titling it 'The Second Encounter'?" Alek had loosened the top buttons at his throat. Elspeth recognized the mark on his skin; caught in her startling passion, she had nipped at him.

Alek rubbed his temple, fighting a headache. He was tired and drained, fighting years of sleeplessness and the constant need of Elspeth. The steady sensual humming in his body wasn't helping his concentration. He clicked off his computer laptop and stood, stretching cramped muscles. Dressed only in his shorts, he padded to the bed in the gallery's lower apartments and lifted the shawl against him. He had pushed Elspeth too hard, and tonight the walls had gone down. Whatever Elspeth felt about him, there was no mistaking her passion or her need to take him down. It had frightened and angered her, raising the color in her cheeks and deepening her smoky gray eyes.

He loved her.

He'd begun to hunt her with rage and then a clinical, cutting revenge, tethering her with the contract. Along the way, he'd fallen in love with her. Maybe he'd always been in love with her since that haunting night in Scotland.

A noise drew him to the empty, darkened gallery. Elspeth, wrapped in an old flannel robe, stood before "Untitled," studying her work. Wool drifted from her hand, as though "Untitled" had drawn her from her weaving.

Alek closed the door, allowing her privacy. He drew the shawl across his cheek, pressing it against his face. The merino wool was soft and light with a life of its own...he wanted Elspeth to want him as much as she wanted the shawl. If he came to Elspeth now, he'd want to make love with her, and though tonight had shown him a flash of her passion, he wanted more than a quickening from Elspeth.

He wanted her awakening.

"All right, Alek. You've had your fun. I'll buy Una's shawl. How much?" Elspeth leaned back against the van's passenger seat and faced the passing scenery. After a week of press interviews and parties, they were on their way to the first exhibit in another gallery.

She could have walked out, dismissing the contract. But she was a Tallchief, bred to honor commitments. Until her obligations were met, Alek had her within reach. He'd waited, and now they were alone. Alek rubbed LaBelle's earring. "The shawl is not for sale."

When she turned to him, her sunglasses like mirrors, Alek placed a dried apricot against her lips. Elspeth had her vices, he'd discovered, and dried apricots were definitely a priority. Hand-feeding Elspeth was an experience he savored. Or was it torture to watch her lips curve around the morsel, her teeth bite into it? She'd actually taken what he had offered. He rubbed her lip with his thumb and sucked an orange tidbit into his mouth. "The shawl requires the legend."

"It's my heritage," Elspeth muttered around the apricot.

"So's the legend. They're a package deal. You give me one, and I give you the other."

"The Paisley mills in Scotland produced excellent work from the early 1700s on. The shawls are pure art. Only a—"

"I admire art," he stated, comfortable with whatever names she would call him.

She stared at him, one sleek black brow lifted in disbelief. "You blockhead."

"Sweetheart. Baby-doll." Alek grinned when Elspeth's mouth curved slightly.

"I'm not a baby-doll. You've got the wrong woman, Alek."

"Have I?" Alek tugged her sunglasses away; he wanted to see her eyes, watch the color change shades with her emotions. When he told her what lay between them, he wanted to see her eyes. "I haven't been with another woman since that night, Elspeth."

Again Elspeth lifted a disbelieving, sleek eyebrow in his direction.

That grated. "You're not making this easy, Elspeth. I'm sharing a bit of Petrovna insight here. My sex life is a private matter."

"Oh, I'm sure," she murmured too easily.

Alek passed a truck and, after checking his rearview mirror, swerved back into the lane. He glanced at her rigid expression, the set of her jaw. Elspeth had plenty to chew on; she might as well hear more. There was nothing like baring his soul to a woman who would walk away from him the moment she could. Okay, he was a sucker for pain, Alek thought as he plunged on. "I loved Melissa. I told her not to come to me, not to enter the war zone, but it was our anniversary and she wanted…us to be together."

Alek tightened his fingers on the steering wheel, his knuckles white with tension. He swerved to avoid a squirrel and dropped back into the terror years ago. "The rocket was a direct hit in the tiny room. It exploded instantly, and Melissa screamed. I'll never forget the sound of—shrieks, blind, terrified, shrieks of pain—"

"Alek…" Elspeth touched his hand; he locked her fingers with his, bringing their clasped hands to his thigh.

He took her hand and brought her fingertips to his mouth. "I'd seen everything by then—hungry orphans, starving elderly, mass graves in war-torn countries. Melissa's dying was—"

"Alek, those things are in the past." Elspeth's voice ran on a thin, trembling thread, snaring him with her emotions.

He kissed her palm, studied her slender, capable fingers. "The past is with us, just like my scars, and I want you to understand. After…I knew what I had to do, to hurt you…to make the break clean. You had your whole life ahead of you, and I had nothing.

Maybe I got scared, so I said what I had to and left you.''

Her wary expression hurt him more than he'd expected. He pulled a small, worn envelope from his pocket and handed it to her.

She carefully opened and eased a tattered woven swatch from the envelope. Her fingers trembled, running over the wool. ''It's mine. I was studying mordants to set the color and used copperas on this. The dye is a heather olive.''

''I found heather sprigs and the swatch stuck to my clothing. The heather crumbled right away.'' He'd crushed it, diving under twisted barbed wire. The swatch was all he'd had left of Elspeth, a silly little bit of cloth that had reminded him of life and tenderness and hope.

She looked down, then away into the mountains, the sunlight skimming her high cheekbones and sweeping down her bare throat. There beneath her lightly tanned skin, a vein pulsed heavily, and Alek prayed it was because she thought of him.

Six

"Alek, this isn't working. You're intruding into my life. *I do not like you acting as though I am your possession.*" The storm outside equaled Elspeth's raw emotions. A week and a half of Alek invading her life, snaring her into sleepless nights, was taking a toll on her nerves. She opened the apartment door to Mark, who had returned to the gallery's apartment with cartons of Chinese food. She helped him place them on the coffee table, then sat on the couch and began filling their plates.

She'd missed the closeness of a family, eating together and sharing small talk over the table.

Alek glanced up from his laptop computer, a pencil shoved over his ear. In a startling change from whatever interested him to complete absorption with her, he spoke quietly. "I have to get this story done. Why don't you tell me what's bothering you? Don't spare my feelings.''

"I *was* telling you, Alek." Thunder crashed as he watched her with interest. "You're steaming, Elspeth. Come on, let it all out."

"Will you two kiss and make up?" Mark complained. "It's safer out there in the lightning storm than in here with you. You've been like this since you got back from that last trip. Neither one of you look like you've had a minute's sleep."

Elspeth placed the points of her chopsticks on his chest. "You mutter when you're distracted, Mark. Alek hovers. You both are—"

She inhaled a quieting breath and began again. "I am not used to being pampered...to being tucked in at night. He physically dragged me away from my work and plopped me in bed, Mark. He brings me a breakfast tray in the morning. Alek actually told a very nice man that he didn't deserve one of my hangings."

She ached from the long day, traveling to the showing with Alek, and she...she didn't want to share herself with Alek, who watched her carefully from what she ate to... Elspeth had just noted that his hair needed trimming and he'd lost weight. Alek Petrovna was not a man to care for himself, his needs untended. Her gaze skimmed him, from dress shirt to worn jeans and socks. He needed a shave and someone to care for him. She glanced at his rumpled shirt, opened at the collar and revealing a soft curl of black hair. She didn't want to care—

"That *nice* man was trying to pick her up. He stroked the painting, put his hands on it while he was looking right down her dress. We're going back to Amen Flats." Alek glanced down Elspeth's loose pink

sweater, her black slacks and her bare feet. Elspeth
curled her toes, aware that Alek's close inspection
raised her senses to a danger level. With him, she felt
feminine and cherished; she didn't like the feeling, nor
the sense that Alek wanted to make up for not being
close when she needed him. Elspeth realized suddenly
how empty her life had been since that night.

Thunder rattled the windows, storm clouds rolling
across the sky outside, and she felt as fragile as the
bouquet of roses Alek had ordered for the apartment.
He'd also ordered the potted herbs running along the
window, their scents giving her peace in an emotional
war zone that was Alek. Restless now near him, she
rose to cut chives, wash and chop them over their
food.

Mark looked at her, then leveled a stare at Alek.
"Elspeth, any time this jerk makes moves you don't
like and you want me to do something, I will. I'm
pretty good in a gym."

She had been afraid of this. Alek could shred Mark
and walk away untouched. "I shouldn't have said anything. I have brothers, remember? Alek is just going
through a phase, and I can handle him."

"A phase...and I am not your brother, sweetheart.
We're going home," he repeated softly, watching her.

Mark's expression said that he had an investment to
protect, if not Elspeth. "Going home? She's got two
more showings in as many days."

"Alek, I am honoring my agreement."

"But you'd rather be home and you know it." Alek
eyed her, a muscle contracting along his jaw. "You
were playing with something you have no idea how
to control."

She lifted an eyebrow. Who was he to tell her what she wanted and if she was flirting? "Don't I?"

She'd scored a hit; Alek scowled at her. "We're going home. Elspeth needs her family, and they need her. She likes to bake." Alek frowned and continued typing.

Elspeth stared at him. There was no limit to his arrogance. How could he possibly know what she needed?

"That's me, just the little homebody. I *love* to putter. Take me out of Amen Flats and I'm just lost without my puttering." Again Elspeth enjoyed the quick flash of anger in Alek's expression.

He reached for his cup of cold coffee, downed it and turned back to his computer. He'd ignore everything when engrossed with an article, and when he was hungry, he ate whatever popped into his hand from cold food to candy bars.

Elspeth finished her meal. Alek continued punching keys and ignoring the food that Mark was devouring. Alek fascinated her, from his high-hell moods to his tenderness with children and the elderly. Elspeth found herself picking up a sliced carrot with her chopsticks; she lifted the morsel to his mouth.

Alek stopped typing, clicked off the machine and slowly turned to her. His lips opened, and Elspeth placed the sliced carrot within his mouth. He chewed and swallowed, and Elspeth slowly placed a chicken morsel to his lips. He fascinated her, restless and concentrating on his writing one moment and then easily managed by the offer of a food tidbit.

Big, tough, impatient Alek Petrovna sat quietly while she fed him, his eyes gleaming beneath heavy sets of curled lashes. "I could get used to this," he murmured unevenly.

"Don't. It's either see that you eat vegetables or deal with Talia."

"Okay. I'll get you off the hook." In a move that she had seen her brothers employ, he stretched his arms up and then laid one across the back of the couch. His hand settled on her shoulder; Alek's thumb lazily caressed her throat. Though she knew his intent, she tried to ignore the immediate response in her.

Finished with his food, Mark cleared away his dishes. "Just take good care of her, Alek. She doesn't look any better than you do. The next time you decide to stake out a woman, count me out. I'm glad you got this one here, though. She's fabulous. Elspeth? Call me if you need me—for anything. You've got my beeper number." After a level, ominous look at Alek, Mark exited the apartment in a crash of thunder.

Alek leaned back against the couch, his gaze locked with Elspeth's as she fed him another morsel. His fingers caressed her thigh, then slid to draw her legs over his thighs. His wary expression reminded her that he'd seen everything, had no delusions about mankind and yet wanted to believe in fairy tales.

"What are you doing?" he asked huskily when she placed the plate aside.

"In the time we've spent together, I haven't seen you eat an entire meal. You eat on the run, Alek, any-thing and everything, hot...cold, and too much coffee. By the time you get to them, your sandwiches are dried."

He nodded slowly. "Okay. If it's important to you, I'll work on regular, balanced, sit-down meals. What else?"

"I doubt you have any idea of what a balanced meal is." Elspeth carefully picked through her thoughts about Alek. First of all, Alek could take whatever she handed him; she doubted she could make a dent in his ego. "You wear socks with holes. You're messy. You shout. You're volatile, Alek. Emotionally expressive. You snarl and threaten and intimidate." Then she flung the worst of the lot at him. "And...you gesture too much. You're much too...dramatic one minute and laughing the next. To top it off, you've been too darn easy lately."

"Gee, I guess it's my Petrovna blood," Alek returned, unbothered. "You can shout back. You can handle it. You can even laugh if you want." Alek tapped her nose with his fingertip, then lifted her to his lap.

"Idiot." She braced herself away from him. He handled her as though he had the right to touch her. "Alek, I am not Talia to tease, or little Megan to be cuddled."

"Shut up, Elspeth-mine. I like cuddling you. You could cuddle me. We could grin together," he teased with eyebrows lifting suggestively.

She looked down at Alek, studied the harsh jutting cheekbones and deep-set, almost slumberous eyes beneath curling lashes that no man had a right to own. Rain patterns on the window shadowed his face, and she knew there was nothing sleepy or laughing about Alek Petrovna. Against her, his body was hot and tense, humming with needs she didn't understand but wanted to match. The storm outside suited her emotions; she wanted to rip away Alek's clothes and—

Elspeth wearily closed her eyes. Alek had moved into her life and turned it thoroughly upside down.

"Don't think about it, love. Just rest." Alek tugged
her head down to his shoulder and stroked her hair.
She could have, should have, moved away, but instead
settled her cheek onto the novel cushioning of warm
muscles and the slow, safe beat of his heart. Elspeth
rested there lightly, curved to Alek. Years ago, she'd
been held like this, cuddled to her father...she couldn't
remember being so safe....

Elspeth awoke to Alek's scent clinging to the pillow
beneath her cheek. Her clothes twisted around her.
She'd slept heavily.

In a heartbeat, Elspeth leapt to her feet and stalked
toward the sound of water running in her bathroom.

She ripped open the bathroom door; the sight of
Alek shaving in the nude stopped her. The profile of
his body was beautiful, rippling cords and hollowed
at his haunches, his legs spread, feet bare upon the
tile. She avoided a full frontal view and skipped to his
legs, bulky at the thigh—the scars angry.

Alek turned to her and lifted his scarred eyebrow.

She advanced, careless that he towered over her,
dressed in nothing but the white foam on his jaw. She
wanted to drag him back to bed...or just have him
where he stood. "Just what do you think you're doing?" she asked rawly. She realized that she had
thrown up her hands and forced them down, making
fists at her thighs.

Her eyes flicked to the foam clinging to the hair on
his chest...then jerked to Alek's flat nipple. She forced
herself not to trace the line of hair going downward—
she grabbed a towel and held it up to him. Alek lifted
that eyebrow again, then slowly looked down to the
intimate bulge in the hanging material.

The atmosphere in the small room shifted and stood still. In the mirror, Alek watched her, his face expressionless. "You slept with me. All night." She didn't believe it was true, not yet.

"Uh-huh. That I did." Alek rinsed his razor and continued shaving as though they spent every night together. Because he had moved, she was forced to shift the towel.

She stiffened at the sight of the delicate pink razor in his hand and took it away from him.

Alek patted his face dry, slashed away the towel and turned to her, hands on hips. There he stood, towering over her, hair damp and spiraling from his shower. Droplets of water shimmered on the hair on his chest and on his shoulders—a deep jagged scar running across his left one. She wanted to place her lips on it and— Elspeth refused to allow the hunger in her; she refused to look down.

"You're not a comfortable woman to sleep with, but I needed to hold you. A simple, old-fashioned, basic need of a man who needs to sleep one entire night with one special woman. I should have spent that night with you, Elspeth. I should have held you close to me and tucked your fanny neatly against a part of me that is in a constant and hard state, thank you very much."

"You could take care of that…need easily enough. You've had enough offers since I've known you." Elspeth straightened, horrified that she had sounded like a jealous lover. She threw out her hand. "You could have slept all night with—"

"You're gesturing wildly, Elspeth. My, my. So I'm not the only one." He took one step toward her, then another, and slammed the door shut behind her, backing her up against it. Alek glowered down at her. "Yes, damn it. I could have had women. But I slept with you. I wallowed in the event. Hell, I probably glowed. I dived into your scents, the texture of your hair, like a love-starved teenage boy, too hot and too hard. You sprawl, Elspeth-mine. You sprawled, took up the bed and nearly made me embarrass myself. You are a restless sleeper, and your hands are very busy. I am not wool to be woven or to be plucked or caressed."

His body heat burned her, ensnared her. "I'm not discussing my sleep habits—"

"Oh, you're not?" he repeated too softly. His face lowered to hers, his eyes savage and blazing. "Get out."

His hardened body lurched intimately against her, and Elspeth flattened to the door, fighting her need to touch him, to soothe...or just pit herself against him and show him that he couldn't walk into her life and shatter it.

"Yes, you little disaster. I'd like to carry you back to bed and keep you there until we've erased that first time. Until you're sweaty and limp and cuddly. Oh, yes, Elspeth-mine. Don't look so shocked. I'd like to lick the sweat from your breasts, watch it gleam on them and pearl on your body. I'd like to slide against you, frontal, side and backside. I'd like to suck and bite and kiss you until you—"

He hesitated, studied her, only to begin again. "Good. You're shocked. I need to be locked to you, in you. With you, Elspeth, until barriers of flesh burn away," he repeated. "But you're going to have to make your own decision. You're going to actually have to take the first step because, if I did...if I did..."

Alek closed his eyes and groaned; he pivoted away from her to latch both big hands on the countertop. The counter cracked, and he cursed. "Out."

Alek realized he'd been staring at the computer monitor while his mind drifted to his neighbor. Elspeth had closed herself away from him and moved through the next showings with cool detachment. His brand-new "necking" car stood in his driveway, unused. A ladybug crawled across the window screen and he followed its progress until his rosebud came into focus. The bud was nothing to compare to the fiesta of color next door, or scented geraniums brushed by the June wind, but it was respectable and it matched his Chevy, waxed and chrome shining in his driveway.

A man had to have more to caress than the big steering wheel of a car he'd always wanted, Alek decided with a sigh.

The *Sentinel* of Amen Flats required little tending, taking shape in Brad Klein's hands. Alek leaned back in his chair. The article could wait. The newspaper boys were hitting their marks without destroying more than three windows and a newly potted vase. Alek's gaze drifted back to the rosebud.

The bud was madder red, the fiery shade that reminded him of Elspeth. Heat lay in Elspeth's work; he'd seen it in "Untitled." He saw it in the new work she'd begun. The vibrant colors softened, swirled, enclosed and burst, her style changing.

School had ended in the last week of May. Amen Flats settled into its Saturday-afternoon routine of lawn mowers buzzing, children yelling and riding bikes and people visiting on sidewalks. Riders hitched their horses to anything that didn't move, and the scent of home cooking lay on the town like perfume. The aroma of baking didn't come from Elspeth's kitchen; she was weaving as if it could carry her away from Alek.

"Too bad, kid. Like it or not, I'm here to stay." Alek traced the Rocky Mountains, rugged peaks attacking the sky. He sucked in the fresh, pine-scented air and the fragrance of herbs growing in Elspeth's garden.

He'd take what he could get from her.

His mind wasn't on the cat-chasing-dog news in Amen Flats, but Elspeth. He rubbed his temples, fighting a headache. She was probably creating one of those sensual masterpieces that dried his mouth just looking at them. He'd played a stupid game with the contract. Now he knew that he'd sink to any depth to be with her, and the thought nicked his pride. Mark's raging sit-down discussion about how to treat women didn't help.

Elspeth's van whizzed into her driveway; a second later, her back door slammed.

Duncan's pickup skidded into Alek's driveway. Duncan pushed out of the cab like a bull out of a rodeo stall. Alek could use a good brawl, and the dark expression on Duncan's face said he'd like to oblige.

"Well. My, my. Things are looking up." Alek moved through the storage crates in his living room, the remodeling of his kitchen, and opened the old back door with enough force to tear one hinge away, then stepped into his back yard. Duncan was big enough and hard enough to take Alek's frustration. Mark had offered to bash Alek for trapping Elspeth in the contract. Mark with his fancy silver shorts and boxing

can's fist slammed into his side and knocked the wind from him. Alek paid him back, and the two rolled across the newly plowed patch of earth where he'd planned his garden. Amid the grunts and the savage sounds of bone meeting flesh, Alek gasped under a wall of icy water.

Duncan grunted and flopped to one side, and the two big men lay there, side by side in a cold pool of muddy water. Birk and Calum roared with laughter, and Elspeth walked with dignity to the water faucet and turned off the hose. Alek enjoyed a good view of her swaying hips before Duncan hauled him to his feet. She walked back to Duncan and Alek, who had looped their arms around each other companionably and awaited their comeuppance. They looked at each other and tried friendly, innocent grins. Things were definitely looking up, Alek decided.

"She's mad," Duncan noted as the flat of Elspeth's hand hit him in the chest and sent him a step backward.

"*Brawling.*" Elspeth's single condemning word lashed out at them. She'd convicted and sentenced the offending males.

"Just letting off a bit of steam, Elspeth-mine. I'm glad you came. Why don't you just go inside my house and make some brownies or something, will you?" Alek watched, fascinated at the lift of her chin, the blaze of her eyes burning him. She moved suddenly, her sleek hair fanning out, gleaming blue black in the sunlight, and his heart flip-flopped. He took in her taut breasts beneath the clinging red sweater with long sleeves and the new jeans that clung to curves he wanted to caress. Neatly packaged, Elspeth's supple muscles attracted him more than would a lusher com-

bination. Everything about Elspeth was feminine, soft
and yet tempered with strength that said she would
hold what she wanted.

Yep. That's my woman, all right, Alek purred men-
tally. He just hoped she wanted him.

Her eyes narrowed. "I'm done with patching bloodied lips and swollen eyes, Alek Petrovna. I've lived
with these three, watched their stupid caveman games.
You're not adding to the trouble."

Alek was floating, high on the sight of Elspeth
aroused to a fine, dangerous temper. He stroked a sleek
strand back from her hot cheek, and her head went
back. She flashed him a look that shot straight into his
gut, twisted it and sank lower to heat and harden and
ache. Alek tucked that look to his heart; she was glorious, a proud, hot woman that he wanted to toss over
his shoulder and run—Alek glanced at the scowling
Tallchief males and decided to wait.

The three brothers looked sheepish beneath her
quick, raking stare. Clearly Elspeth could pull rank
and intimidate with the best. This was the real Elspeth,
Alek mused, elegant even as the shutters went up and
darkened steel gray eyes changed to fire.

"Be gentle, Elspeth-mine. I've got a few bruises
already. Will you kiss them and make them better?"

Air hissed between Elspeth's teeth, the tone a warning.

Good. This was what he wanted, honesty between
them. She was mad and letting it show; in another
minute, she'd broil him. Intoxicated with the heat rising in Elspeth, he'd take a few more bruises from her
and be glad of it. Alek grinned and tugged her hair,
wrapping a strand around his fingers to enjoy and to

torment her. With her, he felt like a teenage boy showing off.

She studied him from muddy hair to muddy boots and back up again as if deciding which piece of him she'd like to sample first.

He hoped it was his lips and pursed them appropriately for her kissing.

Her eyes went black, boiling with temper.

Calum straightened and stopped grinning. "Take it easy on him, will you, Elspeth? He'll be an uncle to my baby."

Without looking at her brothers, Elspeth tossed over her shoulder, "He asked for this. Go bother someone else."

Duncan shifted restlessly, a muddied, rough cowboy towering over her, with a guilty little-boy expression.

"What a woman. Right now, I'd say she could take all four of us and leave us in the mud," Alek drawled, his breath catching as her eyes flashed at him. He winked at Duncan with the eye that was not swelling. "She loves me."

Elspeth muttered darkly to herself, a delight to Alek.

"Uh-uh. If she did, she'd take you down herself. You'd be wearing kilts—like the rest of us with a cold wind blowing up your backside." Duncan grinned at his sister, who had slashed a look at him steely enough to freeze spring. He stepped away from Alek. "Ah...you're on your own, Alek."

"Juveniles," she muttered quite clearly.

"Just boys having a good time. You'd better start sewing." Alek grinned and slowly placed the muddy tip of his finger just on the end of her nose. He almost laughed as she went cross-eyed and quickly recovered, glaring at him.

The sheriff's patrol car pulled up, complete with his latest opera and dogs howling. His bullhorn rattled the windows of every house on the block. "I thought you Tallchief boys gave up brawling since two of you got married. Now, Birk I'd expect it from, especially since Lacey— Never mind."

"They've been missing it, and I'm innocent," Birk called back to him. He waved to the line of trucks stopped on the street. In town for Saturday shopping, people enjoyed a show from the Tallchiefs. Birk watched Sissy Mayors strolling by in her short shorts, and tossed a tidbit to the sheriff. "Petrovna has a thing for Elspeth. What did Lacey do?"

He glanced at his brothers. "I do not trust that little witch past anything. Since she bought that old bordello, she's been twice as bad."

Elspeth groaned, closed her eyes and shook her head. Her cheeks flushed slowly, and she turned a glare on Birk that widened his eyes. "Chelsey is too sweet for you, Birk the rogue. You'd mow her down too easily. Now take Lacey—"

"The hell I will. Elspeth, you try to match me with Lacey, and I'll—"

The sheriff's loudspeaker blared, inciting a new round of howls from dogs. "Oh, hell, Birk. Everybody in town knows that Petrovna is sweet on Elspeth. He's passed up some choice offerings, all heated up and engines running. How's Petrovna doing? Don't hurt him too bad. He's doing a real nice article on western law and Caruso for the paper. He just interviewed me."

"He can hold his own," Calum yelled. "It's good to know the uncle of my baby isn't a pansy."

"Not a one of you will ever taste, smell or come

close to another loaf of my bread,'' Elspeth stated too quietly.

She took one step toward Alek. There wasn't anything sweet or soft about her, but enough passion to ignite them both. She took another step and struggled for control; the shutters began to come down as she pressed her lips together. He couldn't allow her to retreat. He dipped his head to kiss her and found what he wanted, the heat simmering inside and waiting for him. Unable to stop himself, Alek wrapped his arms around her, lifted her against him and gave himself to her care.

He placed his hopes and dreams on his lips, asking her to taste them. He promised her his heart and asked for hers. He sank into the taste of what she had held apart, of the precious core of her—to the softness and the heat.

Elspeth's arms went around his neck, and she took. She tasted like wine and hunger and temptation all in one. There in the spring sunshine, she kissed him until he forgot the limits, the sweetness he wanted to show her, and sank into the heat of what she offered. When the kiss was done, Elspeth looked down at him, her hair spilling around their faces. The world spun and tilted and stopped in a halo of glittering sunshine as her thumbs caressed the corners of his lips, her eyes dark and mysterious. She was all woman, and his heart, the other part of him—

She'd been like this that night in Scotland, and he prayed there would be more times when she'd look at him as if nothing else mattered.

After a time, Duncan cleared his throat. ''Aye,'' he murmured. ''That's what I thought. But I wanted to make certain.''

Elspeth pulled her gaze away from Alek's and turned to Duncan, her face still flushed and her lips swollen. The drowsy look in her eyes did not match the taut press of her body within Alek's arms. Her arms, locked around his neck, loosened; her fingers trembled as she placed them lightly on his shoulder. He held her there, her feet off the ground, and admired her dazed expression, as though she didn't know what had snared her but had enjoyed the taste. He intended to give her more than a taste.

"Aye," Birk and Calum agreed, borrowing the term from their great-great-grandmother.

Duncan reached out a friendly fist to punch Alek's shoulder. "Come out and help us lay fence. We're needing an extra hand. There's a beer in it for you, and Birk has a sweat lodge near the creek. After a nice icy swim in the lake, Sybil won't know—" Duncan glanced down at his muddy, torn clothing and muttered a curse.

Elspeth had shocked herself; the proof crawled up her throat in a beautiful pink, coloring her cheeks. Entranced by the wordless movement of her mouth as she looked at the crowd that had gathered on the street, Alek grinned. "Shocking, Elspeth. Just shocking. Here you are making out with me in broad daylight."

Mrs. Schmidt, who had been Elspeth's first-grade teacher, called, "Elspeth Tallchief, are you all right?"

Elspeth's lips moved wordlessly, and her hands flopped helplessly on his shoulder. Because he was in a generous mood and floating on Elspeth's kisses, Alek called, "She's just fine, Mrs. Schmidt."

"You be nice to her, Mr. Petrovna. She's always been a nice girl."

"Let...me...down." Elspeth braced herself and pushed away from him.

Alek lowered Elspeth to her feet. He'd prefer taking her into his bed.... The struggle for composure cost her; Elspeth straightened her sweater, smoothed her hair and attempted a cool, detached smile. She failed when she glanced down at her sweater to find two muddy patches where her breasts had pressed to Alek's. He admired the sight, peaks pressing against the material and then the wild flush sweeping up her cheeks.

He didn't reach out a hand when she sagged, but let her straighten by her own will. She'd have pushed him back in the mud and then he'd have to wrestle her down into it for a kiss. "Aye," he said, borrowing from the Tallchiefs. "You'll do."

Sun glinted off her lashes as they narrowed, and Elspeth turned to elegantly pick her way across the muddy garden back to her house.

Alek folded his empty arms, ached for her, and tilted his head to admire the fine sway of her hips.

Birk hooted. "Petrovna is in love."

"Petrovnas can be a fast game," stated Calum from experience. "Elspeth is picky."

Duncan looped an arm around both brothers. "She can handle it."

Calum elbowed him. "You'll be sleeping on the couch tonight, older brother."

Duncan winked at him. "Making up is the best part. It's worth a night on the couch."

"She hasn't decided she wants me yet." Alek spoke to himself. He stroked his muddy beard. "I'll have to make myself even more enticing. It doesn't usually take this long to have them swooning over me. Five seconds, tops.''

Birk guffawed at that, and Calum grinned.

"I'd say she's thinking about having your scalp right now. You could work some of that off by helping us with the fence.'' Duncan placed his western hat on his head and braced his legs apart, grinning at Alek.

Alek suspected Duncan worried about Elspeth...that Alek would cross those few yards to her home. "Tucking me under your wing, Duncan the defender?''

"You could call it that. A few years ago, you wouldn't be standing on two feet now. She can rip the earth right out from under you before you know it. I've got firsthand experience, and I'm wearing Megan's oatmeal. From the look of Elspeth, one wrong step and you could be wearing some bruises.''

"It would be worth it.''

"I know the feeling,'' Duncan returned with a grin that brought a quick, pained frown and a finger to his swollen lip. "At least we know you can handle yourself. Come on, girls, let's fix that fence.''

Seven

Elspeth shook. She managed to walk to her kitchen table, poured the alfalfa-mint tea she'd just brewed into a cup. She stared at leafy bits at the bottom of the china and spread her trembling hands flat on the table.

She'd taken one look at Duncan and at Alek; a lifetime of experience with bristling males had told her they wouldn't be civilized. She'd swept out of her home, leaped across a bed of sweetwood herb and had feared that she wouldn't reach them in time.

Alek had stood there with one eye swelling and had blown her a kiss. "Swaggering, arrogant..."

Her home seemed to quiver around her. Thyme and sage, bundled and hanging by her kitchen window, seemed to twirl in her flooding emotions.

Her studio was the same; her loom caught the sunlight from the windows. Skeins of dyed wool hung from pegs and the spinning wheel. Everything was in its place, and yet her life had changed.

She had cared what happened to Alek.

Her kitchen was neat as usual. Her new weaving projects consumed her, as though she were pitting what snarled and heated and brewed inside her against the wool. She reached for a skein colored with madder root—a fiery red—and gripped it in her fist.

Violent. That's how she felt about Alek.

Elspeth sifted through her emotions concerning Alek. No. Violence wasn't enough. Primitive suited her emotions better.

A reluctant glance out the window caused her to shake her head. Alek stood beneath the hose, his ruined shirt hanging on a branch. He stretched his arms high over his head, and Elspeth's mouth went dry, her body instantly quickening.

She wanted to feed upon him. To take and to give, to bear him to the mud and—

She touched her swollen lips, still hungry for the taste of his promise, his dreams...if only he hadn't offered her his dreams....

"Aaagh!" Elspeth lifted her teacup and forced herself to sip slowly. She knew men were boys, and boys liked boasting and brawling. She shouldn't have jumped to defend Alek against Duncan, who used to fight to ease his demons before marrying Sybil. But the sight of Duncan moving purposefully toward Alek sent her flying to rescue Alek.

She ran a fingertip across the rose design of her teacup; Alek made her feel like a rose—delicate, soft, beautiful. She glanced at the shadowed mirror and found her flushed face in it, her lips swollen and ripe.

She inhaled the scents of her herbs to calm her

nerves and found Alek's, lingering on her skin. "Beast. Arrogant—"

Beast. The word echoed in her mind, reminding her of Una's description of Tallchief:

A swaggering, arrogant warrior of a man, accustomed to women doing his bidding and fetching for him. The worst of it was he knew how gloriously beautiful he was, even with his battle scars. I'll bring the beastly, mule-headed giant of a man to his knees...I swear it. He mocks my size and feminine weakness, but there are other ways, softer ways. I have nothing so fine to capture this Tallchief man-beast but the shawl.

The shawl. Suddenly she had to know the legend. Elspeth shook the pieces of paper detailing the legend to the table and began to arrange them. Under a magnifying glass, Una's handwriting defied reading. After a few frustrating moments, Elspeth called Sybil and asked her advice about duplicating the page. Minutes later, Elspeth hurried down the street to the printers and asked them to enlarge and darken the pieces.

When she arrived home, Sybil was sitting on her doorstep with her camera and magnifying lens. "We can shoot the pieces outside in a few minutes with natural light and have pictures in a snap. Meanwhile, I am *not* a happily married woman," she stated. "Your brother is a huge, brawling, full-of-himself boy. He walked right into the house, kissed me with his swollen lip—right while my client Marcella Portway was on the phone, pestering me about her blasted royal Spanish gene. He actually eased me down to the floor and held me there, all muddy and bloody and...Mrs.

Portway raged on about her royal blood while he kissed me silly.''

Sybil blushed. ''There Duncan was, huge, ragged and bloodied and grinning like a baboon. 'Don't blame me. I did it for Elspeth,' he said. The strange thing of it is that he seems to like Alek.

''I could use a good cup of tea. I left them all with Megan, who is teething and not happy about anything. That should keep them from fighting. Duncan is cooking tonight, planning to wine and dine and candlelight me out of sleeping on the couch…and just maybe he will.''

Elspeth and Sybil went inside and Elspeth prepared and served tea. ''I remember when you entered a brawl at Maddy's to defend Duncan.''

Sybil sniffed elegantly. ''I had to. There he was having a fine time when I needed him to rescue Emily. He was the only one who could track her kidnapper and find her.''

''You'd do it again.''

''Of course. Alek shouldn't pick on Duncan just when he's properly tamed. Now show me what you have. I wondered when you'd get around to this.''

Elspeth pivoted to Sybil with a thought that plagued her. ''Do you think a man can be celibate for more than five years?''

''I do. But he'd be a hungry one—'' Sybil's eyes widened. ''Five years. That's about when you went to Scotland, isn't it? Before you changed? Don't tell me that Alek has wanted you for five years— Don't tell me that you knew him in Scotland and you and he and— So that's what's been going on between you. Something happened before.… Oh, yes! Tell me.''

''No. Duncan will get it out of you…there'll be

more stupid, overgrown boys' brawls, and then Talia…I do not want to think about what she would do. She shouldn't be upset now." Elspeth decided not to ask Sybil more questions; she was too sharp, her mind trained to connect hidden implications.

"Mmm. I see what you mean. But Duncan can't get *everything* out of me."

Elspeth shot her a disbelieving look. "He's getting good."

"I can still hold my own. By the way, I know all about Alek's little contract. You know it equated to the Tallchiefs' capturing their brides, don't you? That old macho thing about beating their chests and dragging off their women."

"He's apologized for the contract. He was rather sweet about it. Alek had his reasons." Alek wanted to make her pay, to run her down, push her around and swagger off after his revenge. He ached for a child, a need coursing heavily through him to produce an offspring, to have his line continue in the world after he was gone.

Elspeth swallowed. It must have cost Alek to back up, to apologize, but he had. She shook her head, clearing it. She had to find a way to exorcise him from her life, to peel him away from her heart.

Sybil sighed with dreamy longing. "I get all fuzzy when Duncan apologizes. I don't know whether to take a broom after him for his crime…or to kiss him senseless. The light should be fine now. Let's go take those pictures. From there, we'll use computer tracing. The pictures are just double insurance."

Alek sat on his porch and drew the shawl across his bare chest. He tipped the chair back against the new siding and settled into his thoughts. A brawl, bruises and hard physical labor couldn't tear away his need to see Elspeth. Neither the sweat-lodge steam nor the freezing dip in Tallchief Lake could cool what she had ignited with one sultry look. He knew better than to push Elspeth now. He'd done enough with that damn, stupid contract.

He'd had his reasons, Alek argued against himself.

At ten o'clock, Amen Flats was settling in, lovers getting steamy and older folks holding hands.

The old tomcat who had claimed Alek yawned and curled into a corner. Sporting a chewed ear-and-a-half, the gray-striped tom yawned and yellow eyes looked at Alek as if to say, *Well, this is what to expect, chum...one ear chewed to hell and lonesome on a Saturday night. You get used to it.*

"Speak for yourself." The shawl, light and soft, whispered across his skin, the fringes tangling in the hair on his chest. He rubbed them against him and wished for Elspeth's hair. Alek propped his western boots on the railing, settling in for a long, lonely night. An owl soared across the sky, and Elspeth's front door creaked. She was probably coddling the hungry strays at her back door. Alek grimaced...maybe he was a stray needing a home and he certainly was hungry. He tried to ignore the lurch of his heart and damned his weakness for her.

Marcy Longfeather cruised by in her convertible and blew him a kiss. Gossip said that Marcy could age a man in hours. "Call me anytime. I'm in the book," she called to him.

Marcy held as much appeal to him as cold oatmeal. He'd never liked a woman who slid her hand into his back pocket when he wasn't prepared. A hefty supply of multicolored, super-duper condoms, waved beneath his nose at the local coffee shop, brought out her cold-oatmeal appeal. He preferred— He preferred Elspeth.

Alek glanced at Elspeth's darkened studio. She was probably weaving those mind-blowing hangings by candlelight, the graceful movements of her arms telling a story that would ignite any red-blooded male. Alek groaned because now he knew that Elspeth sometimes wore only a T-shirt to weave. Visions of the taut peaks of her breasts, the gentle, soft weight swaying to her movements, had haunted his sleepless nights.

He inhaled the cool night air and watched newly hatched moths cluster around a street lamp. Caruso's music drifted from a distance away, and dogs howled. Alek smoothed the shawl across his chest. It was going to be a long night.

The tom sniffed the air; he leapt to his feet like a young cat, arched and stretched. With his tail high, he pranced lightly down the steps, headed for Elspeth's house and welcoming female company.

"Deserter." Alek reached for a can of beer and stroked the shawl. His fingers curled to the can, then released it as Elspeth moved quietly up his porch. The single black braid swung down her neat white blouse and dangled at her waist. He admired the loose fit of her gray slacks and wanted to strip her then, taking her on the front porch.

"Here." He tossed the shawl at her. "It's yours. Forget about the contract. You're free."

"You don't like my work?"

Alek spread his scarred fingers and studied them. He didn't want to hurt her on any level. "You're talented. There's not another artist like you. But you're not under any obligation to produce for the gallery. I'll see to it. It was a stupid move on my part.''

"How kind of you. And you're right. It was stupid. Mark agrees.''

Was that a smile lurking in her tone? Because he felt too exposed, too raw and aching, and wanted his pride, Alek plopped the chair to its feet and stood. He pushed his hands in his back pockets to keep from grabbing her. "Well?''

Elspeth's slender fingers flowed over the shawl, and his body jerked into a tight knot. She touched it reverently. "It's beautiful. No wonder Una loved it so.''

"It's yours. You should have it.''

"Thank you.''

She placed it around her, and Alek went weak. He brushed the tangled, fiery fringes with his fingertips and found them shaking. The shawl flowed, clinging to her slender body, fringes catching the soft night breeze. She looked exotic and yet untouched. But Alek had touched her, had taken away something that she would never get back. "You look good in it.''

Unused to compliments, Elspeth bowed her head. When her head came up, her expression sent him reeling. She frightened him, and Alek took a step backward. "I don't want you to feel...obligated on any level.''

Her lips curved, enchanting him, and she slanted him an amused look. "For a shawl? Come on, Alek. I could have taken it any time I wanted.''

"From me? I doubt it.''

"You know, there's just something about taking you down that appeals.'' She took another step toward him, and the look in her eyes caused him to blink. He hadn't expected the sultry look, as if she had chosen to feast upon him and was considering where to start.

He took a step back and found his hips against the railing.

She came close to him, placed her hands on his shoulders and watched him. She was taking him apart, examining him with those smoky gray eyes and trying to see beyond bones and scarred skin. He wasn't a mystery, yet Elspeth kept hunting what ran beneath the surface. The shawl's fringes caught on his skin, lifting with his sudden breath.

"What are you doing, Elspeth?" he asked unevenly, uncertain of himself and of her. In another minute, he'd be lifting her in his arms and devouring her. He had to get her out of here, to a place where she'd be safe.... He sucked in his breath as she leaned closer.

"I'm waiting for you to kiss me, Alek. To see if you're all show for my brothers and the town, or if you really mean it." Her fingers touched his face, smoothing the stubble there.

She touched the earring, and Alek's knees began to weaken. "Games, Elspeth?"

Her mouth curved again, secret and feminine. "Are you going to show me your house? You've been in mine often enough. You've been hammering and sawing until all hours of the night. Something must have changed." Elspeth moved to the door and waited, the slender line of her nape as vulnerable as Alek felt. He opened the door, and she moved inside to the darkness.

Inside his house, Alek's fingers found the shawl, gripped it and tugged her back against him. His arms instantly encircled her, his face pressed close to hers, caught by the fresh and exotic scent of her skin and hair. "You like playing with fire, do you?"

Against his cheek, her smooth one moved in a smile. "Maybe you're the one in danger."

She eased away, and Alek let her go. He pushed his hands in his back pockets to keep from grabbing her.

The shawl whispered secrets as Elspeth studied the house, and Alek sensed that another woman had worn it and had called up a man, beckoning to him. In the dim light, the soft material gleamed and dipped into her waist, traced the slender curve of her hip. Alek washed a fast, hard hand over his unshaved, taut jaw; in another minute, he'd be drooling.

"You've opened up the rooms...there's more space. I'm glad you didn't use contemporary furniture." Her fingers smoothed an old piano, battered from years of use at Maddy's Hot Spot. Alek had liked the thought of happy people, clustered around the old piano and singing to the music. She glanced at the mantel, filled with framed pictures, and picked her way around unpacked cartons. Her fingers trailed over the shells he'd collected and set to catch the dawn's light. She wandered into his office, touched the paper clutter and his computer. She studied his desk—two file cabinets set a distance apart and topped by an old door. "This is the heart of you, isn't it?"

The heart of him thudded heavily, needing her warm and soft against him. Because he was afraid he'd frighten her if he pushed too hard, he asked, "What about going down to Maddy's?"

Elspeth lifted an elegant eyebrow. "And face what you did to me earlier today?"

"No, I suppose not."

"Thank you for that much." She picked up a rock

painted with a child's hand, then moved to the swatch she'd woven in Scotland. She turned and studied the room, littered with bits of his traveling years, bits of people he wanted to remember. When she touched a framed picture of a little Eurasian boy and girl, Alek said, "Marta and Ben. I help them by one of those foster-adoption plans."

"And these?" Elspeth touched other pictures of children and Alek nodded.

There was a picture of an Asian girl, blushing as a bride with her husband standing proudly near her. "Those two were young teenagers, living in cardboard boxes. They entered a medical training program and now they're married."

"With your help?"

When he nodded, she lifted a picture of Doug Morrow, an arm draped around Alek. "The frames are new."

"This is the first time I've stayed in one place long enough for frames. The pictures were getting battered. That's Doug Morrow, a friend. When I was in Scotland this last time—I had some notion of finding a woman I'd met years ago."

Alek shook his head. "It seems so long ago, and it was just months. I thought I'd go there and...find you...see if you were happy. It didn't turn out that way. I was on my way here when Doug got sick, calling me to complete his assignment. I said I would. The assignment delayed my trip here."

She glanced at her work, a blend of earth and sky and mountains wrapped in mist and sharpened by a spear thrust diagonally through it. Elspeth roamed to the pictures of his immigrant great-great-grandparents. "All immigrants of that time have a look, don't they?

Dressed in black, half afraid and half joyous that a new life was theirs for the taking. I can picture Una lugging her precious dowry, some of it in the shawl on her back.''

"Mine came from Russia. They were probably thinking about how soon they could get to Texas heat.''

Heat. Despite the cool night, Alek's palms were damp, and his hands shook. If he touched her— He jammed them deeper in his pocket.

Alek followed her to the kitchen, remodeled and gleaming, too clean and uncluttered. Her fingertip traced an open manual to the pasta machine. "Very nice…a new bread machine and a pasta machine and an electric wok.''

He didn't want her to know that he ached for her fresh bread and that he'd tried to make his own, that he didn't know how to make a home. "I'm not exactly a homemaker, but I'll learn.''

If she found that old stew pot under the cabinet, she'd really think him off center. He loved the idea of that old pot bubbling with enough food to feed an army of kids.

She glanced down at the assortment of kitchen gadgets on the counter. "You're certainly prepared. No more dishes from gorgeous blondes?''

"I'm waiting for a herd of them to turn up now.''

She opened the cupboards to see the old dishes he'd bought at an auction. Talia had teased him ruthlessly; she had relented when she saw how he treasured them despite the chips. "These are lovely. They're from the Winscotts, one of the first pioneers in the valley. They had eleven children and loved each other deeply. The table was theirs, too. Mr. Winscott had to make more leaves and supports as their family grew. He wanted the entire family to sit down at once, every meal, and so they did."

Álek had felt that, the love in the chipped dishes and the handcrafted table, scarred by years of use. He sensed the children eating greedily and then bouncing up from the table, filled and ready to play. It pleased him to eat from the same dishes, to imagine that his children would be settling on his knee to be rocked and cuddled and burped. Lost in that dream, he could forget that the meals he ate were prepackaged and frozen.

"The rocking chair in your living room is the Mulveneys'. Mrs. Mulveney was six feet five inches and of ample proportions. She loved rocking children, sometimes three at a time. All of their children were rocked there, and most of the Tallchief clan, too," Elspeth added, jarring him. He sensed that she had dipped into his thoughts.

The seed packets on the table embarrassed him. He wanted to grow herbs, to wallow in the scent of them in his house as he had in hers. Comfortable in the shadows, Elspeth touched and smoothed and explored—he wanted her touching him in the same way. Elspeth probed into the desperate, lonely heart of him and exposed his raw edges. "Why are you here?"

She touched his cheek, then stood on tiptoe to nibble on his lip. "Questions. Ever the journalist, aren't you? You've been over here, hoarding a collection of things that no one wants anymore. Why?"

"My lifestyle hasn't exactly allowed me to have a houseful of furniture or dishes." That was true enough, but he wanted bits of happiness of other homes. Because he wanted a family and a home and was too proud to admit his need.

Alek gripped her upper arms, then her wrists as her arms slid up to his neck, around it, drawing him close to her curved body. Elspeth, on the prowl, could frighten any man who thought he could control what lay within him. "We'd better go somewhere else."

He'd hurt her now if they made love. He wanted to make this time tender and last until the dawn came and then start all over again. Elspeth moved against him, and Alek hardened instantly. The sound of his voice came raw and uneven as the shawl whispered between them. "Elspeth..."

For an answer, she held him tighter. Alek eased aside the folds of the shawl to lock his hands on her waist. "Elspeth!"

She held him tightly, refusing to be eased away. Her thumb ran along the scar on his shoulder. Then she looked up at him and grinned for the first time. "I've shocked you, Petrovna. Admit it."

He blinked, uncertain if Elspeth had really sent him an impish, five-thousand-watt grin that sent him reeling. Tonight he wasn't certain of anything. The shawl's fringes clung to his fingers as he forced her away gently. "You're inexperienced, Elspeth-mine. You have no idea of what you're doing."

"Not up to it?" Her tease was followed by a quick smile that enchanted him. Her hand lay flat on his chest, toyed with the hair there and slowly, slowly moved downward.

"You wouldn't—" When her fingers skimmed down his stomach, he jerked back against the counter and gripped it with both hands. "Elspeth!"

"Yes, Elspeth. Remember my name, Alek. It's Elspeth.'' Elspeth slowly unbraided her hair, combing it around her. The shawl slid from her shoulders to rest over the back of a chair.

Alek latched his fist in the soft material, warm from her body, and found that he couldn't think as Elspeth began to undress. She unbuttoned her blouse and tossed it to a chair. Alek's mouth went dry when she reached behind her to unfasten her bra.

She tossed the white cotton scrap at him, and he crushed it in his fist. She kicked aside her flats and, veiled by the heavy swath of hair, she stripped away her slacks. Her practical white panties slid down her slender thighs, revealing the dark triangle between her thighs. Alek shuddered, every muscle in his body tightening into a knot.

The moonlight coming through the window slid to caress her body, to outline it in silver as she took the shawl from him. Then she draped it around her and began slowly ascending the stairs. Alek, taut and shaking, traced the flowing movements of her body beneath the shawl, the fringes swaying along the slender, strong backs of her thighs, the cloth caressing the sway of her bottom.

Alek realized that he was alternately cold with fear that he would hurt her and hot with need that rose with stubborn pain within his body.

Then Elspeth paused, looked down at him over her shoulder and lifted an elegant, expressive eyebrow.

Elspeth listened to the movements downstairs as Alek locked the doors. The cats howled near her house, the sound grating on her nerves...not exactly romantic music for her adventure into tasting Alek.

"Untitled" hung on Alek's wall, mocking her. It

was very sexual, a woman's translation of intimacy, colors locking together, exploding— Elspeth groaned silently. She should have known he'd buy the wall hanging, outlined in the moonlight, a monument to what she was about to do.

It was no casual thing coming to Alek, following the needs of her heart and body. She studied the room, bits of other people's lives mingling with Alek's family, his friends. The braided rag rug on the floor, well washed and familiar, probably had once belonged to Mrs. Potts, who was fond of cutting off buttons from ruined shirts and braiding them into rugs. The buttons were likely in the antique blue glass jar. The lovely old quilts neatly folded on a chair ached for a proper bed.

She'd passed a small room, cluttered with tools and lumber and a crib folded against a wall. There was a tiny rocking horse.

Alek wanted a family. While he could afford better, Alek preferred to retrieve old pieces, to lug bits of lives back to his house.

Elspeth pressed the heels of her hands to her eyes. He wanted a home, deserved one.

He'd gone to hell and back when he'd discovered there was no child. He knew more than her family knew about her—

Oh, fine. She'd gotten herself worked up, raging and pacing in her house and mourning her lost powers given to her by her seer and shaman ancestors. She'd meant to set Alek on his ear, to define the rules of his life interrupting hers, and then she'd seen into the very heart of his need to have a home and family.

Oh, fine. She should have walked away. She should have placed their night in Scotland into a drawer—

wove it into her wool or buried it. Some secret part of her, uncontrolled by her will, wanted to tuck that night close to her— Elspeth forced down the panic streaking through her.

Alek had been pushing her and she didn't like it. While her mind didn't quite trust his motives, on another level she needed Alek to prove that she had emotions, that she was a woman and not a shadow. Alek definitely made her feel feminine, exciting.

Was she using him? Definitely. She needed him to complete a restlessness within her. To be cherished and held and yes, loved.

Was she wary of him? Yes. Alek wanted her to have the shawl, giving the prize to her too easily.

Elspeth had never liked easy, or trusted it. She preferred to claim the shawl herself, as a matter of pride. Was he yielding the field to her? Not likely. Alek Petrovna had definite fighting tendencies that excited her own.

Why was she here, in Alek's bed, waiting for him? The answer came back, true and strong. Locked deeply inside her was the need to hold Alek close…to have him so close that nothing could separate them…not the past, or the future he kept pushing at her…. She wanted…no, she needed to be complete once more, as a woman felt with a special man. And for whatever happened in the future, tonight Alek was very special.

She wouldn't be pushed; she would make up her own mind about Alek and what he was to her.

He'd wooed her with his love of family treasures, the simple things harvested into his home. He'd touched her with his children, obviously cherished.

Deep inside Elspeth lurked the fear of Alek leaving her again…devastating her with words. She acknowl-

edged that fear and tended it, even as she knew that
Alek moved gently through her heart. She would keep
that part of her locked safely away.

Yet here she was, waiting—naked—in his tiny cot
for him. Elspeth drew the shawl against her as she
thought back to Una's legend, which she had recon-
structed with the aid of Sybil's photography trick.

When the Marrying Moon is high, a scarred warrior will rise from the mists to claim his lady
huntress. He will wrap her in the shawl and carry
her to the Bridal Tepee and his heart. Their song
will last longer than the stars....

Tallchief had wanted Una to add the Bridal Tepee
to the legend so that the legend became a blend of
their bloods. Sybil had cried and held Elspeth's hand
as the legend was revealed before their eyes. Una had
cried as she wrote, the teardrops blurring the ink. A
hand stronger than hers and untutored with a pen had
drawn Tallchief Mountain and a man and a woman by
the tepee.

In the end, Una had captured her captor, and the
shawl had been her weapon.

A tiny shiver skimmed along Elspeth's bare skin.
The legend didn't—couldn't—apply to Alek Petrovna
and herself.

Elspeth surveyed the spartan room, littered with
Alek's battered suitcases and clothing. She recognized
the huge bureau of the Samuelsons and framed pictures of Alek and Talia with their family. Propped
against a picture of Talia and her sister was a picture
of the Tallchiefs at the wedding. A circle had been

drawn around Elspeth's face, the enlargement resting next to it.

He'd come through years and crossed continents to find her.

Elspeth lifted her head as his footsteps rose surely to the door of the room. He paused, then moved into the bathroom, and the shower ran. The water stopped, then silence.

Alek loomed in the doorway, framed by moonlight skimming his shoulders and down his spread legs. He hadn't given her the concession of a towel around his hips.

She wasn't making concessions, either. "You will not come to this bed with thoughts of your wife, Alek Petrovna. Not with my weaving on your wall."

"I wouldn't think of it." His tone bore arrogance and a taunt and just enough uncertainty to curl around her heart.

He moved to her, filling the room. He'd hurried, droplets gleaming on his shoulders. A deep scar crossed his ribs, another rode his hip and the moonlight caught the smooth expanse of healed burns. Alek appeared battered and toughened by years, his cheekbones rugged and darkened by stubble, his jaw tense. The dim light angled off his broken nose, LaBelle's earring gleamed in his ear and Elspeth ached to feel the soft flow of his curls against her breasts.

She gripped the shawl tightly and forced herself to continue, "That is my price, Alek Petrovna. I will not have you take me with a sense of guilt. I'll know it if you do and I will not forgive you. Pretty apologies won't work."

"Pretty...?" He tensed, the moonlight shafting over angles and taut muscles and cords that ran down his arms to his fists. His feet locked to the pool of moonlight on the old braided rug. The heavy muscles of his legs stood out in relief; his desire jutted into the silvery light, startling Elspeth. Or did her body startle her, desire streaking through her, cords igniting, clenching, heating?

A shudder ran down Alek's body. "I can promise not to hurt you...but I can't promise to forget that night completely." His voice was ragged, rimmed with naked, deep emotion.

"You won't hurt me. I ask that you try to forget."

He took a step. "They say you inherited both seer and shaman powers. What do your senses tell you about me, Elspeth?"

She already knew. "That whatever happens, you will try to please me."

"I will be careful." His promise came firm and raw.

"Do and I'll kill you."

Alek's grin was slow in coming. "Now, that's my girl."

For a moment, Elspeth was startled. She'd never been anyone's girlfriend; she hadn't allowed the possessive tone from anyone, not even her brothers. She found herself blushing as Alek came to the cot and stretched out slowly beside her, his hands behind his head. She lay there, the shawl drawn to her chin, and wondered what to do; her confidence of moments ago had vanished.

"We can lie here and admire your weaving technique, or you can simply take me...I'm yours," Alek murmured, his body heating her side like a furnace. He lifted a challenging eyebrow at her. "Lost the mood? Have a headache?"

"You're taking up all the space." She couldn't

breathe. Alek smelled like soap and man, his heat warming the shawl. Her breast brushed his arm, and he tensed. Alek tugged her over him and wrapped his arms around her. Beneath her, he was all hard power and vibrating male, hot and rigid against her stomach. One hand stroked her bottom leisurely while his other hand prowled dangerously close to her breast.

He tugged at the shawl. "You wouldn't want it damaged, would you?"

She drew the shawl from between them and let him take it. His eyes flicked down her body; his features hardened, a flush rising up his cheeks. There was nothing sweet about Alek, nor in the desperate way he wanted her.

"What now?" he asked with interest after tossing the shawl to a folding chair. "Ready to make your move?"

Elspeth settled closer, placing her flushed face in the shelter of his throat. Alek's hand smoothed her side, lingered along her ribs, then rose to cup her breast. "You're trembling."

He kissed her forehead, her lids. He tasted her gently, brushing his lips across hers, tempting her. She could have killed him for being so tender... for taking time to place protection between them. For trembling so badly that he ruined his first effort, cursed and had to try again.

Elspeth smoothed the taut cords of his neck, his shoulders and the hair covering his chest. As her fingertips brushed his nipple, Alek went taut, shivering. His look at her was fire and desperation, his body burning hers.

She lay quietly as he moved over her. "Open for me, Elspeth," he murmured when her thighs trembled, then closed against his intrusion. "It's all right, love. We'll do what you want, when you want."

Braced away from her, Alek ran his hand down her side, pressing his fingers into her softness, lingering on the curve of her thigh. The night breeze coursed through the window's curtains, bearing the scent of the mountains, an elemental blend of time and passion, and Elspeth gave herself to it, allowing Alek's touch to open her legs.

He held very still, then bent to place his lips upon her throat. "Your heart is leaping out of you. You can touch me."

She placed her hand on his chest, and beside her throat, Alek's mouth curved into a smile. He nipped the side of her jaw. "That wasn't exactly what I meant."

He cupped her breasts, cherishing them, lifting them to torment with gentle bites and then catching the peaks deeper, suckling her until she cried out, holding him to her.

He tensed as she moved, his body intimate against hers. She accepted the tip of him, holding her breath, and fought the slight pain of his intrusion. "Am I hurting you?" he asked.

There was pain, but she wouldn't let him leave her, not now. Elspeth pressed her legs against his hips, her face hot against his throat. "Don't leave me."

Alek groaned and, when she raised her hips slowly, taking him fully, he cried out, trembling. This was what she wanted, Alek close to her, a part of her, despite the slight pain.

His body began to move, hips thrusting down on hers, filling her. She held her breath, aware of the mechanics of sex and yet startled that he desired her.

"Elspeth!" Alek's hushed shout tore from him, his hands clamping on her thighs.

Elspeth smoothed the heavy muscles of his shoulders, rested her palm over his racing heart.

"Elspeth-mine..." Alek struggled for breath, and Elspeth shivered as her body heated, moistened and tempted. Her nails dug slightly into his flesh as she bent to kiss the scar running across his shoulder and the one slicing his eyebrow. Her breasts dragged slowly, softly against his chest, the hair sensitizing her nipples, hardening them. The new sensation caught her, and she moved beneath him.

"Elspeth," Alek began, and stopped when she kissed the scar on his bottom lip. He groaned and held very still. "Do not move. Just don't move."

He trembled, cords standing out in his arms, his throat, his body barely joined to hers. Alek's fist wrapped in her hair, turning her face to him. He took her lips deeply, answering the savage need. He shook violently, trying to lie still, his hands braced at her head. "Don't you dare move, Elspeth."

His desperation was a challenge that she took, lifting her hips to capture him.

She'd forgotten, the weight and heat of him stretching her, and fought the cry tumbling from her lips.

Alek muttered a frustrated curse, then he found her breasts, kissing and suckling them quickly now, his body urgent; the sound of her hunger came, shocking her. This was Alek, Alek soothing her, caressing her, telling her—telling her what? She'd captured him, run him down through the years and tethered him. Elspeth rose to find his face, the pounding within her too loud to hear his words. She stroked the scar on his eyebrow with her thumb and slid her fingers through his hair, locking his to hers. She lifted again, her body taut and pounding, but she had to see him, to watch him move through his passion. Alek was beautiful above her, his face all rugged angles and tense cords. His eyes were brilliant, black and hot as he lifted his hips slightly. He stretched her gently, filling her until she cried out again.

His body plunged into hers, and she tossed him back. Again. Then the frantic, desperate rhythm began, Alek breathing as if his heart had run the fastest race, as if he ran to the edge, waited for her and then shot off into the heat. His cry came from the depths of his soul, as if he'd shattered there, lodged in her.

Just beyond her reach, whatever she sought taunted her. Alek drew her shaking body to him, his heart pounding beneath her cheek. He ran his hand down her back, caressing her and then covered her with a quilt that had warmed other lovers.

Elspeth snuggled close to him, mourned the moment of separation and sighed as Alek kissed her. She gathered him to her; for the moment, he was hers and the shadows were gone.

Una's shawl moved in the night, the moonlight playing over the shimmering colors, the fringes swaying gently in the breeze.

When the Marrying Moon is high, a scarred warrior will rise from the mists to claim his lady huntress. He will wrap her in the shawl and carry her to the Bridal Tepee and his heart. Their song will last longer than the stars....

For a moment, Elspeth fought tears and wished the shawl's legend was true.

Eight

Alek allowed Elspeth to slip from the cot. He fought the urge to drag her back to him—as if he had the strength to do anything but drag air into his lungs and regain his sight.

Elspeth had taken him and left the shawl as if it meant nothing to her. As if making love with him meant nothing.

He lay in the shadows, his arms behind his head, winded, filling his senses with their past lovemaking. Beyond his window, Elspeth's screen door creaked, and the night settled around him.

Alek rose to study Elspeth's dark house; there was no light. She liked moving through shadows, becoming one of them. He reached for a bottle kept on his dresser and poured a quick neat whiskey. He hadn't had a drink since December—when he'd first seen Elspeth in Talia's wedding picture—and he badly needed one now. The glass was halfway to his lips when Alek realized that Elspeth had not climaxed in his arms.

Nor had she on that night in Scotland.

She'd accepted his passion, soothed him later, but she had not fully entered the fire....

Alek sat abruptly, locked his fist to the sheets bearing Elspeth's scent and shook his head to clear it.

He began tracing their passion. He'd been intent on her pleasure that first time, then had lost himself and gone over the edge. He plopped the whiskey glass down on a stack of magazines and licked a drop from his wrist.

Alek forced himself to breathe. Melissa had been more like his sister than his wife. Their lovemaking had been tender and sweet, and Melissa had been shy their entire marriage. They'd been cautious, wanting children, but when wasn't he blazing a career in foreign wars? He'd known the moment he'd poured himself into Elspeth that he'd given her the deepest part of his being....

Elspeth wasn't sweet; lava ran beneath the surface. Yet she had waltzed through their lovemaking twice, never experiencing the full measure. Her heat ran just below the surface untested, and his body knew it.

Alek lay back carefully on the cot, bracing the glass on his naked stomach.

Elspeth had had him and left him. She'd gone back to her safe shadows and left him with the shawl, a reminder that she kept her secrets, and the Tallchief legend, to herself.

Preoccupied with the wrongs done to him and feeling fragile, Alek almost admired the curses boiling out of him. He threw the glass against the wall, glared at the shards mocking him in the moonlight and lurched to his feet.

He jerked on shorts and stepped out of his window and onto the huge oak-tree limb. Two more limbs, and he was within jumping distance of Elspeth's roof.

He stepped into her bedroom window and listened to the sound of her shower. Alek waited, prowling in the room scented of her and the lily of the valley blossoms in the old vase. Moonlight filtered through the window, running across the bed's old, hand-stitched quilt. He scooped her blouse and slacks from the bed, caught the scent of their lovemaking and crushed the material in his fists, flinging it to a chair. Because their precious daughter was about to be exposed—her cool veneer ripped away—Alek draped a lacy handkerchief over the framed portrait of the Tallchiefs.

Elspeth entered the room in a scent of soap and lavender. The sight of her naked body—breasts tilted high, the dip of her stomach, the curve of her hips— caused him to suck in his breath. Alek's hand latched to her wrist. "I don't like being used."

She turned on him, damp hair flying around her bare shoulders. "What?"

Alek stood back and kicked the door shut with his heel; he crossed his arms, fearing that he'd shake her. There was no kindness roaming in him now for Elspeth Tallchief. "What just happened in my bed?"

"I don't know what you mean."

"Anytime you want to play games, honey, just let me know the rules first, okay? You wanted to exorcise that night. Get rid of me, then come home, tidy up and forget the whole thing happened, right? Well, it did. It happened with me."

She frowned and backed up a step when he advanced. "Of course it did."

Alek picked her up and tossed her to the bed, following her down. He held her damp hair in one fist and braced above her. "It goes like this, Elspeth. When you come calling for me, plan to share breakfast with me."

She moved beneath him, the scent of her soap sending him precariously near taking her right then. He studied her. She wasn't afraid; rather, a keen anger had begun to brew. Good. He could deal with her anger, not her fear of him.

She shivered, control skimming along her voice. "Alek, I didn't know there were rules to this."

"You thought you'd just wander over, have a bit of sex with old hungry Alek, lay there, let him take—" Alek bit off a curse, then continued. "You come home, take a nice shower and drop off to sleep, right? Or was it more like, 'I think I'll give Alek whatever he wants and then he'll go away.' I've never been a nice guy when I want something, Elspeth darling. Don't count on my sympathy."

He was just getting wound up. He wanted Elspeth to understand everything boiling out of him. "You play hardball, Elspeth-mine, and I don't like it."

He'd never talked to a woman like this, pushed her, held her forcibly still beneath him. Of course he loved Elspeth Tallchief—that was a given—but a man had his pride. He'd just realized that he'd never given Melissa the deepest part of him, poured into her everything that he was, that he would be.

A fresh tide of anger and frustration ripped through him. Elspeth's face registered shock. He bent nearer to hear her whisper. For the first time, Alek began to realize that Elspeth had no idea of true fulfillment.

"It wasn't like that at all." Her lips quivered in the moonlight, and Alek bent to taste them. "I thought—"

"You thought you'd complete the circle and this time *you'd* walk away, correct?" he shot at her, his heart raw and exposed.

Alek found himself hard, wanting her. Elspeth eyes widened as his desire lay upon her stomach. "Oh, yes. I want you again, Elspeth-mine. I ache with it, hard. Not a little 'Oh, I think I'll get this off my calendar,' but damn hard, right down to my toes and back up to the pounding in my brain, not to mention other parts of me. Baby, this time, you can come along for the journey, too." Alek smoothed his hand down her leg, enjoyed the rippling of her muscles as she tensed and followed them back up to the soft, fragrant center of her.

"Alek!" Her soft cry of panic stopped him; it skittered through her eyes.

He hadn't meant to frighten her. He cursed himself rapidly, silently in whatever languages he could manage. His hands shook as he caught her close, drew her up to him to scan the terror in her light gray eyes.

"You don't know what this is all about, do you?" he asked, studying her shocked, flushed face.

Her flush ran all the way down her slender curves; he could feel it warm against his skin. "Sex. I suppose you want sex. I know the mechanics. I've lived on a farm. Alek, it's late and we've just— I thought you were finished."

Finished with me...the same as before...when you pushed away and left me on that stone, alone and torn— Alek went cold, just sensing the words Elspeth could be thinking. Then he'd ripped her apart with words to protect her, to protect himself.

There were times for words and there were times for loving. For touches and tenderness that Elspeth deserved. Alek found himself smiling down at her; maybe they were both new at the loving game. "This time, I'll do the thinking, okay? Not that your little foray left me much for brains."

Alek carefully placed his lips on hers, fused the shape of his mouth to hers, hoping to stamp the memory of this loving over the others. He kissed her until she softened, hungry little sounds coming deep in her throat. Gently, Alek reminded himself, gently. He cupped her breasts, cherished them, then the softness of her stomach and the mound below.

The hard thud of his blood, pounding at his temples, stopped him; he shoved back the desire to have her too quickly, reminding himself that this was the woman he loved, a treasure opening to him, damply, softly....

Hunger flowed in Elspeth now, arching her body to the sweep of his hand, her arms locked around his neck, her mouth fused to his hungrily.

She made love silently, Alek thought in the last remaining reasonable cell of his brain. He treasured her sounds, wrapped them against him and waited for her to say his name.

Elspeth tensed as he traced her soft opening, spreading the folds delicately with his fingertips to find the moist, taut bud; Elspeth bolted at first, then writhed beneath him, making outraged, frustrated noises. She flung back her head, her hair flowing around her, and raked him with her eyes. The moonlight caught the edge of her teeth, biting into her lip. "Alek!"

There was nothing cool about her now, the heat shimmering in her eyes, her heart hammering against his, lips trembling. Her fingers dug into his shoulders, anchoring him. "What do you want?"

"I want to spend the night with you. Naked. Here in this bed or in mine. I want to wake up to you, to hold you. It's a simple matter." Alek kissed her with the stark hunger raging inside him. He trembled when her lips slowly parted for his tongue, when her arms came out to lock around his neck and her body undulated in a quick, satisfactory movement beneath his.

"Don't push me, Alek," she warned, even as her lips bit his shoulder and her nails lightly raked his back. Her breath swept unevenly, rapidly across his skin.

"Wouldn't think of it," he murmured as he moved away from her, drawing away the old quilt. Elspeth's fingers dug into his arm, and he tensed, bracing himself against the fresh wave of desire. This time, she would know how he felt, shattered upon her just a short time ago.

Alek rested his head upon her breasts, nuzzling them and giving her time to adjust to him again. His hands stroked her breasts, her ribs and locked to the restless, quivering movement of her hips. Or was it he who needed to slow down and gather control? When Elspeth shivered, he opened his mouth on her breast and let her know how much he needed her. She jolted up, her hands ready to push away and then cradle his head against her.

Alek smoothed her restless, heated body from shoulder to ankle. "I want everything this time, Elspeth."

She murmured a protest as his hand smoothed her

inner thigh, moving to cup the fragrant nest of curls.
"No, Alek, don't."

"Don't what? Do you want me?" If she didn't—
Sheer terror swept through Alek, freezing him.

"Yes. Yes, I want you. But like before—"

"Oh, no, sweet Elspeth. I'm not letting you set the
rules this time. This time you won't lie quietly and let
me have you. This time you'll have to step into the
fire with me."

She breathed heavily, her body trembling beneath
his. "No. I won't—"

Yet her body—soft and moist and welcoming—
parted for his fingers. Elspeth's thighs pressed together, her hands shaking on his shoulders as he began
to kiss his way downward. His tongue in her navel
brought a shudder and an unwilling groan. A thumb
sweeping across her hipbone brought her arching upward. She moved with his hand now, flowing restlessly, her fingers anchored in his hair.

He held her still as the first small quivers tightened
around his fingers and Elspeth's nails bit into his
shoulders. "Alek, no. I can't take—"

"Yes, you can. But I'll stop if you want. Do you?"
Alek gritted his teeth, waiting for her answer. For her
and for the future he wanted with her, he would force
himself to do anything.

Her fingers dug into his shoulders, and a ripple shot
through her body, pleasing him. "Don't stop," she
whispered unsteadily.

He smiled at that, rising to sink into the delicious
heat of her mouth, drinking in her unsteady breath.
She gave and gave, demanding more, slanting her lips
against his, and then Alek began his thorough passage
down her body.

When his mouth touched her, Elspeth's hushed cry trembled on the night air. She squirmed beneath his touch, and Alek locked her to him until she trembled and went still. Her body arched to his touch as his lips took her breast, suckling, gently biting it and laving it with his tongue, and then he found her, lifting her to him. Elspeth's body jolted into a taut line, the delicate contractions within her began, giving him pleasure. He held her there, poised on the tip of her desire until the tightening slowed and Elspeth went limp, her hands locked to his damp shoulders.

She barely moved when Alek slid into her, rested over her, kissing her gently. "I didn't know," she whispered against his lips.

He moved his hips, filling her, and a second set of contractions began. This time Alek flung himself over the edge, his body thrusting into hers.

She cried out, fighting him and her, her body flowing beneath him, heating, shifting, tightening. Alek gave himself to the storm, reveled in it until it burst, raging through him. This time, she had taken and given, her heart pounding against his.

Alek cradled her against him, rocking her as the last shudders vanished. He tipped her face up to his and found what he wanted in her expression, a woman who'd been thoroughly loved and had loved back, a drowsy and sated look that filled him with pleasure. He ran his thumb across her soft, swollen lips, treasuring her. "And that is how it's going to be, Elspeth love. No self-sacrifice, no guilt...just the loving."

Still wrapped in her passion, shaken by it, Elspeth smoothed his cheek with her fingers. The touch was light, exploring him as if she'd just discovered him. She skimmed his throat, his shoulders, all the time looking at him with soft, drowsy eyes, her body tangled with his. "Stay."

As if he could stand. As if he was anything but one boneless, fuzzy grin wrapped in rose blossoms. He almost laughed at the thought, but the effort was too much. Instead he smoothed his chin over her hair, letting it tangle, web across his skin. Alek had poured himself too deeply within her to be free, had given her a part of him that he hadn't shared with another woman. Elspeth nestled against Alek, her legs tangled with his, her heart slowing as she slid into sleep.

Elspeth awoke to birds cheeping, the pink light of dawn entering her bedroom window and Alek's mouth upon her breasts. His hands caressed her stomach, her legs. "This isn't fair," she protested even as her body opened to receive his hard one and her lips opened to his.

Alek's hands ran beneath her hips, lifting her, his mouth feeding upon hers. He locked her to him until they moved as one, sharing body and skin and hunger.

She locked her hands to his hair and held him still for her kiss, and then the contractions started. Pleasure rolled through her, taking her. She held on to him, refusing to release him, his body thrusting into hers just as she wanted.

She wanted the primitive heat, the hardness of his thighs, his hands shaking yet gentle upon her heated skin. "You smell delicious," Alek murmured, running his hands down to her ankles and locking her legs around his hips.

Elspeth gasped and braced her hands on his chest. "Alek, I can't—I can't take any more."

"Dare you." His wicked grin set her off, caused

her to fling herself into the fire. His fingers reached between them, and Elspeth splintered into fiery shards. Minutes later, she managed to flop her hands from his sweat-damp shoulders. Alek showed no signs of moving, a single lid opening slowly. "Now, that is how it's done, Elspeth-mine. At least between you and me."

She grabbed his head and kissed him with the last of her strength. Alek settled down upon her breasts, and with a feeling of coming home, of safety, Elspeth stroked his hair and slept.

She dozed and awoke again to Alek's hand shackling her wrist and terror in his voice. "Come on, kid. You're okay. I'll get you out of here."

His legs threshed the sheets, his body taut and sweating. He pushed her away, fists gripping the sheets, feet moving. "I can't take it anymore...what happened to loving kids and keeping them safe?.... Yes, damn it, I'll finish your assignment, Doug. Just don't die...."

Elspeth placed her hand on his arm to wake him from his nightmare, but he flung it away. Tears gleamed on his lashes, trailing down his face. "Damn it," he cursed as if that labeled his pain. Then a brisk burst of a harsh language and a shift to a Latin-based one, probably French.

"Alek." Elspeth smoothed his hair and his cheeks as he tossed beside her. "Alek, you're here now. With me. Alek."

"Damn it," he said finally as if mourning the world while he moved from nightmares to reality. Alek's hand swept out to grasp her hair to tug her close to him.

She saw his nightmares lingering in his eyes. "I'm here, Alek."

"Did I hurt you?" he demanded hoarsely as if he'd die if he had.

She touched his damp lashes and remembered how he had cried with her about the baby. "No. You didn't hurt me."

He sat upright, turning his back to her. He washed his hands over his face hard, fighting the nightmare. "I could have. Damn. I could have."

"But you didn't, Alek." She ached for Alek, needing to comfort him. Elspeth sat up behind him, stroking the taut muscles of his back, his neck. She rose to her knees and folded her arms around him, rocking him gently. He allowed her petting, and she placed her face against his throat and rocked him. "I could get used to that."

"You're here now. Safe with me, Alek. Don't think about tomorrow." The words surprised her, she who had always thought of consequences and of tomorrow and of safety. First for her family, then for herself and now for Alek. Elspeth leaned her head against his shoulder and enclosed him with her arms until his shudders stopped completely.

He turned to her, tracing her face as if locking himself to a dream he wanted very much and shoving away the past. "I hate being weak like this. Sometimes I wake up— Elspeth, I could have hurt you. I wish...I wish we'd met before...when I hadn't seen too much."

"Wishes are for the taking," Elspeth whispered, and kissed him. She wished that he'd never awaken to his terrors again. "Here and now."

"Are they?" Alek cupped the back of her head and pressed her lips to his.

She floated beneath the tender assault, wrapping her arms and legs around him to moor him in the present, safe from the past.

"Sweet Elspeth-mine," Alek murmured, and the kisses changed, heated and they began again.

Alek reached for Elspeth and drew her against him, spooning her body against his beneath the quilt. His hand ran down her curves to the heat he sought. He lost himself in the fragrance of her hair swirling around him. Birds chirped outside her window, and children yelled in the street. This was how he wanted to wake up every morning. He nuzzled her throat, found the awakening pulse with his lips, ignored her sleepy protest and began to kiss her. Her bottom shifted on his lap as she snuggled back to him, sighing.

Alek closed his eyes and let his hands roam over his captive. With luck, he could keep her here all day—he smiled and wallowed in cuddling her against him.

"Well, well," Birk noted with an edge in his tone, and Elspeth tensed, her fingers digging into Alek's wrist.

"I suppose this means a wedding, Elspeth." Duncan's tone suggested tar and feathers for the man who had dishonored his sister.

"What if they're married already?" asked Sybil in a dry tone.

"Not a chance," stated Calum.

"Stop it, all of you," Sybil ordered, balancing Megan on her hip. In a tactic to deter Duncan, who was already moving toward the bed, Sybil plopped Megan in his arms. "There. You will not interfere with Elspeth's life."

"She's our sister," Birk stated in an outraged tone.

Talia laughed outright. "I think they look cute together. I've never seen Alek look so outraged. Isn't Elspeth gorgeous? And sweet. I think she looks sweet. At least neither one of them look like the living dead now."

"I'm going to beat the living crap out of him," Calum stated too coolly. "That contract was bad enough."

"What contract?" Talia asked, pivoting to her husband, the sunlight showing off the tiny mound of their baby.

"Duncan Tallchief, you told," Sybil stated, outraged. She plucked Megan from him and placed her on the bed. The toddler scrambled toward Alek and, with a squeal, launched herself upon him. Sybil stopped Duncan from retrieving his daughter. He glared at Alek as if he'd stolen another female away from his nest.

"I demand to know what Alek has done, Calum. You would keep this from me, a Petrovna?" Talia's tone caused Alek to feel sorry for Calum.

"Tallchief," Calum corrected in a flash.

"Duncan Tallchief." Sybil's tone said she had plans to teach her husband a lesson. Duncan had the good sense to look sheepish, all six foot four inches, two hundred thirty pounds of him.

Alek sat up, propped a pillow behind him and said, "I'll get you off the hook, Duncan. I arranged for a two-year exclusive contract in Denver. She's too good, and I wanted to see her work hanging where people could enjoy it. I also wanted her away from the pack of you, so that I could persuade her that she likes me.''

"You weren't on assignment?" Talia asked.

"My assignment days are over, kid. It was a plain case of wanting to get Elspeth alone, and all of you, standing here right now, are proof of that need.''

"Why, Alek. You're a romantic," Sybil murmured. "And you knew Elspeth before, didn't you?"

Elspeth let out a loud, protesting groan and closed her eyes. He took her hand, but she shook him off.

"We met five years ago when she was studying in Scotland. When Talia's wedding pictures arrived in December, there was Elspeth. I wanted her then and I want her now. It's as simple as that.''

He waited for that one to sink into the Tallchief brothers. Click. Click. Click. All three brothers' scowls locked in place. Alek frowned back.

"Nothing is ever that simple," Calum stated, already digging at facts, placing them in a neat row.

Elspeth groaned and flipped to her stomach, jamming the pillow over her head; Alek placed his hand over the curve of her bottom. He answered Megan's kiss and admired the satin ribbon she pointed to on top of her head. "Pretty, Meggie...Elspeth apparently is not taking appointments today.''

He placed Megan over Elspeth's bottom and let her bounce as though riding her rocking horse. Elspeth groaned aloud as Megan gurgled, delighted.

"She's never been afraid to face us," Duncan stated, outraged. "You, Petrovna. Outside.''

Elspeth groaned again and wiggled up to sit beside Alek. She placed a pillow between them. Megan launched herself at her aunt, and Elspeth cuddled the baby against her. "Go away, all of you."

Just looking at her with Megan started him thinking about— He sat back to admire the picture Elspeth made, rosy and warm from a night with him, a blanket tugged up to cover her breasts. He found a long strand of her hair and brought it to his lips. "She isn't an easy woman, but faced with a shotgun wedding, I'd sacrifice."

"Shotgun wedding. Try another century." Elspeth's snarl caused him to grin. Alek soaked in the sight of her, hair wildly flowing around her, cheeks flushed with outrage and eyes leveling hot, steely threats at all the males in the room. "Petrovna, shut up."

"Yes, ma'am."

After a warning look at Alek, Elspeth turned on her brothers. "Have I ever, ever butted into your love lives? I had plenty of opportunities between the three of you. When you were teenagers, it's a wonder your zippers held the strain."

Alek wanted to lick the gleam on her shoulders, but instead tugged on her hair. "She's feeling a bit testy and worried about my reputation."

"I thought I told you to—"

Birk glowered at Alek. "Huh. What did she do, drag you here? You outweigh her by a good eighty-five pounds."

"My, the testosterone in this room is fairly bubbling," Talia noted with delight, inching away from Calum's restraining hand. "This could be the makings of a new play."

Alek ran his finger along Elspeth's hot cheek and jerked it away before she bit him. "She came after me. This wasn't my plan at all. I'm a regular old-fashioned guy. I'd prefer necking and dating and picnics and the regular route to…ah…a relationship. But there she was, determined to have me, and what could I do?''

Too incensed to speak, Elspeth looked at him as though she'd like to tear him to bits. He jerked when her fingers pinched his thigh. After a quick search and another pinch, he captured her hand and brought it up on the blankets to hold it.

Elspeth's muttering was the frosting on Alek's well-devoured and sated cake. He knew he was glowing and grinning. ''At least she's not indifferent to me.''

''Idiot.''

Duncan snorted, drawing on his leather gloves. ''I've got a field to plow.'' He glared at Alek and then at Sybil, who was smothering a grin. ''I've got work to do. Any time, Alek. Name it.''

''They don't call him Duncan the defender for nothing.'' Sybil gave way to her grin.

Talia straightened the curtains at the windows. She glanced at the tree limbs connecting Alek's open window to Elspeth's. An experienced troublemaker, Talia knew exactly how Alek had traveled to Elspeth's bedroom. ''So, Elspeth. Are you keeping that dinner date with Jeremy Cabot? Or does this change things?''

Elspeth tried to reclaim her hand from Alek and couldn't. ''Alek and I are not going steady or engaged. Of course I'm keeping my date with Jeremy.''

That stopped Alek, who was foraging for his shorts with his toe.

Sybil cradled her cup of coffee and sat on the end of the bed. ''Don't glower, Alek. Mmm. Tell me what you know about Una's shawl, the one she seduced Tallchief with?''

''I did not seduce Alek,'' Elspeth stated firmly, edging away from Alek.

"I found the shawl. Used it as bait." He jerked her back, glowering at her after a full minute of trying to identify one Jeremy Cabot, a man soon to die. "Is that the idiot that runs the office at the feed-and-grain store? The piece of blubber who tries to fit himself into that tiny red sports car?"

She sat very straight and smoothed her hair. "He's always liked me. It's been only lately, since his divorce, that I've thought he might have possibilities."

Talia leaned against Calum, whose expression said he was putting lots of twos together. "You know, this reminds me of home, Alek. Remember when all of us piled into Mom and Dad's bedroom and Dad kept trying to shoo us away?"

"Una's shawl?" Duncan repeated too slowly in a tone resembling a growl.

"Get lost, and take your posse with you. Now." Alek didn't want to deal with the Tallchief brothers right now; they could take him apart later. He took Elspeth's wrist; Cabot wasn't getting her. Elspeth glared at him and tried to reclaim it. She picked up the pillow.

"You hit me," he stated a heartbeat later, and blew a feather from his lips. He slashed a hand down his face and glowered at her, the woman who had swung the pillow with enough force to tear it. He blew away another feather, tumbling down his forehead. Outraged that she would attack him after a night of lovemaking, Alek stared at her. When she didn't act as though she'd apologize, Alek wrapped the quilt around his waist and stood.

He looked out into the morning sunshine. The sheriff was parked on the street, binoculars focused on Elspeth's bedroom window. Beside him stood Elspeth's first-grade teacher, Mrs. Schmidt, shaking her head. A squad of little boys on souped-up dirt bikes stared with blatant interest and open mouths. Alek cursed; the boys would learn soon enough how a woman could make a man act like an idiot.

"That's mine," Birk stated as Alek reached back to grab a kilt that had been flung over a chair. A spool of thread attached to the hem rolled to the floor.

"I'm sure you won't mind me borrowing your skirt, under the circumstances," Alek returned. He stepped into the kilt, ignored the sewing pins jabbing him and crossed the limbs amid hoots and whistles from the Tallchiefs. Once in his bedroom, Alek slammed down his window. The phone ran a second later, while he was debating about which wall to take down. "Yes?"

He knew it was Elspeth by the soft breathing at the other end. She probably wanted the kilt back, but he served her a warning instead. "You date that jerk, and I won't be held accountable."

String circled Alek's ankles, and he traced it from the kilt's hem back to Elspeth's window. Duncan appeared, grim faced, and jerked something between his leather-gloved hands. The thread at Alek's kilt went limp.

Elspeth strained for control. "Alek Petrovna, don't you dare hurt Jeremy. He's been my friend for ages."

Alek crushed the shawl. He intended to disassemble Cabot. "Will all that lard fit into a bucket?" he asked in a too-pleasant tone.

Then he looked at the kilt he wore and smiled grimly. For the moment, he was wearing it just the same as the rest of the Tallchiefs. He began to wind the thread around his fingers. He was keeping as much of Elspeth as he could.

"What's that noise?" Elspeth asked as Sybil and Talia began laughing. Megan squealed in delight.

Alek finished his thread recovery and glanced out his window. "Why, Elspeth-love, I believe that's your brothers' chain saws."

"What?"

"It looks like they're cutting off my access route to your boudoir."

Her outraged gasp did wonders for his bruised ego. Alek slowly replaced the phone on its cradle. Beneath his window, Elspeth, dressed in a faded flannel robe that exposed her legs magnificently swooped upon her brothers. The revving chain saws died as they backed away from her accusing finger and found themselves against her house.

Though Alek couldn't hear the words, from her expression, they weren't pleasant ones. The brothers' expressions changed from outrage to frustration. Duncan began arguing with her, Birk threw down his western hat and Calum shook his head. Talia and Sybil stood on the porch and laughed. Elspeth threw up her hands. She pointed to the new flower bed the brothers had tromped.

"Huh. Look at that," Alek mused as Elspeth stalked to the water faucet and turned the hose on her three brothers. After they were dripping and Sybil and Talia doubled over with laughter, Elspeth began pacing in front of them, her flannel robe flying around her legs. Duncan, Calum and Birk stood rigidly against the wall, until she pointed at them and scolded. One by one, they spit a distance. Elspeth shook her magnificent mane, threw up her hands and stalked into her house. "I love it when that woman gestures. She's showing a real flair for it," Alek murmured.

The three brothers tromped and huffed and cursed and in the end packed up their chain saws.

Suddenly Alek felt much better and took the stairs two at a time on his way down to make breakfast.

He whistled while he fixed his cereal. After plucking away several pertinent pins from the back of the kilt, Alek sat down and propped his feet on another chair. He listened to the birds chirp, the revved-up teenagers' trucks prowling on the street and settled into a happy cloud of morning-after—

His back door opened and slammed. "Alek! Where are you?" Elspeth's tone was not sweet.

"In here, my love. Would you like breakfast? Have you come to court me or to drag me off to that shotgun wedding?" He was groggy on dreams, daft on making love with Elspeth and mellow with contentment. There was just something about seeing his lady love protect him. "You know Amen Flats isn't really that boring—"

When cold milk and soggy cereal ran down his head and onto his shoulders, Alek shivered. Then he grinned and licked a flake from his cheek. He leered at the gaping flannel robe and the curve of her breast. "Things are certainly looking up, Elspeth-mine."

"Jerk." She ripped his shorts from her pocket and dropped them on his head.

"I'll treasure that endearment forever." Alek sat very still as Elspeth lifted the carton of milk and slowly poured it over his cereal and his shorts. He tilted his head to better appreciate the slope of her breast. "Are you going to make me spit, too?"

He got a delicious view of a taut, dark nipple when Elspeth threw up her hands. "I used to make them

settle their differences that way—spitting contests to
see who could spit the farthest.''

''I love a passionate, dominating woman,'' Alek
murmured, and leered up at her. ''Let's try whipped
cream next time.''

''Whipped cream...'' Elspeth's hand reached for the
bed sheets, hovered and then she decided to leave
them. She dusted the feathers from it and remembered
how outraged he'd been, feathers drifting around his
black, shaggy head and shoulders.

She picked up the abused pillow, and Alek's scent
clung to it.

A wave of stark longing washed over her, startling
her. She couldn't want him again. Not after last night,
her body still aching from his. Yet images of Alek
flashed through her mind, forcing Elspeth to brace herself against her emotions as she always did. She
quickly made the bed and took a long, thorough
shower, and the images returned. Alek, dressed in
Birk's kilt, created a memorable picture. Complete
with breakfast cereal and extra milk, he looked delicious. He had sat very still while she poured, then
smiled hopefully up at her with milk dripping off his
nose.

His little-boy expression had changed too rapidly
back to a dark, passionate one. He'd wiped his face
with one big hand and leveled a glare at her. ''You
date Cabot and—''

Elspeth had reacted instantly, hooking one foot beneath the legs of his chair and pulling, sending him
sprawling down in a mass of muscled, hairy legs and
tangled kilt. She'd placed her bare foot on his cereal-
spattered chest. ''Hmm. Threats. Take a note, Alek.

Don't ever threaten me...I have lived with arrogant, threatening males all my life. I have experience in dealing with them."

Then, disgusted that Alek had provoked her and lay grinning as if he'd single-handedly won a football game, she had tried for an even tone. "I think I need to get out more," she had stated elegantly before returning to her home.

She'd broken every rule that she'd ever made—losing her temper with Alek Petrovna. There was no reason she shouldn't date Jeremy and add to a growing list.

Elspeth rummaged through the lacy lingerie she'd stuffed into a pretty flowery box and selected a white lace bra-and-panty set. Her body told her that she'd strained every muscle while making love to Alek, and a few she hadn't known existed. "And that is how it's going to be," he'd said after their lovemaking.

There was nothing sweet about Alek's lovemaking, not at the center of it, while he held her on high on that fiery, throbbing pinnacle and still demanded more— Who was he to make rules about their lovemaking? To say what and how and when?

She couldn't forgive him for unleashing her emotions, for exposing her need of him.

"Shotgun wedding," she said, repeating Alek's light concession. She had no intentions of getting involved with Alek.

She was involved. For starters, she never wanted Alek waking to his nightmares alone. He should be held and tended and loved.

Elspeth groaned. She knew herself, the old-fashioned steel built into her. She ran her hand across her mother's quilt, the one she'd been holding that terrible night long ago in the kitchen.

Alek Petrovna had come from another time, from another world in which she'd given herself.

She'd changed. Or had she?

She'd changed, the proof lodged in her body.

Elspeth placed her hand over her eyes and sat upright. *Elspeth…* She recalled his murmur, close and hot against her. She didn't trust Alek Petrovna; he was far too experienced at games and always pushing her, prodding her about what she'd locked inside. The shawl's legend was none of his business. She'd tossed it and her romantic dreams away after returning from Scotland.

Elspeth shivered and reached for her jeans, drawing them on and zipping them. She sucked in her breath and glanced at the light scrape marks on her stomach caused by Alek's morning stubble. The rough denim material rubbed against the sensitized flesh of her thighs, and Elspeth groaned.

This morning, Alek's back had shocked her, pink lines showing where her nails had scraped him. A rush of heat shot through her, and Elspeth groaned again. She quickly drew on an old blouse she hadn't worn for years. Alek had demanded everything, kissing her intimately, touching her. He'd handled her gently, firmly, committed to extracting the ultimate from her.

Elspeth let out an unfamiliar, long, frustrated groan.

She shook her head. Sex with Alek shouldn't have gone so far, nor taken her so high, nor should gentler emotions tug at her now.

Elspeth threw up her hands. What did she know about sex? She'd been unprepared for the shattering, and no amount of preparing could have shored up her walls, her protection.

It was eight o'clock. Elspeth shivered and swept the lacy handkerchief from her family portrait. At least Alek had that much decency before he planned his raid.

Downstairs, for the first time in her life, her loom held little interest. She was too restless. Elspeth forced herself to sip her morning herbal tea and then work her hair into one long braid. The sounds coming from next door said that Alek had set out to remove another wall—or tear his house apart. She listened intently and decided she liked Alek Petrovna worked up and frustrated.

Elliot Pinkman, an older man needing to supplement his retirement income, came to till her garden and haul away brush. "Mornin', Elspeth. You're looking in the pink. Flushed, sort of. You been baking?" Elliot sniffed the June air. "Nope, can't smell that good bread of yours. You sure look worked up. Alive. Full of it. Haven't looked that way in a few years."

"I've...I've been moving my loom, Elliot. You know how big it is. I've got to get back to it." Elspeth quickly made her retreat and glanced at the mirror. She placed her hands on her hot cheeks and released the taut, frustrated "Aargh!" to the shadows of her home.

Elliot knocked at her door. "I could help you move that loom, Elspeth."

"Thank you for asking, but it's all right now," she lied. Nothing would ever be the same again, not with Alek dipping in her life.

Jeremy called, clearly aware of the morning's events. He wanted to confirm their dinner date. Jeremy hesitated slightly before asking her if she had a "thing" for Alek Petrovna. Her "We're neighbors and Talia is his sister," pacified Jeremy, who had been hovering around her for years, even during his marriage.

This morning, Elspeth decided to ignore her garden, ignore her waiting loom and Mark's messages on her answering machine. She slapped sandwiches into a backpack and drove to Tallchief Cattle Ranch.

The time had come to visit her parents, resting high on Tallchief Mountain. When she'd returned five years ago, she couldn't bear taking her shame to them—that she had loved a married man and had taken his child.

Her mother had always told her that a special love waited and Una's journals had supported that belief. Elspeth had returned with crushed dreams and chose to mourn her baby alone. Though she thought of them often, her parents' love had been so perfect that it seemed they should rest, undisturbed by Elspeth's dark storms.

She'd missed the visits with her mother, as daughters do, and now it was time to share her life with them.

Like a violent summer storm on the mountains, Alek had changed her life yet again. Her parents needed to know about him.

Alek. She refused to surrender to him easily. Years ago, she'd tasted heaven in his arms, certain that life would grow richer and love would come to call. Those dreams were dashed too soon and that trust was hard to regain.

Did she trust Alek? Not quite. He pushed too much, moved too quickly and wanted too much. She wasn't ready to give her deepest heart, the privacy she kept as her fortress. She doubted that now she could give that part to anyone...

A man who could and had changed her life, Alek wanted everything. Elspeth clung to her safety, weaving it around her like a shield. As a girl, she'd lost her parents, and then Alek.... She feared another loss would take her deeper into the shadows....

She needed this visit to quiet the sadness within her. Her parents had missed so much of their children's lives and now it was time....

When she arrived at Tallchief Cattle, Duncan had saddled Delight, a sturdy brown-and-white mare. He'd always known when she needed to ride up the mountain; they shared the Tallchief intuitions.

As he watched her strap on her chaps, Duncan's expressive eyes told her he worried but that he understood. He nodded to her and held out the reins. Elspeth placed her western hat on her head, nodded to her brother before placing her foot in the stirrup and rising to the saddle. Duncan didn't say anything, nor did she; the Tallchiefs understood that dark moments roamed within them and needed privacy. She took the trail to Tallchief Mountain, passing through the shadows of the pines up a rocky stretch and over meadows filled with grazing Tallchief sheep.

It was the first time she'd taken the trail to her parents' graves in those five years.

Nine

Chipmunks ran up the red bark of the pines, and rabbits crossed Delight's path as she carried Elspeth upward. In an aspen clearing, Elizabeth Montclair, Elspeth's great-grandmother, had met the son of Una and Tallchief. Liam Tallchief, a half blood, had fought his captors who wanted him to dishonor Elizabeth. To save her sister, Elizabeth had agreed to shed her pride, marry the savage in his customs and take him into her body. Then Liam had followed her to England to revenge his pride, his seed taken from him unwillingly by the English heiress. She'd given up everything to be with him, to return to Tallchief land.

The mountain sun burned through the trees, and a lizard baked on a lichen-covered rock. Scarlet Indian paintbrush blooms quivered in the wake of scurrying ground squirrels.

Elspeth lifted her head and sighted a cliff where

LaBelle Dupree, her grandmother and a reformed international jewel thief, had hidden her treasures. LaBelle had been a bit of a tomboy, something like Fiona, always into trouble, and she'd loved intrigue. Nothing satisfied her like plucking fortunes from the wealthy. Until Jake Tallchief had turned up at her fancy soiree and blackmailed her into marriage. Jake had only wanted to capture her, to prevent her from hanging or worse, and tuck her under his wing. LaBelle, once faced with a man she couldn't push to do her bidding, had fallen deeply in love with him.

Now LaBelle's earring was Alek's.

Elspeth slid the reins through her fingers and glanced up at the clear blue June sky. Her ancestors had loved deeply, and she would settle for nothing less.

Alek had carried the woven swatch with him for years.

Elspeth ran her hand across her damp lashes, not wanting to believe the tenderness in Alek's arms, the gentle, reverent way he touched her.

A doe bounded across the path, startling Delight. Elspeth calmed her in a soft, gentling tone. The sound reminded her of Alek, whispering wild, exotic things to her, treasuring her with his body....

A hawk swooped down in a grassy meadow, reminding Elspeth of Alek. In a cave beyond that meadow, Pauline Dante, the first woman judge of Amen Flats, had been held hostage. Matthew Tallchief, her childhood nemesis, and a sheriff's deputy assigned to protect her from threats, had tracked the kidnappers and rescued her. There in the meadow, he'd won her heart by reciting Greek mythology.

Elspeth stood in the saddle, absorbing the mountain's familiar sounds and scents. Her eyes swept the valley below, a blend of rich fields, winding roads and the small town of Amen Flats. She stretched, her muscles aching from Alek's lovemaking and from riding. Elspeth inhaled the pine scents and knew that she'd never pitted herself against anyone, any challenge, like Alek.

She'd never felt more alive.

She believed in her senses, in what they told her before the happening; they'd told her that Alek would be coming and that he would change her life.

Lovers' whispers swept through the pine branches, and Elspeth shivered because they sounded familiar, the tone the same as Alek's and hers.

Delight grazed in the meadow while Elspeth settled near her parents' graves. She folded her arms over her knees and let the tears roll down her cheeks.

She'd created a safe nest, and now he'd come to tear her loose.

The wind whispered along her body. It caressed the tendrils of hair near her face, and she remembered her mother's words, *Love isn't calm, Elspeth. It's fierce joy, rising out of your very soul. Love can shatter and hurt and, if it's real, it will take the wear and become stronger. There are no guarantees, nothing but the tenderness in a man's eyes that's just for you. When your time comes, honey, take a chance.*

Elspeth crushed a bluebell stalk. Alek's black eyes had been very tender. He'd placed his face into the hollow of her shoulder, a gentle, sweet gesture from a hard man.

Elspeth held the wildflower bouquet and thought of the heather that Alek had given her that night. She'd taken one chance with Alek Petrovna. Could she withstand another?

You sense things, probably because of your seer and shaman blood. Duncan has a bit of the gift, but not as much as yours. You'll know, Elspeth, when the man is right. You'll feel like you're walking on air when he looks at you. There's a fever in your blood that is only for him.

Elspeth had been too full of thoughts about Alek; he'd washed away the premonitions she'd come to expect. Even now, she saw flashes of him wherever she looked, big arrogant and bold, pushing...pushing....

Elspeth placed her forehead on her arms, braced over her knees. Alek moved too quickly; he was too passionate, too ready to laugh or to rage...or to kiss her as if all his dreams were wrapped up in her.

Your heart will know, even if you deny him, dear. The Tallchiefs are a complex brood, and I've always known that love wouldn't come easy to you.

At five o'clock in the afternoon, Amen Flats's Main Street began settling in for the weekend. The scent of apple pie and backyard barbecues hung in the June air. High-school boys in their spotlessly waxed trucks and cars cruised up and down. The butcher hauled an extra order of hamburger into the local drive-in. Trucks and cars were already parking near Maddy's Hot Spot, and the sheriff had slept in that morning to prepare for Friday night and payday on the ranches.

At eight o'clock, the ballfield lights would flick on for the start of the first softball game. Families would sit on blankets lining the field, and babies would sleep through it all.

A hay baler prowled down Main Street, on its way

for repair at Powell's Machinery. Forced to move aside, a tractor ran up on the sidewalk, the driver cursing and slapping his battered Stetson. Dirty from working in the fields and building fence, a truckload of college boys home for the summer whistled at Sexy Sue, who wore a gold chain around her waist and had just gotten a brand-new rose tattoo on her ankle. According to gossip, Sexy Sue had pierced more than her ears, and the boys were drooling to know just what.

With Megan strapped to his back, Alek sorted through his thoughts. He'd grown up in a town just like this, his teenage hormones lusting after another version of Sexy Sue before Melissa.

When it came to Elspeth, maybe his hunger hadn't changed. Alek stared at Jeremy Cabot leaving the feed mill in his red sports car. Jeremy did not return Alek's unwavering stare. Alek managed not to flinch when Megan's wet fingers investigated his ear and a certain warm dampness spread down his T-shirt. When Cabot's sports car shot out of sight, Alek cursed the intricacies of diapers with sticky tabs; his engineering attempt had been admirable, if lopsided.

Outside the newspaper office, Alek crouched in the midst of the dirt-bike squad. Bundled to his back while Sybil shopped, Megan alternately cooed and giggled and jabbered at the boys surrounding her.

Alek liked the feeling of the toddler on his back almost as much as he liked her in his arms.

"They're girls. I can shoot off a ramp, fly up ten feet, spit another ten feet and still come down on both tires." Jimmy Lattigo, the biggest of the ten- to twelve-year-olds, wanted a steeper ramp to jump his bicycle.

"Who says we're girls?" Ace Wheeler demanded.

"You're lucky you don't drown when all that spit flies back in your face."

"Jimmy is a show-off. Watch this." Mad Matt, his baseball cap on backward, glared at Jimmy and spit a perfect arc into the street.

"Nice shot, Matt. I always thought the best riders were the most careful. They finished, while the ones showing off laid on the pavement, bleeding their guts out." Alek tightened the sagging bicycle chain for Killer McGee. The raging discussion was a mix of air gauges, wheelies, tire treads and Annie Jones, who wanted to kiss the entire gang.

Alek had been amid other children, hungry, damaged ones. The grins on these faces said that no one was hungry and the biggest problem was soap and fleeing Annie Jones's mushy kisses. It eased Alek to know that in Amen Flats, most parents took care of their children and that they could sleep at night without fearing for their lives. There were images of children he would never forget.

"He's been in wars. He knows everything." Shark Malone's freckles caught the afternoon sun. Shark didn't know that Alek had failed the diapering rodeo twice before succeeding—somewhat.

Alek reached to ruffle a boy's unruly hair, and another small boy—Tyree—timidly placed his hand in Alek's. His mother had made Jimmy take Tyree, and Jimmy wasn't happy about a kid brother in tow. Alek knew the feeling; as a boy, he'd been mortified when stuck with Anton and his sisters.

A horseback rider came down the center of the street, and people came from their offices and stores to watch.

Alek stood slowly, keeping Tyree's hand in his.

Maybe he needed the boy's support; maybe he needed to take a breath before he passed out. Electricity played along his skin, and his pulse rate zapped into overdrive.

Megan squealed with delight and bounced on Alek's back as she recognized her aunt.

Elspeth sat straight, shoulders back, the wind tugging at her dirty and torn blouse. Each movement of the horse caused a soft movement of her breasts. Her hair, loose around her shoulders, rippled and gleamed, black as a crow's wing. The chaps covering her jeans were as worn as her western boots. Her gloved hand rested on her thigh, and the other skillfully managed the reins.

Beneath the straight brim of her black western hat, Elspeth's eyes were steady heat, searing Alek's. She stopped the horse directly in front of him. There wasn't a shadow touching her; she was all steel, all woman and knew what she wanted.

Alek sucked in his breath and knew that what Elspeth wanted, she would take. Maybe it was Una's shawl...maybe, just maybe it might be him. His brain swarmed with dreams and hopes, while a solid ache lodged low in his body, turning his thighs into stone.

Elspeth's mare held still as the squad hopped on their bikes and circled Elspeth on Main Street.

Birk's pickup, laden with a portable concrete mixer, slowed to a stop. Calum, laden with grocery sacks of Talia's latest craving, placed the sacks on Birk's hood. The brothers stood side by side, legs spread, arms across their chests, their faces impassive.

"She always was the best horsewoman around," someone murmured behind Alek. "Her mother rode like that. Straight back, eyes that could see into a man's soul and find the dirt in it. She was a judge right here in Amen Flats. I saw her mother wound up, one day, and Elspeth right behind her. The two of them came after Lacey MacCandliss's mother. You could feel the spit and fire coming off them when they rode into town that day. Everyone knew that when Pauline Tallchief rode like that on horseback and came into town by herself, someone had stepped over the line. Though only a bit of a girl, Elspeth was right at her side, riding straight backed and looking like steel. Never knew what they said to Ms. MacCandliss, but she didn't treat her little girl as bad after that.''

Lee Braker picked up the Tallchief story. ''The Tallchiefs all pulled their weight when they lost their folks. Sometimes they're plenty hard to understand because of those times. Every one of them has that Tallchief steel, clear through. Elspeth took on her mother's chores right then and never complained. She was a champion trick rider when she was fourteen and making a nice penny at it, too. Or else she was at her loom, earning another penny, or in the kitchen trying to keep her family fed.''

As Elspeth sat straight, watching Alek, he knew he'd pay hard for loving her. Deep down, there was the steel that had kept the Tallchiefs together, and they'd fight when pushed. But from the look of Elspeth now, the fights would be out in the open, not in the shadows of the past. It was worth the battle. She didn't give an inch, her expression unreadable, and Alek wanted it that way; she had a right to her privacy.

Tyree's eyes were enormous as Alek walked with him to Elspeth. The four-year-old boy clung to Alek's leg, peering up at her. ''He's afraid of the horse,'' Elspeth noted curtly.

Alek slowly took in her hat, the faded pink blouse, jeans and boots. "Did you get it settled?" he asked, even as he knew the shadows had shifted in Elspeth.

She'd gone to the mountain, searching for answers and a measure of peace. He ached for her, because she'd torn herself apart along the way. Alek wanted to reach for her, to wrap her safely in his arms, but knew she'd have none of that tenderness between them now. Sunlight slanted down the set of her jaw. Sometime during the day, she'd cried, a tear streak dragging across her cheek.

Elspeth ignored Alek's question; she'd answer him when she was ready and not before. She tipped her hat western-style, and went dizzy with the sight of Alek. On the afternoon after their loving and subsequent cereal dumping, he was dressed in low-riding jeans, a faded T-shirt and a teething infant's drool on his shoulder. He stood there, combat boots locked to the pavement the color of sundown, his jaw set, a tense muscle working beneath his dark skin. Slashing cheekbones, soaring black eyebrows and beautiful, curling lashes ran into a nose that had been broken and then to a tight, scarred, unforgiving mouth. She preferred that mouth in its natural sensual curve or widened in a grin that softened his face. When he fused his mouth to hers, assaulted her senses—

She gripped her thigh with her glove and remembered Alek's big hands soothing her. Raw-boned, big and tough, there wasn't anything sweet about him— until he tasted her, because that's surely what he did, tasted. There in the dying light, shadowed by the mountains she loved, Alek stood amid the children he deserved. The infant strapped to his back could have been his own. Alek wanted a family and he wanted her. Fear shot through Elspeth, and she gripped the reins tighter, startling Delight.

She wouldn't know how to keep him when the excitement outside Amen Flats beckoned to him. She couldn't bear loving him one day and then finding him gone the next.

She didn't know how to trust her emotions; she'd kept them locked and safe too long.

"We're planning a Fourth of July soap-box derby," Alek said, and she knew that he wanted something from her that she wasn't ready to give. The currents were there, running through Elspeth's eyes, though her face remained impassive.

"I've never ridden on a horse like that. Can I ride on your horse?" Tyree asked shyly, and Elspeth shivered in the late heat of the day.

Alek realized suddenly that Elspeth kept her distance from children this age. She looked strong enough to take anything now, and he decided to push her a bit more; Alek wanted her eyes to flash and smoke at him. He bent to lift Tyree to his hip. "She's got a hot date tonight. She might not want to right now."

Elspeth shot him a look that would have made her brothers take two steps back. Instead, Alek took one toward her and pushed again. "I bought the Kostya place."

The moment he'd seen the old ranch, he knew it suited Elspeth; laden with flowers and vegetable gardens, the yard spread into fields and the fields spread into mountain meadows. He could see Elspeth rocking a baby on their front porch, running after a toddler and swinging a child.

He could see her in the old house, busy at her loom

or walking and spinning on the huge old wheel on the front porch.

Alek's heart skipped a beat as he saw her in the old bedroom, dressed in yards of old-fashioned nightgown and waiting for him.

The mare pranced backward; Elspeth's soft mouth firmed, sunlight catching on the edge of her jaw, spilling down to her breasts, flowing with the horse's restless, sidestepping prance. "The Kostyas haven't wanted to sell their ranch."

Smolder. Steam. Heat. Alek pushed her again. The lady had a chip on her shoulder, and he liked prodding it into a precarious tilt. "I'm from Russian stock, and they knew a Petrovna once. They like the idea of ties to their homeland continuing their ranch and want to retire into town. I traded them this house and any modifications they want. They're in their new motor home, headed to a South Dakota reunion of their native village."

Elspeth narrowed her eyes. "What are you going to do with their ranch?"

"Grow things." *Hold you. Kiss you. Love you. Marry you. Make children with you. Adopt children and give them homes. Keep them safe and then love you more.*

"You're not a rancher, Alek. It isn't easy."

"I'll learn what I have to. I'll make mistakes, but I'll learn." *I've made mistakes with you—I'll learn what makes you happy.*

Delight pranced beneath Elspeth, and she ran a gloved hand down the mane's neck, soothing her.

Alek stood and waited for her to make her call; he realized that he hadn't known the meaning of fear until now. Living in war zones, lit by rockets and bullets, hadn't prepared him for the freezing terror that she might not want him on a permanent basis.

If she didn't, he'd get drunk first and fall apart later and pick himself up to try again. She'd have a hard time getting rid of him. He locked his boots to the pavement and waited.

Elspeth's brothers walked to Alek. Birk lifted Megan from Alek's back and cuddled her on his hip. "Say 'Birk,' Meggie. Birk is your favorite uncle. You're wet, kid. Uncle Alek needs diapering lessons, doesn't he?"

Calum snorted and placed his hand on Alek's shoulder as they watched Elspeth manage the mare easily. "Women," he said, as if the word explained the intricacies of the universe. "Elspeth the elegant can take the heart out of you when she rides. She hasn't in years."

She's got my heart now. Alek crossed his arms over his chest. Because if he didn't, in another minute he'd be up on that horse, taking her out of town.

Elspeth smiled at Tyree, a strand of hair whipping along her cheek and flowing into the wind. "Her name is Delight, and she's the gentlest horse on the Tallchief spread. Her grandmother was my first horse, and they both loved little boys the best. Do you really want to ride with me?"

"I...I guess so." Tyree was too scared to know that Elspeth rarely came close to children this age; Alek ached for her.

Tyree's thumb was almost in his mouth when his big brother pushed it down firmly. "If you wet your pants, you're in double-dutch trouble, shrimp."

Tyree turned slowly to his brother and from his look, his brother would pay for that one day.

"I've never ridden in a soap box. Do you think I could ride in yours?" Elspeth asked Tyree, distracting him from the wet-pants shame.

Tyree's eyes went wide. "You never? You can sure ride in mine."

Alek lifted Tyree in front of Elspeth and envied the little boy. She placed her hat on his head and wrapped one arm around him. With the other, she guided the mare through her paces, circling the street slowly, then trotting, then stopping, shifting directions and repeating the fancy steps.

Alek went lightheaded just looking at her. The dying sunlight caught on Elspeth, her hair swirling around her, and his heart stopped. Somewhere violins played—he was certain of it—and rose blossoms fell like rain. Maybe it was rain, sparkling in sunlight. Maybe it was moonlight and angels singing. He tossed in butterflies and magic fairy dust and listened to the uneven flip-flop of his heart. He dragged in a necessary breath of air and hoped no one heard it come out as a lovesick sigh. He locked his knees, because they were getting weak at the sight of Elspeth's taut body, moving as one with the mare, controlling her.

"Welcome to the pack, Petrovna. You're in love," Calum remarked dryly. "You're also drooling. The thing about all this is that from now on, you won't have an idea what hit you. By the way, did you know Megan wet your back?"

"Babies, laundry and a spare tire around his belly. Having to explain a beer at Maddy's and why the dishes weren't done. It's all downhill from now on," Birk added, and returned Megan's wet kiss.

"Getting up at midnight and waking up the grocer when she wants pistachio ice cream with kraut."

Calum rummaged through the grocery sacks. "Good. I didn't forget the pickled artichoke hearts."

"Gag," Mad Matt commented, his finger in his mouth.

"I think I'm going to swoon," Alek stated, meaning it. The Tallchief brothers' eyes widened, and then they began to laugh, rolling laughter that turned the townspeople's attention to them.

Mrs. Schmidt began to weep, and Maddy wiped a tear from his eye with a bar towel. He gave the towel to Mrs. Schmidt, who blew her nose on it.

An old cowboy, bent by years of ranch work, drew out his harmonica and began to play "The Yellow Rose of Texas."

Alek leaned back into the shadows and knew that if Jeremy Cabot put one finger on Elspeth, he was—

Jimmy peered up at Alek and asked, "Who's dead meat?"

Elspeth struggled out of Jeremy's arms for the twentieth time that night. The effort cost her; she ached from head to toe and back again. She'd discovered that a man's hands could be sweaty and soft. Then the tiny muscles within her body reminded her of her night with Alek. There was nothing soft about Alek, all hard angles and strong, rippling muscles...he'd demanded and took, and she'd given and demanded more, hungry for him.

Jeremy's flabby body pressed against hers again; it seemed as if she were fighting a living, sweaty swamp. She'd regretted her impulsive date with him from the moment he placed his hand on her knee—which was an immediate event, once they were in his car. Jeremy's sneaky looks at her thighs beyond her new short skirt disgusted Elspeth, almost as much as his eating habits.

Sideburns did nothing for his chubby face and fat lips. His shirt barely closed over his round belly, a middle button severely strained. She'd liked him while they were in school, but Jeremy had truly gone to pot and to pork. Somewhere between shy Jeremy with glasses and this Jeremy with busy hands, he'd lost that sweetness that she remembered.

"Let's not say good-night just yet," Jeremy crooned, sneaking another appreciative look at her thighs. "You are a strong woman, Elspeth. Uh...I don't suppose you'd ask me in for a drink?"

"No, I don't suppose I would." If Jeremy tried one more move, he'd find out just how strong she was. He was her first experience with a man who— She realized suddenly that Alek hadn't forced his hands on her. When Alek leered, something rose out of her that wasn't disgust, rather the need to pit herself against him. In one day, her male menu was certainly varied— from Alek to Jeremy.

She eased up and out of Jeremy's tiny sports car, her horse-riding muscles protesting every move. "Good night, Jeremy. It's been an experience."

"But honey—" Jeremy glanced at Alek's porch light, which had just flicked on. Alek came onto the porch and stretched, then folded his arms across his chest. "Uh...I'll call," Jeremy muttered, and sped away.

Alek stared at Elspeth through the night and a bird swooped between them. She stared back, and a ripple of excitement shot through her. She decided against talking to him, rehashing her miserable first date with Jeremy, and walked slowly to her door, aware that

Alek's gaze followed her, daring her to start something with him.

"Have fun?" he drawled in a Texas tone that sparked her temper.

"Of course." She wouldn't let him know that the evening rated a total zilch.

"Lady, you've got an attitude. Next time, let me know when you want to go out."

"What makes you think you'd get top billing?"

This time, Alek's voice was menacing like an approaching thunderstorm, with all the lightning bolts ready to zap. "Like I said. You've got a real attitude."

"Suits me," she returned airily when every muscle in her body reminded her that Alek had made thorough love to her the previous night. Elspeth decided she would pick when and where, and Alek could look all he wanted. There was just something about Alek that created in her the need to walk in a leisurely manner, letting her short skirt work slowly up her thighs. Mail-order catalogs definitely had advantages in tiny Amen Flats; once she'd started ordering an updated wardrobe, Elspeth had had to force herself to stop. She really enjoyed short skirts against her thighs.

She shot Alek a look over her shoulder and watched him sizzle, his brows jamming together fiercely, his body taut. Elspeth stopped outside her door and blew him a kiss, just as he had done to her.

If he would have just come to her, she could have— But he didn't, and that nettled Elspeth.

Whatever Alek Petrovna was, he wasn't flabby or unexciting. Just looking at him gave Elspeth pleasure. Pleasure was one thing, excitement another, and desperation to have Alek kiss her yet another.

Once inside her house, Elspeth passed by her loom

and realized suddenly that today was the first time she had not spent hours weaving or spinning or carding.

She groaned, her muscles aching as she made her way up the darkened stairway. Once in her chamomile-scented bath, scrubbed free of Jeremy's busy hands, Elspeth leaned her head back against the wall and closed her eyes.

At nine o'clock in the evening—after one hard, long day and the night preceding it—she should have been exhausted. She wasn't. Usually in this mood, she would be at her loom…but it didn't soothe her tonight.

Alek had stood in the midst of the boys with Megan strapped on his back as if he'd last forever. As if he'd come to her to stay. As if nothing could keep him from her. His wide grin had caused her heart to flip-flop, and the answering twinges in her thighs as she rode told Elspeth that she wasn't finished with Alek, not just yet.

He'd bought the Kostya place, a beautiful homestead with natural meadows and fields plowed by mules. It bordered the Tallchief land, and Duncan had been trying to buy it for years. The Kostyas were a beautiful elderly couple, steeped in their Russian background and mourning their son, killed in a minor revolution. Alek would appeal to them, a man needing a home, scarred by life and pain, ready to laugh, ready to love—

Elspeth groaned and shook her head. She was high on fresh air, playing with her lambs and freedom. She'd needed the day on the mountain, the visit to her parents' graves and the reminder that their love had touched her life. She soaped her leg, lifting it to survey the strong yet slender line. Alek had possibilities, if properly trained.

Distance, she decided. She needed proper distance from Alek to balance what she needed. A friendly relationship wasn't possible, not now. He was pushing her too much, offering to sacrifice himself to a shotgun wedding, a willing victim of the Tallchiefs.

Alek Petrovna would have to learn how to behave.

She ached in every muscle possible, and yet she wanted—

Elspeth rose, dried slowly and lay upon her bed. Alek's scent caressed her, and she pressed her face to the pillow they'd shared. Elspeth flopped to her back and watched the moonlit ceiling of her room and groaned. However she'd strained her body today and made a fool out of herself by showing off in front of Alek, she had to face him again. Today she'd reclaimed a part of her life and she wanted to tie up one last loose end. Alek had no right to give her Una's shawl, to make it so easy for her. She had left the shawl because the *giving* bothered her. *What was hers, she would take.*

Tonight, Elspeth was up to reclaiming the shawl and whatever else was hers. If Alek interfered...she smiled into the night and hoped he wouldn't make it easy. She wasn't an easy woman and she did so enjoy challenges, the hunter in her lifting to the scent even now...

Alek could be ruthless, withholding what she needed; another man would have come to her tonight and tried an apology. But not Alek—he only offered to be her victim in a shotgun wedding.

She could have strangled him for that.

Elspeth dressed slowly in black shorts and a black T-shirt. At eleven o'clock in the evening, Alek's lights were off. Elspeth watched as a sleek black convertible pulled up in front of his house and Alaina Michaels, complete with bottle in hand, waltzed up to Alek's porch.

He rose out of the shadows on the porch; Alaina's hips swayed beneath her short dress as she moved toward him.

Elspeth suddenly decided she needed to top off her day with a glass of wine.

She went outside, lit her candles, sat on her front porch and plopped her moccasin-covered feet up on the railing. She rocked back in the chair, tilting it against the wall and decided Alek could be replaced anytime, anywhere.

She sipped her wine, trying to ignore the tussle on her neighbor's porch. She tried to convince herself she'd find another Alek Petrovna tomorrow; she'd just go out and pluck one just as sizable, just as exciting, off the shelf. He was a common-variety stud, confident of himself—damn, she hated his confidence. No, she hated his teasing more.

All in all, little kept her from bounding those few feet to Alek's porch and ripping Alaina's willing body from his.

Elspeth inhaled. Alek's body was hers. She'd claimed him five years ago. "Dibs," Elspeth muttered, and poured her fourth glass of wine. She kept trying to ignore Alaina's whimpering sounds and Alek's sexy rumbling.

She closed her eyes and melted at the image of Alek, naked and aroused.

Alaina's convertible squealed off into the night, and the sheriff's car cruised by, sopranos nicely muffled. He trained his spotlight at Elspeth. "Everything okay, Elspeth?"

She lifted her glass to him. "Just peachy."

"You okay?" he persisted, clearly worried that Elspeth Tallchief was having a glass of wine.

"My neighborhood livens up this time of night. Sometimes the cats squall and it's hard to sleep," she returned as the sheriff's spotlight hit Alek, also sitting on his front porch.

"Petrovna, how's my feature article coming—you know, the one about me?"

"It's done. Who won the game?"

There was only going to be one winner in the Alek-Elspeth match and that was her.

"Had to leave it early," the sheriff called. "Some teenage boys with too much beer in them decided to face down Apache, that old buffalo. They made it up a tree, where he's got them pinned. I'm going back there to check that no one gets hurt. If I have my way, they're staying in that tree until their parents collect them in the morning. I'll have someone call you on Monday. My boy is a top player in the town league, you know. We won big time. They need a shortstop. Maybe you could try out."

"Maybe I could. I'll be waiting for a report on the game."

"Maybe you could help me out next time I need a deputy quick. The Tallchiefs usually help out. Duncan's got a real name for it. I hear your dad is a sheriff."

"He's retired and growing orchids. I'll be there if you need me."

The spotlight swung back to Elspeth. "Caught Calum naked out on his porch again. He was picking a bouquet. Looked guilty as hell when I spotlighted him. Had to pull Lacey off Birk. Seems he didn't like what she said to Chelsey Lang, and now the almost-engagement looks shaky. Guess I'll be going then. Uh...Elspeth, it's a couples team. What do you say about trying out, too? You're in shape...I saw that today. Nobody could ever ride like you, except your mother. Something to see, all right.''

"I'll think about it," Elspeth lied, then she took her glass into the house to answer the telephone.

Fiona went right to the reason for her call. "What happened today? I called Calum. Uh...I'm in a bit of trouble here in Wisconsin and needed some... uh...advice. He's helping me."

"What kind of trouble?" Elspeth smiled; Calum had left a message on her machine. Fiona had pushed an attorney's nerd-boy son into newly poured concrete and sat on him—with only his head above the surface—until it hardened. Nerd-boy didn't like the handcuffs he'd been tricked into wearing, or the concrete overcoat. At twenty-nine, Fiona was moving more quickly now, and Elspeth sensed that her sister had almost finished her wandering.

Fiona explained curtly, then switched to Elspeth's life. "This guy Petrovna, Talia's brother. He's tough, Elspeth. I met a journalist friend of his, who told me a lot about him. He's been there, done that. I really wouldn't...mess with him if I were you, Elspeth. He's not your type. I hear he has Una's shawl. If I were there, I'd get it back for you. Calum thinks that earring Alek is sporting is Mom's from LaBelle. I don't care what Duncan says, I think I should come home and rescue you. You're too sweet, Elspeth. Too elegant to deal with a guy like that. He's nothing like Talia at all. There's absolutely no reason for him to be in Amen Flats, and I don't believe that newspaper malarkey for a minute. There's our family honor at stake, you know.''

Because Elspeth had had enough of other people in her life for one day, she cut Fiona's advice short. ''Yes, why don't you come home? Joel Johnson asked about you the other day. He misses you. Says Amen Flats is dull without you. Micah, Steele and Taggart said they hoped you'd never come home—but they were very nice about it.''

''Those nerds. You know how I—''

Elspeth smiled and lifted her glass in a toast to herself. ''Don't worry about me, Fiona. Or Una's shawl and Mom's earring. Just come home when you can. Megan is growing fast, and Birk is teaching her to say he's her favorite uncle. Duncan is happy. Talia is blooming and driving Calum nuts.''

''I like that. Calum never lets anything get to him. It's fun to see Talia broadside him. They were so beautiful when they got married in December.'' The silence at the other end of the line said that Fiona did miss Amen Flats despite all her declarations of never coming back to wither away in a boring dirt town.

''I went to see the folks today.'' Elspeth ignored the stab of pain.

''I hope you took a bouquet of bluebells. They were Mom's favorite.''

''I did. I love you, Fiona.''

''I love you, Elspeth.''

''Aye,'' they said together, and hung up slowly, without saying goodbye.

Birk's pickup skidded to a stop outside, and she watched him stalk up the walkway. She met him on the porch. He wasn't mulling over Chelsey in Elspeth's house or spending the night on her couch. She wasn't baking his favorite bread in the morning to soothe him. Tonight she had another agenda and a date she was determined to keep.

Birk nodded to Alek, who nodded back and said, "Nice night."

"Depends." Birk plopped down on Elspeth's front steps and slammed his Stetson against his hand. "Man. For two cents, I'd take Lacey over my knee and paddle her."

"The last time you tried that, you lost. You're a lot slower than she is. She went right over the top of you."

Birk glared at her. "She knew that branch wouldn't hold me. You know what she told Chel? Never mind. You'd just laugh. I'm not in the mood for advice tonight." He frowned at her. "Hey. Do I smell Chablis or a wine cooler? You?" he asked, frowning at her.

"Me. I'm not giving away advice tonight or making you a snack after my kitchen is all clean, and I'm not cutting your hair. I think Chelsey has good sense. I like Lacey. Go away."

"Uh-huh." His response said he knew more than she did. "I'm headed home for a brew and a bath. Take it easy, Elspeth the elegant."

She loved her family, but tonight she wanted them off her front porch and off her telephone. Birk's pickup sailed out into the night, and Elspeth glanced at Alek. He hadn't moved, his bare feet still braced up on his porch.

"Nice night," he said again, and stood.

His stretch caused Elspeth's mouth to dry. The porch light caught the powerful sweep of his shoulders, glanced off the ridges of his stomach and highlighted his thighs. She realized she was straightening to see more of him and closed her mouth abruptly. After Alek entered his house, the porch light clicked off, leaving her alone with her thoughts.

Elspeth watched moths circle the streetlight. First of all, Alek had a shawl she wanted and an earring that was also her inheritance. She shook her head because it was getting a bit light and concentrated on Una's legend.

When the Marrying Moon is high, a scarred warrior will rise from the mists to claim his lady huntress. He will wrap her in the shawl and carry her to the Bridal Tepee and his heart. Their song will last longer than the stars....

Alek glanced at the clock in his living room. At two o'clock in the morning, he sat in Mrs. Mulveney's old rocking chair, his jeans unsnapped at the waistband, and waited. From the look in Elspeth Tallchief's steely eyes as she'd ridden into town, she'd decided to reclaim what was hers.

He tried to give her the shawl, and now she'd have to take it...and him, if his luck held.

Jeremy was lucky Elspeth had left his sports car when she did. Jeremy wasn't the real problem, and Alek curled that comfort around him. Jeremy had simply intruded on a very private battle, one that Alek intended to win.

Elspeth's endless legs in a short, hot, red number had lodged an uncomfortable hardness low in Alek's body. If making love to Elspeth happened a second night, he didn't intend to wake up to the entire Tallchief clan and end up in kilts and feathers.

Like the summer thunderstorm brewing on the mountains, Alek sensed that Elspeth would make her move tonight—if Alaina's visit hadn't put her off. Somehow he doubted that anything could put Elspeth off from what she wanted. Alek hoped she wanted him.

Outside, the wind whipped at the rosebushes he had planted in the front, and upstairs he heard the first creak. Alek smiled; he hadn't expected Elspeth to use the tree route. He rubbed his earring, listened to her progress across his new roof, and then a board in his bedroom creaked.

Alek bent to pick up the blanket roll and the picnic basket he'd prepared. Then he slipped out of his house into the night.

Ten

Elspeth pulled her van into what used to be the Kostyas' driveway; she parked next to Alek's pickup. She placed her hand on his hood, which was still warm.

Moonlight filtered through the old oaks sheltering the house. Out on the mountain hillside, sheep seemed to float over a hill. Cattle grazed in the fields, and Yakov and Yuri, the Kostya mules, looked at her from the corral. A white-eyed sheepdog ran from the sheep to her. "Hello, Fadey."

Fadey panted, accepted her ruffling of his black-and-white pelt, then bounded back to his sheep. Protective of the Kostyas, Fadey wasn't a dog to give his affections lightly or to trust trespassers on his property. The dog knew Alek well to have let him pass. So Alek had been coming here, making friends with the Kostyas, had he?

Elspeth crushed Alek's note in her hand. She'd

found it beneath a rose, lying upon his cot. "The shawl isn't here," he'd written in that bold script that few could read. Nothing could keep her from Una's shawl tonight, nor from Alek. After a stop at the newspaper office, a call to Talia and Duncan, another sip or two of wine, Elspeth knew that Alek Petrovna had barricaded himself in the Kostya farm place.

Only Alek would know that she wanted this homestead desperately and he'd plucked it from her. Though she loved her house, she'd dreamed of having this farm, of tending the sheep and milking her cows. She'd dreamed of placing her mother's things amid new ones. She'd thought to make the Kostyas an offer, but she'd been...tied up with life. She phrased the thought carefully. She hadn't taken the time, and now Alek had scooped a dream away from her.

She bent to pet Sophy, the barn cat winding around her feet, and studied the darkened two-story house with the opened front door. The Kostyas didn't trust electricity, and a lamp glowed within the old house, spreading a square of gold upon the front porch.

Elspeth ripped off the note pinned to the front door: "Make sure you shut the front door and blow out the lamp. Sorry I missed you."

"Aye. You'll be sorry, Petrovna." Elspeth went back to her van, retrieved a flashlight and her tartan plaid—if he played games in the mountains, she'd need the warmth. She quickly braided her hair into a single rope, then began looking for signs of Alek's passing. His boot prints were too big to miss, tromping through a newly plowed field, headed straight to a glade near a stream.

The man couldn't grow anything but roses. How did he expect to take care of a farm? As her father had taught her, Elspeth turned off the flashlight and let the moon guide her, noting a bent stalk, a freshly broken twig on the path to where her mother and she had often gathered sumac berries, goldenrod, wild rose hips and blue lupine flowers for dye.

She hadn't tracked in years, since before— Elspeth pushed that time away, on her way to run down Alek.

Elspeth entered the shadows of the pines, slipping through them to watch the bubbling stream. She reached up to pull a black, curling hair drifting from a pine cone; she lifted it to the moonlight. "You need a haircut, Petrovna."

Higher on the mountain, an owl shot high into the sky. Elspeth bent to trace a boot track and another, then stood and straightened, drawing the tartan around her. Alek was headed to the meadow that she'd just passed the day before. From the distance of his footprints and the depth, he was loping up a mountain.

"You'll have to run faster than that to keep ahead of me, Petrovna," she muttered, inhaling the clean mountain air. Nothing could keep her from running Alek into the ground.

Alek wasn't an easy man, but he didn't have to make the catching so hard, Elspeth thought, pressing her hand to her side and panting. Every muscle ached, including some she didn't know she had, until Alek pushed her over the edge. He liked edges, did he? She intended to give him plenty of them.

She moved quickly over rocks and fallen logs, tracing his path. Every muscle ached, her head throbbed and Alek had Una's shawl. She stepped into the meadow, panting, sweaty and dragging herself every step. *She'd caught him!*

* * *

Elspeth paused at the edge of the meadow, the light of predawn shimmering in the dewy flower field between them.

He'd been waiting, praying she'd be safe.

His heart lurched just looking at her cross the mountain daisies almost reaching her bare thighs. Did she come for the shawl, neatly folded and tucked in the basket? Panic skidded up his back and coiled low in his gut. He wanted her to want him more than anything she'd ever desired in her lifetime.

Elspeth took her time in coming to him, and with each step Alek forced himself to breathe. Almost black, her eyes locked with his, the dim light catching her high cheekbones, glistening in the length of her blue-black hair. He saw her take in his bare chest, the scars on it, the hair arrowing low to his jeans. Alek placed his hands in his back pockets, afraid that he would touch too soon when he wanted her to come to him. To love him. To hold him and let him love her. He'd settle for half a love—his for her—and yet knew that Elspeth would have nothing so easy.

On her way to him, through that sea of daisies, Elspeth was proud and ready to fight. He'd linger on the sight all the days of his life. The tops of her bare thighs glistened with dew; Alek sucked in air and remembered the strong feel of them beneath his touch, wrapped around him. He waited for her to speak, to make the first move.

She slanted a glance up at him, not making it easy. "You have the shawl."

"It's yours. Take it." Would he ever forget the look of her, a huntress on the prowl, ready to take him down? He clung to the hope that maybe, just maybe, she wanted him more than the legendary shawl.

She circled him slowly, dragging her fingertip around his waistband until she stood in front of him. Her fingertip reached to touch his scarred lip lightly. "Where did you get this?"

He caught the scent of her, one he'd remember until eternity. "Minding an orphan, stuck in the middle of no-man's-land and scared as hell. I was running, carrying Danny, and went down in shrapnel. Danny made it out without a scratch. I had a stitch or two."

In another minute, he'd be dragging her to him. He glanced at her breasts and wished he hadn't; her shirt was damp, clinging to her and showing every curve. Her nipples peaked against the light cloth, and Alek's mouth dried. He strained to keep his mind on her questions, but his body was strained, as well.

"Did you adopt him?"

Whatever roamed in Elspeth's sea-gray eyes told him that she would choose what happened between them. He kissed her roaming fingertip. "He's enjoying a family here in the States, adopted and safe."

"How did you break this?" She touched his nose.

"Back in Texas and again in Germany."

Elspeth touched the scars on his neck and cheek. Alek shuddered just once; it wasn't easy feeling like a Christmas package about to be opened and inspected. "Do my scars bother you?" he asked hoarsely, surprising himself.

"I like texture," she murmured, tracing the smooth old scars along his cheek and throat.

He snorted at that. "Texture. Now, that's a name for it."

"Interesting texture," she corrected, and his heart went still, waiting.

Her fingertips drifted over his bare chest lightly, circling each nipple. Her feather-light touch roamed to his shoulder, skimmed his back and trailed down his spine as she moved around him, giving him nothing but her heat and the maddening scent of her body. Her finger trailed over his wrists, touched his palms, locked to his pockets. He shuddered as her lips touched his back, soothing an old scar caused by shimmying under a wire barricade.

"You made me come looking for you, Alek. I know the look of a planted trail, and that's exactly what you did, breaking branches as you went, swaggering heavy enough to plant a good print. You should know, the bear and cougar on Tallchief Mountain aren't exactly friendly."

"I passed some of the wildlife on my way up here. They seemed friendly enough." He'd worried, guilt biting him until minutes seemed like hours. He'd timed the moment her van arrived at the Kostyas' former farm and the time it took her to cross the meadow. He'd traced her progress with his binoculars. She was good, stopping to mark his passing, trained by her father. The Tallchiefs should have let her go with them, tracking on the mountain that night her parents were killed. Elspeth had been put in her place, and Alek wanted to give some of that back. He knew how he'd feel if he were left behind. She'd not been allowed to go with them that night, but tonight she'd prove to herself that she could. Yet if anything had happened to her, he'd—

He arched against the stroke of her lips on his back.

He needed to breathe—he'd stopped when she began touching him. He sucked in air, filled with her scent.

She stood on tiptoe, leaning against him, her lips against the corner of his mouth. Her hands smoothed up to his neck and locked around him, fingers playing in his hair.

He wouldn't grab her, drag her closer yet to him. Then he did, hands splayed across her long back. "Come here, sweetheart," he whispered against her lips, and caught the taste of wine and woman and desire.

"I'm here." Elspeth bit his lip, kissed a path to his earlobe, and her tongue toyed with his earring. "You couldn't make this easy, could you?"

"And have that family of yours arriving on our doorsteps?" he scoffed. He breathed deeply, savoring the twin press of her breasts against him. "I've got plans that don't include them."

She smiled against the curve of his throat, her fingers digging slightly into his shoulder. "Tell me."

First I'll tell you I love you and watch that sink in. Then, because you'll look so flustered, I'll damn myself and go all the way, telling you all my dreams. Instead, Alek bent to scoop her bottom in his hands, dragging her body upward. She locked her legs around his hips, her arms looped around his shoulders as he hoped she would.

"If we go down, you land first," she whispered. "I didn't come all this way to be crushed."

"I'm hoping you came for just that reason." Alek tossed away his smile. "Trust me, Elspeth." *Trust me with your love, trust me to love you.*

He kissed her in the faint light, told her he loved her with his lips. She gave him back heat, hunger and what he needed. Alek slanted a look down at her wicked smile. She filled him—quite simply filled him with pleasure just looking at her. He felt tipsy on pride, daft on dreams and full of himself. "So you tracked me, did you?"

"Did you doubt that I could?"

Pride was there in her voice, and despite the fears shrouding him, Alek grinned.

"Arrogant, intellectual gypsy meathead." But she locked her hands to his cheeks and fused her lips to his. It was a rough taking, hunger dancing on her tongue and sucking, tempting his desire until he trembled and went weak kneed. He felt like a chocolate to be savored before the having.

The having. "I love it when you talk dirty, Elspeth-mine. You keep doing that, and we'll go down. Did you come for the shawl?" he asked roughly when he could drag his lips from hers.

Would her pride let her say the words that he needed? Would she admit she needed his body, if not his love? He saved her pride by taking another kiss and lowering her to the blanket he'd prepared.

He spread her hair upon the old quilt, one stitched by loving hands and one in which children had slept, lovers had talked intimately. The shadows had them now, dawn rising on the rugged crest of the mountains.

Then Elspeth lifted against him, her hands gripped his hair, her mouth hot on his. Her hips moved restlessly against his sweeping hand. "Hurry, Alek. I can't wait."

"Not this time, love," he managed to say, and wondered where he got the strength. His pride barely in control, Alek needed some sign she cared, that there might be a chance she'd take him to her heart. He smiled grimly, quickly, mocking his uncertainty. He needed a measure more to salve his pride. He smoothed the soft line of her stomach and lower, the excitement racing in him, battling with the punishing stab of desire.

"I came for you," she whispered against his mouth, setting flame to the tinder burning in him.

"Did you?" he had time to whisper before dragging her to him.

Her hands flew between them, touching him, igniting him. She gasped as she pushed away from him and quickly shed her clothing. Alek groaned, shucking his jeans and cursing when they lodged at his ankles, halted by his boots. Her hands flew to touch him, to cradle the softness gently and stroke him until he groaned outright. They stared at each other, panting, dragging air into their lungs, then Alek managed to drag off his boots and kick away his jeans. He bent to take her breasts, to cherish them.

"Alek," she cried out wildly, locking his head to her.

He touched her intimately, felt her pouring into his hand, waiting for him, gasping. Alek jolted when she touched him again, this time with possession, dragging him back to her, over her.

He'd go blind, locked in the pulse of her, lodged deeply as they rolled from one edge of the blanket to the other. Elspeth cried out, her hips lifting quickly to him, her arms and legs gripping him to her.

Alek lost himself in the scent of her hair, in her body taking his, the drag of her breasts against his chest, nipples taut. He suckled hard, surging deeper into her, so deep he lost himself and gave himself to her. Poised in the heat, skins aflame, bodies locked,

Elspeth pried his head from her breasts and forced him to look down at her face.

Elspeth was flushed, hot, ripe, succulent...sweet, tender...necessary Elspeth.

"Say my name, Alek Petrovna. Say it," she demanded unevenly, her body rippling beneath his, quivering with the effort of holding the heated flight away, until she got her due.

He tried to focus, his arms trembling with the effort of giving her what she wanted...what did she want? If she wanted the world, he'd give it to her. "Elspeth. Elspeth. Elspeth. Love...my love."

She clenched him with her legs, claiming him, her hands wrapped in his hair, her breasts shining damp and peaked in the sunrise. Alek allowed himself a quick look downward, to her stomach quivering against him, to the pulse of her straining against him. Then there was no time for thinking, for taking images into his mind, for dissecting the whys and the whats. Passion came curling out of him, squeezing him, and still he kept hold of Elspeth, caught the dimming of her eyes as she loosed her desire, caught it, held him, their bodies, heartbeats raging, rushing as one.

Alek cried out her name, pledged himself to her and poured himself into her.

The rippling constrictions had already begun deep within her, and they went flying into the dawn, pitting their strength into the ultimate release. He quite simply shattered, giving her everything. He watched, fascinated, as she took pleasure into herself, her eyes bright with it, riveting him, until his eyes closed in his own pleasure.

When Alek could force his eyes to focus, to see Elspeth drift lightly back to him, to go wonderfully, beautifully limp and damp against him. She managed a weak kiss when he offered it, allowed herself to be caught close and fast. Alek listened to the beating of their hearts slow. "Elspeth," he whispered against her damp brow, and smoothed the curve of her hip, keeping her near, their bodies joined.

"You watched." Her voice dragged like velvet on him, warm and rich with lovemaking.

"You were beautiful." Again, another treasure to tuck in his memories when they were old and rocking their great-great-grandchildren on the front porch.

"You didn't swoon," she stated slowly in a tone that made him grin. Elspeth Tallchief was a very satisfied woman. "My brothers bet each other that you wouldn't swoon with my kiss. I wanted a really good swoon."

"I'll try when I can see again," Alek promised with a kiss. "Talia told me about the famed, mind-blowing Tallchief kiss. I'd say you've got it."

She grinned up at him. "Just the kiss?"

His hand skimmed appreciatively down her hip, squeezed her softness. He wouldn't give her what she wanted; she'd have to take it from him. "You're a fast learner. What if I were delicate or sensitive and you came at me like that? Why, I'd be shocked."

The lift of her eyebrow mocked him. Her hand flopped from his shoulder and slowly, slowly slid to his ear. "You're wearing my mark, Petrovna. Remember that. You said Elspeth."

"Elspeth-mine." There were rules to this game; he was no easy lover, nor one to walk away. "I'm sorry about the first time."

She traced the earring thoughtfully. "I understand now what happened to you. You're a passionate man,

Alek. Not one to give himself lightly. When we met, you were hovering between two worlds.''

"Something like that. They got tangled at the wrong time, and I hurt you.''

"Now that we've got that straight...'' She smiled and skimmed her hand downward until he sucked in air. She touched him just at the spot of their joining, and Alek surged, desire renewed. Elspeth lifted, braced her elbow across his chest and touched him again, smiling enchantingly down at him.

He toyed with her hair, fragrant upon him. "Be careful, little girl.''

She laughed at that, startling him. She bent to flick her tongue over his nipple, and Alek caught her chin, brought her curved lips to his and whispered, "Elspeth. Elspeth. Elspeth. Have I told you that I love you?''

She tensed against him, and he held her tight, lodged deep in her body, their passion humming gently, ready to ignite or to die. Her eyes flickered, wary, her fingers digging in his shoulder. "You don't have to say that, Alek. It isn't necessary.''

He took her mouth, dragging her against him, fighting for his dreams. "But it is. I'll probably pay dearly for saying it, for loving you, because when it comes right down to it, Elspeth Tallchief, you are a greedy, greedy, savage woman. I didn't stand a chance.''

He let her chew on that tidbit and held himself still when he wanted to make love with her.

She toyed with his earring and shot him a challenging look. "You're saying that I enticed you. That I gave you little choice but to make love with me. Here. Now.''

He nodded. "Little choice. You've run me down.

There was little I could do but let you have me after all your effort.''

"Petrovna, you're half the size of a house. Don't tell me I've winded you." She grinned, teasing him. The sight dazzled him; he fell into it, wallowed in his sheer joy.

"Not quite," he said, satisfied that she wasn't denying him. Or that something more than desire could be moving through them. Then, just to keep the balance right and in his favor, he began loving her all over again.

In the midst of the daisies, Alek stood, sunlight flowing over his bare shoulders and making Elspeth catch her breath as it spread across his chest. She'd awakened without him, groggy from lack of sleep and high on the lovemaking that had crept into her very bones. She awoke craving Alek, moving her hand upon the empty, wrinkled blanket, awoke to Una's shawl covering her.

She'd panicked, icy with fear. Could she trust herself? While Alek seemed to know exactly what he wanted and was ready to declare his love, she moved at a slower pace, needing to sift through her emotions.

If she gave herself too freely and gave too much because Alek pushed her, would she ever be certain that the choice was really hers? There was the heaven of the past hours—lying with Alek, challenging him, meeting his passion and her own—and then there was fear that her hurried decision could harm them both. At dawn, she'd trusted what moved between them. But would it last when put to the test? He'd walked away before—

In a frenzy, Elspeth tossed away the shawl. She'd

dressed hurriedly, ready to run Alek into the ground if needed, and then to give him the lesson of his life. She surged out of their bed, ready to hunt, and then she saw him picking flowers, and her knees went weak.

Of course, he'd had her twice the night before she tracked him to the mountain and twice more as dawn became morning. No wonder her thighs quivered and her knees almost buckled. No wonder her heart raced at the sight of him. *I love you....*

Love had happened to her brothers and would come to Fiona when the time was right. The Tallchiefs were bred for loving families. But she'd never imagined Alek loving her. Elspeth fought for the visions that would come to comfort her, and all she could see was Alek standing in the morning sun, holding a bouquet of wildflowers out to her. She blinked, waiting for an image to tell her what to do. She felt the thumping of her heart, racing against her breast, the softness of her body where Alek had been and a light, flowery, lacy sense that she was a woman, all woman, and desired.

Alek looked as if he'd been rumpled, steamed, and had during the night. The look suited him, she decided.

As if to test her mood, Alek held out the bouquet of wildflowers shimmering with morning dew. "Good morning, Elspeth-love. You're thinking hard enough to scare me."

"You could use a good dose of scare." What was he doing? *Trust me...I love you.*

Then Alek smiled, a whimsical little smile as if he were wishing something from her, and her fears went tumbling into the wildflowers. There he was, everything she wanted. Cocky, irrational at times, grumbling, laughing, passionate—a huge, tender, delectable morsel. Her heart sailed out of her, desire slamming into her, tightening her throat, dancing along her skin. Elspeth began to run toward him. Her T-shirt landed in a patch of bluebells. She hopped on one foot, tugging off one moccasin, ran two steps and tugged off the other.

"You're on my land, Petrovna."

Who did he think he was to leave her alone in their bed, the scents of loving snaring her before she woke fully? Oh, he'd have to pay for that one, she decided. She unzipped her shorts on the run and shimmied out of them.

The sunlight glinted off his teeth, this huge bear of a man she'd come to claim.

"Pay for being on your land, am I?" He stood there holding his bouquet and grinning like a boy who'd just won the prize.

She flew across the meadow. She wanted to plunder and take; it was her right, she'd run him down.

"You know you are. You know exactly where you are and what happened here. You've researched the Tallchief family. You knew everything." Elspeth leapt upon him, and Alek grunted with the impact and caught her close as he reeled backward. They went down in the field of flowers.

She pinned him beneath her. She straddled him as she had before and knew that he'd let her take him down. She sat on him, her palms on his chest, and studied him, this new Alek that she'd captured.

"You're full of yourself, Tallchief. What are the rules on this one?" Alek asked as he tucked a bluebell into her bra.

"You'll have to pay the price for being on my land and for stealing the Kostya place from under me." She tugged a whorl of hair on his chest. "And that awful contract."

He brushed the hair from her cheek, his expression tender. "I want a long-term contract with you. One that says you'll be waking up beside me every morning." *Elspeth...I love you.*

Unable to dance along that dangerous dream, Elspeth slid back into reality. "You really shouldn't have bought the Kostya place, Alek. I wanted it."

She was glad he let her change direction.

"It looked like home to me. You can bring me a blueberry pie or come milk the cows—" He sucked in his breath as her fingers went to his jeans snap. The angle of his jaw hardened. "Watch that."

Too bad. She had her own agenda. He'd stepped over the enticing line and looked as necessary as the wildflowers strewed across his chest.

Elspeth ripped away her lacy bra; she arched and stretched and looked down to see what she wanted— the heavy hunger shadowing Alek's face, the taut, carved edge of his cheekbone and firm dip of his mouth as he fought for control.

She skimmed the flat of her hand down his chest, following the V of hair lower, until Alek's hand gripped her wrist, staying her. "Take it easy, Elspeth-mine. I'm feeling sensitive this morning."

She fell upon him, fused her mouth to his and gasped as his arms came around her, hard—just the way she wanted. She wanted Alek to hold her as if he'd never let her go.

He rolled her over, unzipped his jeans and sprawled heavily upon her.

She was waiting, eager, locking her fingers to his

hair as she dived into the kiss, the hunger of his mouth, feeding upon it, nipping his lip.

Alek groaned unevenly, tore away the scrap of lace separating them—she didn't give him a chance to pause to reconsider. Elspeth reached to glove him, to bring him to her.

Later, when her bones had melted from their passion, Alek smoothed her body, gentling the aftershocks of their lovemaking. "Elspeth-mine, you're seriously denting my ego. I've just made love for the first time with my boots on and my jeans around my ankles. To pay for that infraction, you'll have to go out with me in my Chevy. We can neck—"

She tensed, rummaged for enough strength to lift herself. "You mean a date, Petrovna?"

"With my best girl. I'll pick you up. We'll cruise Main Street, stop at the drive-in for burgers and shakes, cruise some more and then neck ourselves blind."

They were lying in the meadow, the morning sun bright overhead, and at any minute all of her brothers could appear on horseback.

"Just neck?" She grinned before his hand cupped her breast and his tongue laved the hardened tip. She skimmed down to taste his nipple.

After a quick lurch of his body and a groan, Alek reached to bring her lips to his. "You're getting really good at this, Elspeth."

Eleven

"My Russian is definitely shaky, but Alek studied it and he's always correcting me. Alek never speaks Russian to you?" Talia asked, her tone incredulous. Seated at the same table, Lacey and Sybil looked at Elspeth, waiting for her answer.

"Not to any of us," Sybil offered. "He's a complex man."

"Hmm. No more than the Tallchiefs." Talia tapped her fingers on the table. "Let me think about this."

At Maddy's Hot Spot piano, Patty Jo Black sang a husky, sensual rhythm-and-blues number after a day of canning green beans. A sign hung over the door on Tuesday night—No Husbands Allowed Or Males Of Any Kind. No Boring Smart-Children Stories Allowed. Maddy's luscious-nude paintings had been properly covered by sheets. Maddy had placed paper doilies beneath the tables' bottles of plastic roses, some with price tags dangling in the breeze from the air-conditioning.

Maddy buzzed by with a tray of iced-lemonade glasses. He sidestepped Miss Loretta Mulveney of the pioneer Mulveneys and owner of Amen Flats's only bookstore. Miss Loretta had wanted Maddy for years, since his first wife left him, but he was wary of aggressive women. He jumped; lemonade glasses clinked as Miss Loretta sneaked him an appreciative pinch on his backside. She batted her lashes at him and he flushed. A beefy ex-football player, Maddy pirouetted away from Loretta on one toe like a ballet dancer. To his credit, he never lost one glass on his tray. He plowed righteously forward to the protection of his bar. Miss Loretta picked up her lemonade and sashayed to him, decked out in a gauzy new number that looked like a drifting tropical bouquet.

At seven months into her pregnancy, Talia smoothed the small ball of her stomach in the short flirty skirt. She plopped her practical flats—Calum had studied the construction of shoes and wooed her into wearing them—on another chair and rummaged through her thoughts. "I love my Hessian boots. Love tromping in them. Calum said if I'd wear these double uglies now, he'd wear skintight leather pants after the baby came—just while I was teaching him Petrovna family dances. Hmm...Alek never speaks Russian when he's really, really wanting to make a point to someone who doesn't understand it."

Talia's long blond hair flew out as she turned to Elspeth, one finger raised. "He wants the Tallchiefs to see him coming. He's being very careful with the Tallchiefs, so they understand his exact motives and feelings for you, Elspeth. He wants to make certain that you do not misunderstand anything that he is intending to do, or anything about his feelings. Trust me, of all the Petrovnas, he can be the most…secretive— an element that isn't typical of any of us. Devious, yes. Secretive, no. I called Mother and told her that Alek had been a bad boy—that he wanted you and that he engineered that whole Denver contract business to be alone with you. I told her that he'd found Una's shawl and that he wouldn't let you have it. She's incensed. I almost feel sorry for him when my parents come…they'll be here before the baby is born.''

Elspeth thought of Alek, and her heart shifted into high gear. She remembered their lovemaking all down the mountain and in the old Kostya place throughout the night. He had taken exquisite care arranging her upon the old bed in the guest room, smoothing her hair across the old pillow decorated with embroidered flowers. Elspeth could sense when he wanted her, desire lurching within her, only to find his eyes dark and hungry. She'd cut his hair, trimmed the heavy, curling mane and fussed with it until she was pleased and he'd tugged her upon his lap. Sunday loving, he'd called her once, tickling her as they went down in the old barn filled with cows they'd just milked.

''Do you want the shawl?'' he'd asked again, poised above her. Somehow she'd managed the truth, dying for him.

''No, I want you, Petrovna.''

She'd learned that Alek Petrovna's law—always finish what you start—also referred to lovemaking. He had wonderful stories of other lands, outrageous ones about his family. The Petrovnas could ignite at any minute, shouting and throwing up their hands. Their mother, Serene, had ancestors that dated back in Texas history to the Alamo. She fought for what she believed in, a tiny, calm woman devoted to her family, all of whom towered over her. Alek Petrovna, Sr., a tough, raw-boned Texan, melted when he looked at her.

But Elspeth had had her measure, too, listening to the humming of his desire, the way he said her name. Her Alek. *I love you.* The words rang softly in her heart. Could she trust herself? Could she trust him?

They had met just exactly five years ago this month; she'd had her life torn from her, and now he was giving it back. *I love you.*

There were quiet times, too. Like the moment Alek came up behind her, holding her in his arms as they overlooked the Kostya fields. It was good standing with him, the late-June breeze playing with her hair and Alek, solid and warm at her back.

He'd left her at her doorstep on Monday morning with a mind-stopping kiss and gently pushed her inside her door. She'd gone to sleep well-loved, aching, exhausted, smoothing her mother's quilt and with the taste of that kiss and the look in his eyes.

She had drifted through Monday in a golden fog. She'd thought about surprising Alek, and a quick glance proved he wasn't home. At six o'clock that evening, she'd grinned at the light rap on her back door, and then Alek swept her out to his Chevy, burgers at the drive-in, a cruise down Main Street and back again. Alek had kept her hand on his thigh, firmly locked in his fingers, which he had kissed and suckled intermittently. Necking in his back seat left the windows fogged, Elspeth breathless and Alek playful and full of himself...until he pushed her into her house, alone and yearning for him. Sometimes old-fashioned males just didn't cut it, Elspeth decided, and when you took Alek apart, he ranged right in the old-fashioned-male depot with her brothers.

Elspeth frowned slightly and traced the lip of her glass of white wine. His look—she couldn't mistake that closed-in, level look at her—suggested he'd made a promise and that he'd be moving quickly upon it. *I love you....*

She wouldn't be pushed.

I love you....

Why did he leave her breathless and aching at her door?

What game was he up to now?

She didn't trust him; Alek had skimmed his hand down her shoulder, to her wrist, then to her hip and thigh as if promising to make good his need for a longer contract—as if he'd be coming for her and wanted her to know it.

She sensed that about Alek. That he was coming for her very quickly— Elspeth frowned. She'd take her time deciding what was right for her. After a lifetime of the Tallchief brothers, she wouldn't be pushed.

A concession—no, a loving—on Tallchief Mountain, at the farm, in the barn, on the meadow—the back of her van would never seem the same again—a concession was all she was making at the time.

Alek had that look. He'd made up his mind to it, locked his teeth into it, and he'd gnaw at it until he got his way.

Elspeth glanced at Sybil, who had been too quiet all evening. "Are you feeling all right?"

Sybil studied Elspeth. "You should know. You usually know when something is brewing with the Tallchiefs...when Calum brought Talia home the first time...when Duncan—"

Elspeth caught a quick image of Sybil, rounded and glowing. "You're pregnant!" Elspeth exclaimed, delighted.

"Yep. Again. Three months gone." She lifted her wineglass, filled with lemonade. "A small concession I've been making for three months, right here, every Tuesday night. Duncan knew immediately, almost as soon as when we—" She stopped and blushed. "When we…"

"But you like a glass of white wine—" Elspeth stared at Sybil, just realizing that she'd missed the entire event.

"Elle, old girl, you're losing it. Even I thought she was pregnant," Lacey crowed, propping her work boots up on the table. "When he wasn't worrying about you, Duncan wore this goofy grin—nobody grins goofier than the Tallchief males. Calum—you can't tell much about Calum these days—he's always grinning. That idiot Birk actually picked me up and kissed me. One of those lip-sucking, mind-blowing Tallchief kisses. The ones he uses on his harem. I dumped a gallon of paint on him, and he stood there, sputtering and grinning. 'Lacey, I think I'm going to be an uncle again. Don't I deserve it? Don't I just?'"

Lacey wiped her mouth as if wiping off his kiss. "Jeez, give those guys babies, and they turn into a pile of daisies."

"Don't look so shocked, Elspeth," Talia murmured with a grin. "I'd say you've been so…busy that your seer and shaman abilities have been shafted."

"A real demolition derby," Sybil added, her topaz eyes sparkling.

"Poleaxed." Talia's grin widened. "Didn't know what hit her."

Lacey smirked. "Yeah. Poleaxed. I'd say that suits her about now."

"Calum has another Tallchief cradle hidden away. Sybil has the original, but Tallchief made several others and sold them. Calum is so proud of himself that I couldn't bear to tell him I found it." Talia beamed at Elspeth. "You Tallchiefs are so easy. You've got all these dark storm clouds swirling around you, and you're pushovers."

Sybil gave her a long, cool look. "You're a Tallchief, Talia."

Talia smoothed her tummy. "Yeah. And happy of it."

"Calum found another cradle?" Elspeth shook her head to clear it. She remembered thinking that Calum would soon be finding another cradle.

"Has the Celtic circle and the Tallchief feather markings. It's beautiful. The guys are at the house now. They're probably glowing with how they've kept Calum's secret." Talia's eyes misted. "I love that guy."

"They didn't totally keep it," Sybil murmured, her eyes lighting.

"No! Duncan told you, didn't he?"

Sybil smoothed her coppery chignon and smiled. "Darling, what do you think I was after, the night I got pregnant?"

Elspeth stared at her splayed fingers, locked to Maddy's scarred table. She usually saw everything, images moving through her, and Alek had shattered those visions and replaced them with ones of him. "I think...I think I am going to have to be very careful."

"Very careful," Talia and Sybil and Lacey repeated too seriously, and then began laughing outright.

"Should I tell her?" Sybil gasped.

"Do it." Talia smoothed her tummy again. "It's all right, baby. Auntie Elspeth may scream a little, but—"

"What?" Elspeth demanded, not certain she wanted to know.

"Today at oh...say...eleven o'clock, one tired Alek Petrovna gifted Duncan Tallchief—your eldest brother and therefore the one acting in your father's stead—with two horses and a flock of prize sheep. It was only two horses and a few sheep, Elspeth. I'd think you'd be worth more. Yes, after a day on Tallchief Mountain and a night at the Kostyas' farm place, Alek was definitely floating."

When her mind started clicking again, Elspeth groaned, placed her arms on the table and sank her head down to them. "Do you know how it feels to have an entire town know everything?"

"Details, Syb," Lacey demanded, setting down her beer mug.

Talia grinned. "I knew it. Junior is just as old-fashioned as Pop. Mom said she sometimes felt that Dad was a steamroller once he'd got it in his mind that she was the one for him. Of course, she gave him the idea in the first place. The horse and sheep are a version of the Petrovna bridal price. Tallchiefs aren't the only one with traditions."

Elspeth allowed herself another groan. She should have understood Alek's look; she should have stopped him.

Talia's laughter rippled over the room. "Syb, it's your decision. Alek is merely following our family tradition and showing that he wants you and that he'll take good care of you and that he sets your value at a few sheep and two horses."

Sybil rubbed Elspeth's shoulders and continued, her voice humming with laughter. "It was all very formal. Duncan stood there, tall and formidable, his arms crossed over his chest. By the way, darling, Duncan and Calum and Birk were all watching your progress up the mountain Sunday morning. It was a regular spy mission with phones ringing, regular reports and binoculars. I believe the words 'She nabbed him,' were used. He said, 'Didn't have a chance with her on his trail.' Birk said something about he and Fiona being the last of the mavericks. He sounded as if he were mourning the passing of an era."

Elspeth rubbed her aching temples. "Sybil, I love my brothers. But I could kill them."

"Don't worry about Birk. He'll be picking up another marriage prospect next week. He'd be all duded up and hot to trot," Lacey stated. "Get on with it. I'm all ears."

"So back to the High Noon of yesterday. There Duncan was shooting bullets with each stare and Alek leading the horses while herding the sheep. They're lovely sheep, Duncan said—"

"Sybil..." Lacey urged impatiently.

Elspeth sat up and lifted one finger. Maddy swooshed to her with another glass of white wine.

"It was really lovely and formal. A male-bonding thing. There wasn't an ounce of giving in Duncan or in Alek. I could barely keep Megan quiet, and then she launched herself at Alek and he cuddled her. He stood, combat boots locked to the porch, all tall and hard and tough and determined male, and cuddled Meggie on his hip."

Sybil took a sip of lemonade before continuing. "Duncan was weakening by then, but he leveled questions like a gunslinger at showdown time, and Alek answered them carefully, exactly. One of them was quite exact—'She cut your hair?' Alek said you did and at last Duncan nodded and said, 'Aye.' Then he added a threat about what would happen if Alek broke your heart. By that time, I was crying. After that, they both went to chop wood, just swinging axes away as if they wanted to brawl and knew they'd better not. Wood flew everywhere. It looked like a lumberjack contest. I found Duncan later, alone in the barn. His eyes were wet, he was hugging one of the sheep and he said he thought he was developing allergies and that there was too much hay dust in the barn.''

"Ha! Allergies, my foot!" Lacey exclaimed. "He cried because his baby Elspeth was leaving his nest."

Sybil arched a brow. "Don't you ever say anything like that around him, Lacey. He's delicate and needs protection, but especially now. He's been having morning sickness.''

Elspeth managed to speak. "I believe that Mr. Alek Petrovna has a lesson to learn. He should have discussed this with me first—what exactly did Alek want, Sybil?''

"Your hand in marriage. He wanted permission to court you, and sure enough there you were cruising in his Chevy last night.''

"You're absolutely right. He should have asked you to marry him first…didn't he?" Talia clearly was not happy with her brother.

"He did not. He's pushy, Sybil. I haven't decided whether I like the man or not. At the moment, I do not believe I want anything to do with Alek. Other than to teach him a lesson.''

Sybil leveled a look at Elspeth. "There's a big difference between *love* and *like*. I always love Duncan, but sometimes I really don't like him.''

Lacey licked the beer foam off her upper lip. ''Birk dumped poor Chelsey Lang. I have no idea why. She's such a sweet, old-fashioned, homey-type girl, too. Looks fertile…massive mammaries and big hips, just like what you'd think a Tallchief would want—no offense, Syb…Talia. Yep, I'd have thought Birk would have wanted that one. Instead he dumped her. Men.''

Lacey's tone put the male species in a box with cockroaches. The four women shot Maddy a dark look that sent him scurrying toward Miss Loretta. When he realized how close he was to her proximity, he reeled back, knocked over two liquor bottles and caught them. He kept a wary eye on Loretta as he wiped his bar.

While Elspeth dealt with just how much Alek had invaded her life and embarrassed her, Alek tossed a beer to Duncan. Alek almost felt sorry for Duncan, a man called ''Mother'' by the law; he'd risked his life to rescue kidnapped children and now he felt he was losing his sister. With Emily baby-sitting Megan and doing her homework at Duncan's, the three brothers sprawled on Calum's candlelit porch, wrapped in the citronella scent. Olaf and Thorn lay in the front yard, watching the Tuesday-night traffic of one truck, two bicycles and three cars in the space of one hour.

Calum propped his boots beside the other three sets on the railing. ''I added the horses and the sheep to Elspeth's portion of Tallchief cattle.''

''I'll keep them until Elspeth decides what she's going to do with you, Alek. She knows Una's legend concerning the shawl. She'll tell you when she's ready, Alek,'' Duncan said.

Alek didn't want the legend coming to him from anyone but Elspeth and when she was ready; a man had to have some pride. Whatever the Marrying Moon was to the legend, it was his right to know. It had been five years since he'd first heard Elspeth sigh the words, and he could wait a little longer.

"She's keeping her secrets to herself. You Tall-chiefs are a secretive lot,'' Alek noted, toying with a baby rattle. It nettled him that the woman he loved, who he wanted to marry him and who had given her-self to him several times, could hold him at a distance when she wanted. Elspeth could have collected the shawl at any time and walked away with it, yet she hadn't.

He ran his thumb over the cool, damp aluminum beer can. He didn't intend to fail Elspeth a third time. Scotland and the damned Denver undertaking had been pure stupidity.

"I think ladies' night at Maddy's should be out-lawed.'' Birk cuddled a teddy bear while Duncan ar-ranged the tiny plastic horses around the crib mobile he'd been assembling. "Uh-uh. Trouble.''

Alek, Duncan, Calum and Birk looked down the tree-lined street, past Mrs. Monroe's yard of roses, past the teenagers smooching on the Joneses' porch swing, to the four women storming toward them.

"Aye. Trouble,'' Duncan and Calum stated to-gether. Calum reached for Birk's teddy bear and the mobile and placed them inside the house. The men propped the backs of their chairs against the wall, rocking on them as they crossed their boots on the railing.

"Alek, did you check with Elspeth about courting her?" Duncan asked carefully. "Did you talk to her before you talked to me? Ask her to marry you *before* bringing those horses and the sheep to me?"

Alek watched Elspeth steam toward him, the streetlight outlining her taut, curved body; her hair flew out from her shoulders, rippling in her passing. Desire shot straight down to his loins and pounded there. "Haven't had time. Brad Klein got sick, and I stepped in at the paper. Went out to cover the new plant nursery outside of town and helped pull a calf from the Stevenson's guernsey. I meant to call, but my truck broke down four miles out of town. By the time I got home, Elspeth was already barricaded at Maddy's."

Calum, Birk and Duncan stared at Alek. "We owe you. That's an outraged female posse coming."

"They're after Alek," Calum said finally. "We'll have to keep you here if you try to run. We can't have them taking out your lack of manners on us."

"Save yourselves, sweethearts." Just looking at Elspeth caused Alek to suck in air, steadying his light head. She looked better than the last time he'd seen her—which was when she'd tried to drag him into her house the previous night, after hours of necking. "I'm a saint," he murmured, and damned his righteous idea that the next time they made love, he'd have Duncan's permission to ask her to marry him. "A real saint."

Birk guffawed at that, spewing out his last sip of beer.

Elspeth, dressed in an emerald green sweater and jeans, marched up the steps to the porch, followed by the other women. While Elspeth stood beside Alek's chair, hands on hips, staring down at him, Talia placed a hand on Calum's shoulder to stay him. Sybil did the same to Duncan, and Lacey placed the tip of a broom handle on Birk's chest.

Elspeth's lips opened and closed, fascinating Alek.

"Yes?" he invited in a drawl. He floundered, went dizzy at the sight of her outlined in the street lamps and flickering candlelight.

Duncan, Calum and Birk slashed him a dark look. All four women acted at once: Elspeth reached for a bag of potting soil, ripped it open and shook it over Alek. Talia poured beer over Calum's head, and Sybil did the same to Duncan's lap. Lacey swept her foot beneath the back legs of Birk's chair, and he went down cursing. Then Sybil reached for another bag of potting soil and shook it over Duncan's head; Talia took it from Sybil and shook it over Calum's and Lacey dribbled beer straight down into Birk's face.

Elspeth lifted a watering can. "What's in this, Talia?"

"Water. Plant nutrients. Do it." She stood back, dusting her hands as Elspeth quickly doused Alek and dribbled the rest over her brothers.

The women shook hands. "Good job, Elspeth."

Duncan blew a clump of potting soil from his hair and slid Alek a dark look. "You should have—"

Alek swiped away the mud and ran his hand up the back of Elspeth's taut leg to pat her bottom. "I know."

He wanted to pack her over his shoulder and run with her. She swatted at his hand and lifted her nose. "This debris stinks. I'm going back to Maddy's."

"Uh...honey, precious, Talia...don't you think you've had enough activity for tonight?" Calum tried a hopeful smile.

"This gives me an idea for a play. I'm going back to Maddy's to sketch it out on a napkin, big boy."

"Sybil, you're coming home with me," Duncan stated, struggling out of his chair.

Alek studied the shape of Elspeth's firmly pressed lips and went lightheaded as he remembered them prowling down his chest. "You're a fine-looking woman," he said, meaning it.

"Jeez, Junior. Your fangs are showing. You're drooling," Talia muttered. "How dumb can you be? You're in real deep manure here, boy."

Elspeth inhaled slowly, as if tethering her temper. "Someday, Petrovna, someone is going to knock you off that overstuffed ego and grind you into the ground. The next time you get an idea that you and my brothers will settle my life, I'd appreciate a little notice."

He lifted his eyebrows. "I believe I've served adequate notice that I'm interested."

"Interested? You're on thin ice here, Petrovna."

"Home, Sybil," Duncan insisted, trying to hold his own on the porch.

"Nope. I'm not," Sybil returned lightly, and placed a firm finger in the middle of his broad chest. "See you in the morning."

Duncan glared at Alek. "He's an ill-manned oaf."

Olaf bounded up the stairs, certain that his name had been mentioned. Thorn joined him to sip the beer wasted on the porch. Talia's kitten and puppy romped across Birk's flat stomach on their way to play with Olaf and Thorn. The sheriff came by, sopranos at full blast. "Maddy wanted to know if you men are okay, and if you'd keep your women here."

"Tell him we're on our way back," Elspeth called,

looping her arm with Sybil's as they began to walk back to Maddy's.

"Well, hell," Alek muttered, surging to his feet. None of this was going the way he had planned.

"I wouldn't—" Calum said behind him.

Alek began singing "You Are My Sunshine" loudly, strolling after the women with his hands in his back pockets.

Elspeth pivoted and leveled a finger at him. "You're pushing me, Petrovna."

"That I am, darlin'. That I am," he admitted, undaunted.

The sheriff cruised by and Alek motioned him over. He took the loudspeaker microphone from the sheriff and lifted it.

Panic rippled across Elspeth's pale face. "Alek, don't you dare—"

"Elspeth Tallchief, I've made mistakes, but I'll learn. I'm here to stay and I'm nuts about you," Alek broadcast to the people lining the streets. She'd have to learn about Petrovna capers, Alek decided and grinned. Petrovnas could be wild, excitable, unpredictable. He didn't intend to give his love anything but the real Alek. The one she'd made love her.

She began to mutter amid the other three women, who were laughing. Birk had rolled off the porch onto the lawn, holding his sides and laughing. Calum was loping toward Talia, and Duncan was walking down Main Street, sighted on Sybil and twirling his lasso. An expert at cowboy rope tricks, Duncan stepped into the rope's circle, hopped out again and back in. He looked at Alek, who nodded and took the rope, performing the trick.

Calum walked by with Talia snuggled in his arms,

clearly on his way to a making-up event. Birk and
Lacey glowered at each other, then both crossed their
arms across their chests and looked away.

Faced with determined women, Duncan and Alek
passed the rope back several times, each matching the
other for tricks. Sybil cursed darkly. "He knows that
Will Rogers stuff gets to me. I turn into putty when
he does it."

Elspeth couldn't take any more. She marched up to
Alek, grabbed the rope from his hands and tossed it
into the bushes. "There. You're finished," she said,
placing her hands on her waist.

Glorious, he thought. Wild and glorious. Soft and
sweet, delectable...his lifetime love, because he'd
never love another, she'd taken him too hard and too
deep.

He caught her to him, bent her over his arm and
fused his mouth to hers. She was caught by surprise,
and her gasp went into Alek's mouth, followed by the
flick of her tongue, tasting him. Then her hands
streaked to his hair, keeping his lips on her hungry
ones. "Ah, you're a passionate one, Elspeth-mine.
And you love me. Admit it," Alek managed to say
when he had to come up for air and took her lips again,
this time lifting her feet off the ground.

When he set her toes back to earth again, when his
heart was racing with need of more than a kiss from
his love, when he decided he'd better leave her or he'd
shock Amen Flats then and there, Alek released her.
He held her arm as she balanced, eyes glazed, mouth
juicy and ripe with his kisses and hair gleaming like
satin under the streetlights.

Then he managed to stroll away, though his knees
weren't too steady.

Elspeth's voice shot at him from the sheriff's loud-speaker, "Wait!"

Alek inhaled and stopped. She had her pride; he had his. She'd have to come to him this time. He turned slowly to see Elspeth sauntering down the street. Alek jammed his fingers into his back pockets. He placed his boot on the curb and waited. "She's going to destroy whatever I've got remaining in the way of pride," he muttered, meaning it.

Elspeth sauntered down the street, long legs outlined in the streetlight, her hair swaying at her hips. She stopped in front of him. "We don't have a thing in common, Petrovna."

Alek steeled himself, suddenly cold in the June night air. He stared down at her and didn't trust himself for one heartbeat. "You're what I want."

"Why?" There wasn't an ounce of yielding in her, and he respected that.

Why? Because he needed her as he needed air. Because his heart raced at the sight of her; his pulses kicked into high gear with just a scent of her. Because he saw her in his dreams and in his future. Because he'd be a shell of a man without her. "I'm here, Elspeth. I'm staying in Amen Flats. I'm dependable and I'll be here when you need me."

"You can't gather me up like you gather bits of other people's lives to you." She traced the scar on his lip with her fingertip. "I don't like being pushed and currently I'm more than embarrassed...I'm good and mad."

"You're afraid I'll leave you...that I'll hurt you again. I won't. You've lost your parents. Let me give you mine. We had something then and we have it now." So much for pride, thought Alek. With Elspeth, he had none. "It's in my nature to push. Waiting for you to make up your mind is damn hard."

"Poor Alek." She served him with a soft, taunting smile.

His temper flared at that. "I could show you poor Alek pretty quickly without this audience, darlin'."

"You talk big, Mr. Petrovna." There it was, that flashing, dangerous, enchanting grin. Then she placed her arms around his neck, leaned against him and gave him the famed Tallchief kiss. It challenged, pushed him to the limit, moved into his body, ignited it and traveled up to cloud his brain. Hormones, he tried to think, keep the hormones on a level— Oh, hell…he sank into the kiss, hands locked in his back pockets because he knew he'd grab her and make off with her to the closest private spot. From there, he couldn't trust himself at all.

Her assault left him in a boneless, drooling, hormonal heap. When he could think again, Alek congratulated himself for not taking his hands out of his pockets.

Twelve

"**P**ushing," Elspeth decided as she opened her kitchen door. Tiny heather plants quivered in the early-morning light, resting on the doorstep, right next to Alek's boot.

He didn't look sweet or in love. Shadows ran under his narrowed eyes; a muscle clenched in his cheek, and the taut skin covering his cheekbones gleamed in the sunlight. "You're a hard woman, Elspeth Tallchief," he shot at her, and slanted a hot look down her body. "These are for you."

Unable to resist, she swooped to run her hand across the tiny plants, each with a cluster of tiny purple-pink feathers. "They're lovely, Alek. You shouldn't have."

"I should have." He looked as if he'd like to take her mouth, devour it.

She'd been weaving without her bra, losing herself in her circular creation—smooth colors and textures beginning, blending, curving and ending as they had begun. She'd been thinking of Alek and sipping herbal tea to calm herself. Now with Alek in reaching distance, calm slipped out into the morning sunshine. He bent to kiss her hard and hungry, leaving her shaking, dragging air into her lungs.

"Heather won't grow here, Petrovna," she managed to yell at him over the sound of his revving pickup.

He grinned back at her. "I know. They're for your parents, up on the mountain. It reminded Una of Scotland, and maybe they will grow."

Elspeth washed her hands over her face and closed the door to lean against it. Life with Alek wouldn't be calm or sensible. She should just take the heather and run Alek down and give it back to him.

She eased open the door to the tiny plants. They probably would flower best in the full sunlight next to her parents' graves. She couldn't wait to plant them and hurried to dress.

"Not much time for weaving anymore, huh?" Duncan asked as he held Delight and handed the bag with the heather seedlings up to Elspeth.

"I'm managing," she returned, not ready to admit anything to Duncan. She'd been working on one design in which a man and a woman stood close together walking through the circle of natural colors. She'd woven an arrow straight through the piece, as if it carried them into the universe for all time. That was how she saw Una and Tallchief, loving for all time.

Duncan angled a wary look down at her. "Still mad at me?"

She didn't answer, but held up her scarred thumb

and smiled. How could she stay mad at Duncan when he wanted the best for her?

She spent the day on the mountain, planting heather. When she returned after dark she was too exhausted to do anything but fall into bed.

The next morning, she heard Alek's boots on her front porch. He looked tough, angry and worn. She wanted to hold him.

"That damn mountain is dangerous," he shot at her, his tone shredding any tenderness instantly.

Hold him? She wanted to throw something at him. "I go where I want."

His smile was pure evil promise. "Things will have to change, Elspeth darlin'. Anything could happen to you, and I don't like having my guts tied in knots. Next time you want to go, I'll ride with you. We'll make it a couple thing."

"Says who?" she shot back, still pretty proud of the way she'd planted a Tallchief kiss on him in the street.

His hot, hungry kiss told her exactly who and what and why. When she was well into floating, Alek inhaled, gripped her arms to set her back a pace from him and plopped a large pink-wrapped box in her trembling hands. "I'd say we have plenty in common. You're not a failure, Elspeth-mine, because of the baby. The failure was mine in not keeping and tending you. I won't make that mistake again."

She shivered and wondered how she kept from dragging him into her house and having him on the kitchen floor. No man had the right to look that edible in the morning or to understand one of her darkest secrets. Now she saw she'd hurt him, excluding him from sharing the planting of the heather, his gift to her.

I love you....

Elspeth didn't wait to examine her wavering emotions as she usually did. She simply reached out and grabbed his worn work shirt. She returned his hot, eager kiss and, gripping her present firmly, stepped back to slam the screen door between them.

Hot eyed, he stared at her through the mesh screen and looked as if he could tear it from its hinges. "Well, what's it going to be? Will you come to my house for dinner tonight? Or are we going upstairs right now?"

"I don't know if I can love you, Alek Petrovna, Jr." Elspeth went in the direction of her thoughts and not his questions.

"It's your call. It doesn't stop how I feel, heart of my heart," he answered, head at an arrogant angle, not bending an inch. "Dinner at six."

How could he deliver such a sweet sentiment and look hard as nails? When he had gone, Elspeth plopped into her kitchen chair and opened the package. The antique Celtic broach, a circle with a pin through it, was perfect for her tartan. Una's shawl was neatly folded beneath it.

She wiped away the hot tears brimming to her lids and knew that if ever a man hunted for the soft spots in her heart, Alek was a deadly shot. The heather seedlings just might grow on the mountain that had reminded Una of Scotland; they were beautiful, perfect little flowers catching the sunlight.

Now Una's shawl shimmered beneath Elspeth's trembling fingers; the legend whispered through the shadows, circling her.

When the Marrying Moon is high, a scarred warrior will rise from the mists to claim his lady
huntress. He will wrap her in the shawl and carry
her to the Bridal Tepee and his heart. Their love
will last longer than the stars....

Vegetable lasagna was not as easy as the *Men Who
Know They Can't Cook Cookbook* boasted. Alek
should have tried something easier for his first at-
home, courting-Elspeth dinner. He ached from riding,
digging new fence-post holes at the Kostyas', from the
butt of a playful young bull and from clearing out an
overgrown garden perfect for Elspeth's herbs. Meanwhile, he kept up the telephone war to get a hot tub
at the Kostyas'.

Alek carefully picked away a crust of the burned
lasagna. Being an impatient man playing a patient,
thorough game for keeps wasn't easy.

He hadn't a clue how to settle down, how to make
a relationship work.

He'd realized during the day that he'd never had to
try—Elspeth was a trying woman. He'd never had to
work to make Melissa trust him, believe in him when
he told her he loved her. He did love her, but in a
tender way that a man loves a woman he's grown used
to, an easy, uncomplicated loving.

When Melissa died, Alek knew that he'd never love
again. That there wasn't enough of him left to give
another woman. Yet he had loved Elspeth from the
moment he met her, eyes flashing, hair gleaming in
the bonfire, balancing a village child on her hip.

She wasn't an easy woman. Elspeth had been hurt
early in life. He'd hurt her again. He wasn't geared to

slow paces and wary women, but he'd learn for Elspeth.

Alek braced himself against the counter and muttered in Russian, venting his dark mood. The light
touch on his shoulder caused him to jerk around to
face Elspeth. "Alek?"

"Elspeth, I love you. I always have." He looked
over his shoulder to where she stood, elegant in a
short, dark red dress. He admired the lean, soft line of
her, the length of her legs down into the strappy little
sandals, then back up to the tiny gold beads in her
ears. There. That was that. "You can chew on that,
spit it out if you want, but it doesn't change things. I
love you. Unless you tell me to stop, I'm going to
keep on telling you, until you believe and trust in me."

He'd expected her withdrawal, the shifting of her
expression, drawing it in, hiding her emotions from
him. Tallchiefs held their emotions to themselves,
plowing slowly through them to reach an ultimate decision about exactly how they felt. They'd learned
how to do that early in life, to protect the family that
could have been torn apart at any time. Pride kept him
from asking how she felt about him, about a relationship—hell, a life with him. He plunged on recklessly,
letting his bottled thoughts fly at her. "This is serious,
Elspeth. For keeps. We've come full circle. How I feel
about you isn't going to change. I intend to bring you
flowers and heather and broaches and anything else I
want."

He tugged her into his arms and held her; she wasn't
going anywhere, not just yet. He counted every heartbeat she did not move from his arms.

"You jump," she finally whispered against his
throat.

"Jump?"

"Pounce. Sometimes I feel as though I'm in the walking wheel—a huge spinning wheel—rather than walking to and from it. I'm in the walking wheel, spinning around with no idea of what hit me."

The wisp of a smile lurking on her lips sent his hopes soaring. Alek picked her up, kissed her hard because he had to and, when she nodded, he carried her up the stairs to the grand old four-poster bed he'd purchased from the Wheelers. It was a lovely old thing, sitting under a blanket in the barn, and Alek had lost his heart immediately.

Then Elspeth's lips burned, igniting him. Her body feverishly answered his, in tune to his needs and her own.

By the middle of July, Elspeth gave up weaving and began her first vacation, much to Mark's distress. "What? You're quilting? What's quilts have to do with anything? A vacation? Honey, we've got clients screaming for your work.... Remember that tiny piece, the one you made on an old pitchfork? It sold to a millionaire. And the breastplate design with feathers? There's a rich buyer circling it. Come on. Now's the time to jump into the fire and run with sales."

Elspeth thought about the fire in her lately and how she'd changed. She swung a Navajo drop spindle from a length of thread, watching it go around. "It's my first vacation, Mark."

He hesitated, clearly balancing income against her needs. "Okay. Give me a call when you're ready. If I've learned one thing about working with artists, it's that they have to have time to focus."

The problem was that Elspeth's focus had changed,

and the work flowing beneath her hands was traditional, what her mother had taught her, and her
thoughts were filled with Alek. In the quiet moments,
she began piecing together designs for a quilt she'd
always wanted to make, one her mother had begun
and hadn't finished.

Alek had moved to the farm, renovating it. He kept
himself there, holed up and away from her, until she
had to come after him. Or until he drove his Chevy
up her driveway. He stood outside her house, leaning
against the car and looking tough and unreasonable.

Alek wanted a home. He wanted her.

Because she enjoyed him, liked working with him
on the ranch, Elspeth found herself in his arms at
night, not wanting to leave him. She needed the comfortable loving, the feeling of freedom with Alek, to
push back, testing herself.

Alek liked to hold hands, slow dance and push her
into dark corners. He'd look at her, and she'd feel his
leaping hunger, that lazy, warm slide of nerves and
cords locking in her body. Alek delighted in teasing
her and kissing her senseless. Tormented to the fullest,
Elspeth had sailed a kitchen plate at him. She'd actually dumped a salad over his head, when she'd just
dumped a bucket of milk over it the day before.

He liked homemade bread, devoured it and then
turned to consume her, the flash fire running so fast it
took her breath away.

The tender moments left her reeling, when Alek
took her in his arms, slowly, purposefully as though
nothing could deter him from loving her. He contained
his urge to push her, to commit to him, though it simmered beneath the surface.

The Tallchiefs accepted Alek in Elspeth's life, and

she met the Petrovnas. "This is her, Mom," he'd said at the farm, holding Elspeth's hand securely.

"Tall," Serene Petrovna had said, walking around Elspeth to inspect her.

"A match," Alek Petrovna, Sr., had stated, reaching out to snag Elspeth and to kiss her cheeks thoroughly. He guffawed at her surprise and thrust her back to Alek's arms. "We'll be your neighbors until Talia has her baby. Mom wouldn't be anyplace else, and we're camping at Alek's house. Sort of fun, just having the basics. Serene and me still fit into the same sleeping—"

He rubbed the spot where Serene's elbow had caught him and winked at Alek. "You're not getting any younger, Junior. And you're getting a hell of a lot slower than what I remember— Ah!" he exclaimed as Serene's elbow connected again with his ribs.

"I'm home, Dad," Alek had said in a quiet, old-fashioned way that brought tears to his mother's eyes. He wrapped Elspeth's hand in his and brought it to his lips.

"You always get what you go after, son. Just like all those war stories."

"I'm playing for keeps, and sometimes the story takes a bit more patience to get the right finish," Alek had returned, looking at Elspeth.

Patience. The minute Alek and Elspeth were alone, he forgot patience and had her behind the bales of hay. Then, when she could think again, Elspeth pushed him down and reminded him that she wasn't an easy taking. She ripped a button from his shirt, which Mrs. Petrovna noticed immediately. Elspeth wished she could rip off Alek's silly grin and her blush as easily when Mr. Petrovna laughed and eyed Mrs. Petrovna.

After a cruise to the ice-cream parlor in Alek's Chevy, the retired Texas sheriff began doing rope tricks for his bride.

"Did you grow up like this?" Elspeth asked Alek as Mrs. Petrovna strolled into the house with Mr. Petrovna right behind her.

"I was lucky. You were lucky, too, having a family who loved you." His eyes told her that he knew she'd been damaged and that he'd try to make it up to her.

"I was afraid, Alek. Horribly afraid I'd fail to do something and that it would separate the entire family. Fiona was only ten, and my brothers were taking more responsibility than they should have. I never wanted to do anything but weave. I've always loved it. I liked being able to sell what I'd made and people enjoying what Mom had taught me." She leaned against him, his arm around her. Alek was comfortable, when he wanted, holding her hand.

"They handled it. You all did." Alek leaned down to give her a friendly, understanding kiss.

Elspeth let him hold her against him, rocking her, right in daylight, right on the sidewalk. "Don't you dare ask me anything about the Marrying Moon. I get the feeling I'm a story and not—"

His kiss was not tender, but demanding and hungry. Alek left her in no doubt about his intentions.

There were moments when Alek waited for her to say something, for something to pass between them, but she couldn't release her heart, not yet. She'd loved her parents deeply and lost them; then that Scottish night had lingered in her thoughts. Alek would sense her turning from him immediately, and his expression would cloud.

By September, Talia seemed ready to burst. While

she took her condition with a grin, Calum the cool was the typical nervous papa-to-be. The Petrovnas treated Elspeth as if she were their daughter; Alek's and her relationship settled into an easy simmer, punctuated by long, passionate nights when they could manage to be alone.

"Me, a Petrovna?" became familiar to Elspeth, as did the sight of Mr. Petrovna caught in a passionate argument with his son. In the end, after all the yelling, there were the hugs. Alek Sr. kissed his son and laughed at the arm wrestling and shoulder-butting between them. There were moments when both men watched Elspeth with the same intent, black-eyed, closed-in look as though waiting for her.... "You love her, Alek," Mr. Petrovna said when he thought she wasn't listening.

Alek's reply had come back instantly, firmly as his gaze drifted to her. "I do."

"Good. She's a strong woman, son, and not too certain of you."

Elspeth had sucked in air, not wanting to listen further. Before she could move, Alek had spoken to his father. "I made a mistake with her. I won't again."

She'd been a mistake. Elspeth felt the floor drop out from under her. She stood, icy cold, ready to run— then Alek surged to his feet and tugged her to him fiercely. There was no denying the hunger of his kiss or that he needed her. He had locked her to him. "Now get this, Tallchief. I love you. Got it?"

Elspeth cried that night, uncertain of her emotions when Alek was so committed to his. She tasted the words on her lips, tried them in the silence of her bedroom and let fear take her. She couldn't trust herself, not just yet.

From Mrs. Petrovna, Elspeth learned how Alek had
always been an impetuous rascal, but no more than his
brother and sisters. Elspeth could see him as a little
boy, filling his sisters' pockets with worms and then,
in his tamed moments, braiding their hair, as he had
done Elspeth's. Of all the Petrovna children, Alek
seemed the most lonely, the one always seeking what
happened beyond the hill and wanting the truth of it.

The truth of it. Alek had moved into her life, her
heart. When he placed her hands on his face and bent
into them, giving himself to her, she went weak and
the thought frightened her. Sharing her life, her
thoughts, with another person who'd grown to understand her so well, frightened Elspeth. She'd grown up
shielding her fears to protect her family.

When she wavered, not trusting the visions within
her, the moments of Alek laughing at her or an older
Alek, faced with taming an unruly brood that could
ignite at any minute.

She didn't trust the image of Alek lying in bed with
her, a ring on his finger.

Or the image of her wrapped in the shawl, the Marrying Moon round and high in the sky and Alek walking toward her...

A keen sense of panic slid into Elspeth, soon to be
noted by Alek. If he couldn't torment and tease her
out of the moment, he became grim and aloof, a cool
outrage that terrified her.

When he saw a child, there was no mistaking the
poignant longing in Alek's expression. There was no
mistaking the love he had for the children he'd fos-
tered and supported in other lands. He shared their
accomplishments, their growth with Elspeth and
hoarded the letters with his pictures of them.

Alek loved. He simply loved people and life and nurturing, growing gardens, planting trees, raising sheep and cattle. Baby, a motherless calf that Alek bottle-fed, followed him around the ranch, and he tucked her in each night. Then Abby, Jules, Rommie and Lincoln arrived, calves bawling for his attention. Alek collected animals like he had collected children, fitting perfectly into the former Kostya farm. Fadey had gone with the Kostyas, leaving a pup—Sergio— with Alek. Sergio promised to be a better sheepdog than his parent and clearly loved Alek.

Elspeth borrowed scrapbooks filled with his stories from the Petrovnas. She cried at his printed images, the horrors he'd seen and shared with the world. Alek caught her in her weaving room, the scrapbooks opened on the floor in front of her.

"Hey! What's this?" he asked urgently, sitting on the floor to draw her into his lap.

She pushed at him, raw with the fresh discovery of what he'd seen. "Leave me alone."

"What? So you can make more walls, keep me out? Me, a Petrovna?" he demanded, outrage hissing through his low, dangerous tone.

"You want too much, Alek. I don't know that I can give you what you want," she burst out, tears streaming down her face. She flailed at him, and he caught her wrists, kissing them. She resented him; he did this to her, making the tears come. Since she'd met him, she'd been nothing but uncertain. She'd changed, and he'd been the cause.

"Oh, baby. Don't cry. You're wonderful. Just seeing you, loving you, makes me happy."

She let him comfort her, because she could do little else. But in the end, she knew that one day she'd come to a dangerous edge. As she stroked the shawl, she knew that whatever edge waited for her, Una had pondered the same decisions, picking her way carefully.

Maybe it was that premonition that caused her to weave a Tallchief tartan, to think of Alek while she worked, at home in her shadows and peace. The explosive Petrovnas consumed quiet, and Elspeth often surprised herself by forgetting everything but a passionate exchange on a simple matter.

They were on her porch swing, holding hands and watching the September evening dust the streets. Fall came quickly; it scented the air and touched the leaves. She held her breath when she gave him the parcel, wrapped in brown paper and twine.

He swallowed, clearly delighted. "You made this for me?"

"You've been giving me enough presents. The heather made it through this year, and I adore it. Open it."

His fingers trembled when he tore away the wrappings and held up the plaid. He turned to her, one fist gripping the plaid and the other hand reaching for her. Alek jerked her to him and buried his face in her hair, his body trembling. "I'll wear it. Thank you."

"Not on your suit at my next showing, Petrovna." Already she saw him, a fine bit of swagger to his walk, hair wild around his angular face, touching the tartan resting on his broad shoulders.

He held it up to the sunlight, admiring it. "I'll wear it and the kilts you'll make me to go with it."

She had to laugh. "You're pushing and full of yourself, Petrovna."

But the kilts were already dancing on her fingertips, waiting to be made....

"Look in the box again, Alek. You've missed something."

"Mmm. More," Alek exclaimed with the delight of a little boy approaching a chocolate cake. He picked through the wrapping and smoothed the swatches of Tallchief plaid. "For my kids overseas," he murmured, running his fingertips over them as though the wool were polished gold, handcrafted and glowing. "They'll like these."

"They're only bits—" He'd humbled her, so thankful for so little.

Alek's finger on her lips stopped her. "You've given them and me something special, Elspeth-mine. You're wonderful."

He told her with his lips that he adored her, which only frightened her more.

The second week of September brought a cold wind from the mountains; the aspens now shimmered in brilliant orange shades. Elspeth finished two fresh designs for Mark, who rejoiced that Alek hadn't totally killed her creative urge. Using a triangular frame, she created Tallchief Mountain, surging out of the rest of the design, and dusted it with heather.

Oh, she had urges, all right. Big ones, where Alek was concerned. Elspeth frowned at the roses blooming in the September sun. She'd stayed home to take a call from Fiona before going to the rodeo. With October approaching, Fiona called home more often, reminded of their parents' deaths.

Delight waited, tethered to Elspeth's back porch by Birk—just in case she wanted to ride, showing off for the Tallchiefs. She planned to ride to the rodeo, but not the showy trick riding or barrel racing she'd done growing up; she wanted to show off Delight, representing Tallchief Cattle Ranch.

As usual, Fiona was late and in trouble with an attorney's son, a regular nerd-boy, she called him. It had all started as a protest on the steps of his father's offices—a man who was in favor of wiping out an entire colony of endangered reptiles to build an industrial park. Fiona had padded herself to look heavily pregnant and, when the newspapers arrived, managed to look like the had-and-deserted by the attorney's son.

Following his kidnapping of her, nerd-boy had actually had the nerve to kiss her; he'd actually had the nerve to tell her she was beautiful pregnant and should reconsider her old-maid state. He'd eyed her appreciatively and told her she looked fertile and he wanted healthy children.... Fiona had hit him over the head with a chair, knocked him unconscious and then was faced with guilt and nerd-boy's outraged fiancée. She missed home suddenly, and Elspeth smiled, sensing that Fiona would soon arrive in Amen Flats and not alone.

"Aye," Elspeth said with Fiona, no need for goodbyes between them.

Mad Matt skidded his bike tires on Elspeth's driveway and called through her open screen door, "Miss Tallchief, you better hurry up. Alek is going to ride after the next two guys. Talia said you'd want to see him ride Diablo."

Elspeth stopped on her way to the door, heart pounding. Alek was a good rider—they'd raced horses, and she was faster, lighter in the saddle. Amen Flats's rodeo wasn't for an average rider. The westerners in Amen Flats had been brought up on saddles and bucking horses. Diablo was a mad-tempered horse, formerly owned by a man who'd abused him; Diablo had broken bones of the men who tried to ride him. The horse was what the old-timers called a "killer". He knew how to jump on all fours, bend his back and come down twisting. He knew how to ram against a fence, catching a cowboy's leg, and once he got a cowboy in the arena alone—

Elspeth let out the breath she'd been holding, caught by the terror on the last cowboy's face. She didn't think; she just grabbed the shawl she'd been holding, sensing a dangerous edge just as Una had long ago. Elspeth wanted the safety of the past wrapped around her, because Alek needed her protection.

"Go ahead, Matt. I'll be there in a minute."

The boy leapt on his bike, spewing dust on his way out of her driveway. "You'll have to hurry if you want to see him."

"I'll be there." Elspeth grimly strapped on her chaps over her jeans. With Delight under her, she'd be at the rodeo before Alek rode, and could save his neck. She slid into the saddle, stuffed the shawl into the saddlebags and bent low in the saddle.

Alek wrapped his glove in the rope, preparing to ride Diablo. He gently lowered himself. The horse was good and mean, just what Alek wanted. After this rodeo, Diablo was his; the horse had been maltreated, and Alek would give him a home. The horse already liked him in a mean-evil way, a case of mutual respect of man and beast. In a way, Diablo reminded Alek of Elspeth, hard clear through and breaking before bending.

He loved her, damn it. Loved her with every bit of his heart, his dreams.

She gave him only so much, and then the doors closed. He had dreams of her walking to him in that shawl, with the moon big and bright in the night sky. Of the Bridal Tepee behind her...of their life in front of them.

Being patient had just about ripped him to shreds. But he could do it, letting off steam once in a while, and right now Diablo seemed just mean enough to suit Alek's dark mood.

From the rough grandstands, Alek caught his mother's fears, the grim pride of his father and Talia's hesitant smile, Calum at her side. Everyone had someone, and Elspeth wasn't giving in easily.

He focused on the horse and lifted his hat to see if Talia's good-luck satin ribbon was still in place; Elspeth's swatch was in his pocket. He'd carried it through wars and he'd been safe enough. Then Alek lowered himself gingerly, firmly, onto the saddle, and Diablo bucked in the stall, edging around to try to crush his rider.

"Easy, boy." Alek gentled the horse as he had earlier. "When this is over, you're going home with me. You watch your side of the fence, and I'll watch mine. You'll have plenty to eat and maybe a few girlfriends along the way. But you won't have to worry about being hurt. Elspeth will have you eating out of her hand in no time, just like me."

Diablo reared again as another horse streaked by, the rider wearing a flash of red and gold. Elspeth stood on the saddle, her arms raised high and the shawl flapping behind her, drawing the audience's attention.

She dropped, and Alek almost lost his grip on the riding rope, quickly reclaiming it. His heart wasn't so easy to retrieve. Elspeth appeared low on the other side of Delight, supported by a stirrup and her grasp on the running horse's mane.

The audience stood to its feet, screaming, cheering as Delight rounded the arena in an easy gallop. Alek, worried about Elspeth, eased off Diablo and up onto the stall; relieved of his rider, Diablo settled down immediately. "What is that woman doing?" Alek asked Duncan hoarsely when he could speak.

"Saving your neck." Grim lines bracketed Duncan's mouth. "Taking the pressure off you. They've been waiting for her to ride for over five years, and now they have what they want. They won't care if you ride Diablo or not. She's giving you a way out, to save your pride." Duncan jumped down into the arena, followed by his brothers and Alek.

"Is that so? She's going to feel some pressure when my hand hits her backside. She could get hurt." Alek's heart plummeted to his boots when Elspeth edged up into the saddle and stood on the back of the horse, standing as it circled the arena. Just as suddenly, she dropped from sight and appeared at the other side, her moccasins skimming the earth, and then she swung up again.

"Don't distract her, Alek," Calum said quietly.

"She's out of shape. She almost didn't haul herself up in time. One hoof on that shawl, and her neck could be broken." Birk's face was as taut as his brothers'.

Elspeth quickly balled the shawl into her saddlebags as though recognizing the danger. Then she began the series of swings to the ground and back up into the saddle, pitting herself against the animal, concentrating on every trick.

"She's giving it everything she's got, just like she always did," Duncan noted. "But even a rider who practices every day shouldn't try that routine. She learned it from Mom."

The brothers shot Alek disgusted, threatening looks.

Wrapped in sheer terror that Elspeth could fall, that a hoof could kill her, Alek could not move. His boots were rooted to the arena floor, and he felt the blood drain from him. If she fell, he'd be there; if she didn't, he wanted her to know she'd purely raked the heart right out of him.

When Elspeth was seated on the saddle firmly, the shawl withdrawn from the saddlebags and now around her shoulders, Delight circled the arena in an easy canter. Alek walked out into the middle of the ring, slapping his hat along his thigh every step. She circled him slowly, the shawl flaming in the sun, as richly colored as the aspens on the mountains.

The dyes should have faded in Una's shawl, yet the colors remained strong, just as his love would remain for Elspeth. The shawl had been well loved and taken care of, just as he planned to do with Elspeth...if she didn't break her neck first.

"You're in for it," Alek snapped, meaning it. He slapped his hat against his chaps. Riding the edge of fear had set him off. "I can't find one bit of patience in me right now, lady. You'd better get off that horse now. You're an evil-hearted—"

"Save the sweet talk, Petrovna," she shot back, her eyes flashing steel at him. "You ride that killer horse and—"

"You would say that to me, a Petrovna? I finish what I start." Alek's leather glove shot out to grab Delight's reins; he glared up at Elspeth, not shielding her from his anger or his need. "Say you love me. Come out and say it. Say you were afraid what happened to me, just like that day you came running to save me from Duncan. You loved me then and you love me now. We've loved each other since this all began...we're a part of each other, lady, and you know it.''

Delight pranced, sidestepping as the shawl fluttered around Elspeth's rigid body. ''You're a hard ride,'' she said finally, employing a western term that meant he wasn't an easy man.

''I won't leave you. You won't wake up some morning and find that I'm off to cover a war. I won't hurt you. I'll love you all the days of my life and then some. I'll give you children, if you want, and I'll be by your side when you need me. You might not like hearing the truth, but I'll always give it to you. I'll be your best friend, if you'll let me, and ready to love you with my body in a heartbeat. You're moving in with me, and the next time you decide you're going to try something like this—'' He fought the cold ripple of fear skidding along his skin, not wanting to think about the next time.

Tears shimmered in her eyes, dropping to the shawl. Fear rasped in her voice, her face pale with terror. ''Promise me you won't ride Diablo. Promise.''

Alek took a long look at the woman he loved. It would cost him a measure of pride to walk away from the horse. But with fear riding Elspeth, his pride meant nothing. She'd been through so much, and he hadn't been there for her. But he was now, in every heartbeat.

Alek reached up, grabbed the shawl and hauled her down for his kiss. He had to know that she was all right, that she tasted the same, smelled the same, looked at him with that same dark, mysterious, heavy-lidded stare after he kissed her.

"It will cost you," he said finally when her lips were ripe from his. "And you'll promise me that you'll never ride like that again, not until we've—a together 'we'—have talked about it."

She blinked and glanced at the pink bow tied neatly in his hair. Alek didn't want to explain Talia's good-luck charm. He slapped on his hat, walked back to a fence and swung up on it.

Elspeth followed on Delight. "Alek! Where are you going?"

He took off his hat and lifted it to the silent, watching crowd. Spellbound, they'd seen him grovel and break Petrovna's law. They knew he loved Elspeth and that she'd come around. But right now, none of that helped, not while he was wearing a big jagged hole for his heart. "Ladies and gentleman. I am going fishing. And hell yes, I like to wear pink ribbons in my hair. Hell yes, I love stubborn, muley Elspeth Tallchief. If she rides like that again, I'm holding the whole damn town accountable."

He hopped off the fence and walked away, still caught by the terror of seeing Elspeth swing from her horse. Alek dashed away a tear with his leather glove and let his Russian curses roll over the sound of the cheering crowd. He'd lick his wounds in peace; he'd done it before.

So much for his patience. So much for his pride.

Thirteen

"*What do you mean, Alek is a champion rodeo rider?*" Elspeth demanded that evening as her brothers sprawled on her front porch. Talia, Sybil, Emily, Megan and the Petrovnas—minus one Alek Petrovna—were stuffed with burgers and potato salad and awaiting the freshly churned ice cream to ripen in the wooden bucket. The ice cream would be topped with Talia's double-rich, super-chocolate-frosted cake.

At almost seven months into her pregnancy, Sybil had eaten her cake before her bean burger and potato salad. At the baby-finish line, Talia picked at her food.

The hair on Elspeth's nape lifted as she rounded on her brothers—the rangy, raw-boned, hard-minded, untamed Tallchiefs wearing smirks. She pivoted back to Mr. Petrovna. She began again more quietly, spacing her words. "Is Alek a rodeo champion?"

"My son is a born-and-bred Texan, no matter what

foreign countries he's been in," stated Mr. Petrovna proudly. "When he was just a pup, he started hiring out to ranches during the summers."

"He can outride any man around," Duncan, an expert on the subject, offered. "Not the fancy trick-riding stuff, just good old bull and bronc riding."

Elspeth pivoted to him. "He's not much in a race."

Birk snickered; Elspeth shoved his plate of chocolate cake up into his face. Lacey burst out laughing, and Birk, in turn, pushed her mouth into the cake. She licked her lips and grinned through the circle of chocolate covering her face. "That was worth it, bub."

Calum cleared his throat. "I believe Alek prefers to ride behind you, Elspeth. There's…ah…certain advantages in that. And when he's feeling abused, he likes to pit himself against a real challenge, not one he wants to kiss. I'd say Diablo was what Alek needed at the moment. We had a hard enough time unloading that horse at Alek's after the rodeo."

"My boy will have that bronc eating out of his hand in no time." Mr. Petrovna licked the frosting-covered finger Megan held up to him. "I haven't set up a tepee in years. When I figured he'd be needing something to hole up in until he wanted to…until he calmed down, Duncan told me to borrow yours from his barn. Yep. That was something there at the lake…Junior looking hard as iron and twice as mean as that killer bronc."

Mr. Petrovna didn't know about the tepee, about how the Tallchiefs had started bringing their brides to it, reviving Una's legends. First there was Duncan and then Calum, and Elspeth had always known Birk would be the next to find his true love. She glanced at Duncan and Calum and found them looking at her, kneading the same thought. To Mr. Petrovna, the tepee served as whimsy, a family toying with their birthright, nothing more. Later they'd tell him, but not now, while Elspeth picked through her relationship with Alek.

She'd wounded Alek, torn the heart from him once, and time had passed, smoothing the edges for both of them.

She resented his damn contract, and he'd pay for that when they argued...because Alek Petrovna purely savored a good argument and Elspeth intended to let him sharpen his teeth on the bones she tossed at him.

Her mother had always said that the making up was worth the fight and that arguments cleared the fog between lovers. Elspeth smiled; Alek had torn her castle walls down, and he deserved a nip or two.

Elspeth looked straight at Sybil, nestled against Duncan, then at Talia, a tall, cool blonde in the midst of the Tallchief clan. Elspeth's brothers had pushed away the shadows; they'd found love, fought for it.

Images of other children danced by her, and she turned to Birk. He'd be finding love soon, because the rogue of the lot, he'd been searching longer, plowing through likely women with a charm that didn't give them a chance. One day he'd find a woman who didn't care for his charm and wouldn't have him on a platter, and then his hackles would lift—because if the Tallchiefs liked anything, it was a hard ride. He'd find Una's rocking chair and the woman to go with the legend, and then he'd be at peace.

Elspeth's gaze drifted to Lacey, and she corrected the thought. Birk would be blissfully happy, because the woman he chose was not likely to be a peaceful one; she would have her own shadows.

Fiona would come tripping to Amen Flats, tired from battling the world. And then she'd hunt Una's sewing chest, with its tatting shuttles, shoe button hooks and doilies and bits of her life. The buyer had wanted the tiny chest intact with its lovely feminine clutter, and Una—to save Tallchief land—had given her heart in the lacy heap. But still she'd loved the chest, as would Fiona.

"It cost Alek not to finish that ride," Birk stated. "Any man who'd walk away from something he'd started in front of a rodeo crowd has it bad."

Mrs. Petrovna stroked Elspeth's hair. She tugged Elspeth to a stool in front of her and began to braid her hair. "You see, honey, Alek has all sorts of rodeo belts and medals. You only saw his journalism scrapbooks. I kept all of his other things separate."

"They were a good match—that horse and my son. He's been feeling evil lately," Mr. Petrovna said.

Elspeth took in a long, steadying breath, and let Mrs. Petrovna finish her hair. Edges, she thought. Just like Una's edges—when she'd made her decision based on love and the man who had placed himself in her care. Elspeth smiled to herself. Tallchiefs weren't easy to capture, and she'd given Alek a good run, while she wound through her shadows to come full circle. Nothing had changed since that night in Scotland when he'd strolled toward her, wearing a grin that would knock the senses from under any reasonable woman. A second go-'round, and Alek had stepped into her shadows, tearing her from them. He'd taken away the distance she'd placed on her life, replacing it with himself. She'd tasted his dreams and found them true, and still she'd hovered in her shadows, until he made her so greedy for him that she'd stepped out.

Then the horrible, heart-stopping, icy fear when she knew Alek would ride Diablo. She'd hesitated outside the arena, sitting on Delight. Then Alek—his face hard and grim—had lowered himself onto Diablo. With Alek in danger, she had had no choice but to show her love. He'd given her everything, his dreams and hopes and his aching past; she couldn't imagine life without him—and she'd given him nothing, not a crumb.

The image of Alek lurched into Elspeth's mind— Alek slapping his hat along his chaps and stalking toward her looking twice as mean as the horse he chose to ride.

But now the time had come to claim him well and good.

She intended to run Alek Petrovna down and—

She stood when Mrs. Petrovna said, "Come here, Talia. It's been so long since I've braided your hair."

Elspeth remembered the pink bow glistening in Alek's curls. "What about the bow?"

Talia smiled tightly and eased herself onto the stool. "It's my good-luck charm. He always wore my bows and usually won."

Elspeth stood still, remembering Alek in the arena, how firmly he spoke his vows—vows, she decided. Alek had made his vows to her right there in the September sunshine with a crowd of people straining to hear. *I'll be your best friend...I'll love you all the days of my life and then some....*

She'd come to the same edge as Una, to a moment when the awakening changed, deepened, ripened and clung.

She quite simply loved Alek Petrovna. He was hers; he'd always been from the first moment. Images flashed through her as she rode toward her love—Alek, laughing outright. Alek, impetuous, burying her in a mound of wildflowers. Alek, playing with her—her friend. Alek, telling her how much he ached for the war-torn countries. Alek, her tender lover...her love...her future.

Her mind racing forward to the moment when she faced Alek, Elspeth walked to Delight, tethered and grazing in a wild field near her house.

Watching her from the porch, Duncan shook his head. "I don't know if I can make it through all this."

Sybil patted his hand. "Darling, you're just emotional now. In another two months, you'll be just fine."

"She's hunting what she wants. She just needed time. It will all come together." Calum spoke from experience; he'd placed his shadows aside with his wife's help. He took Talia's hand and drew it to his lips. "Honey, are you okay?"

Talia pressed her lips together, her knuckles white as she gripped Calum's hand. "I want my black boots...now!"

He plucked her up from the stool in a heartbeat and stood holding her in his arms. He looked as if he wanted to carry her off to keep her safe and wasn't certain which direction to take. Talia kissed him and grinned. "Hi, Pops. Just see that I get my boots and don't let the doctor bully you into taking them off—Ohhhh!"

"Boy. Don't you dare faint. Not while you're holding my daughter," boomed Mr. Petrovna.

"She's having the baby now. Here." Mrs. Petrovna, who had been keeping her hand on Talia's stomach, beamed. "I knew it. They're coming two minutes apart. Talia is unpredictable. I knew she wouldn't give us proper notice and that she'd pick a time when the doctor was out of town. This baby is on its way...fast."

"For once, this isn't my fault. It's Calum's. I thought it was the excitement and the hot dog at the arena.... *I want my boots!*"

Birk placed one hand on the porch railing and used it to swing down to the lawn. He landed at a run, heading straight for Calum's house.

Duncan turned to Sybil as if seeing her potential danger for the first time. "You wouldn't do this, would you?"

"Darling. I'm predictable as rain. The Petrovnas are another matter." She grinned at him over her shoulder, just enough to make him question what she'd just said.

Mrs. Petrovna and Lacey helped Calum carry Talia into Elspeth's house and bed. Mrs. Petrovna hummed between giving orders. Talia tugged Calum down on the bed beside her and started cursing him in Swahili. By the time another pain hit, Mr. Petrovna started the Russian music blaring. "To help my little girl. She always loved this music," he explained.

Birk arrived with the boots, and Calum placed them on Talia's feet. "Man, I can't wait to wear these things again, Tallchief. You'd better make good with your promise to wear those leather pants while we're dancing to that music. Look at him, Mom. Isn't he cute? Right now, he's trying to remember everything in all the books he read—the methodical stuff, steps one through—"

Then she screamed, bearing down. Calum went white and took her hand. Talia gasped, grinned weakly at him, and said, "Well, I've got my boots on. Let's get this gig on the road. Mom has done this before. She's an experienced midwife. Calum, don't you dare pass out.''

Emily, almost sixteen, took Talia's other hand. "I'm going to be a doctor. Or a vet."

"Now is a good time to learn," Talia said, gritting her teeth. "You'll take care of Calum for me, won't you? When he passes out?"

"You bet. Hey, I like the boots."

"Aren't they fine? We'll get you a pair— Ohh! Calum, you are a low-down—"

When the Marrying Moon is high, a scarred warrior will rise from the mists to claim his lady huntress. He will wrap her in the shawl and carry her to the Bridal Tepee and his heart. Their song will last longer than the stars....

Elspeth dismounted and tied Delight to a tree. The mare whinnied as Elspeth hugged her for reassurance. She took the shawl from her saddlebags and wondered how the treasure, so fragile and light, had stood the poor use of the past months.

Yet it shimmered magically in her hands, just as it must have done in Una's when she'd claimed Tallchief. The shawl was a part of Elspeth's life, what had happened and what would grow deeper.

The words in Una's journals attested to how much she loved Tallchief, how the legend was a blend of their lives and how it had come true.

Elspeth didn't need her tracking skills to find Alek this time. The tepee shone in the moonlight, gleaming in the shadows of the trees. On Tallchief Lake, mist hovered over the black waves and whispered of other loves; on a moonlit night, it floated and curled around the reeds, swaying in the restless wind.

Elspeth braced herself against what Alek might say. He'd been hurt today, a passionate man wanting more from her than she'd given. She moved from the shadows of the pines into the moonlight lying on the mist; the cool, damp layer curled around her, whimsically choosing its path.

Suddenly Alek stood before her, his legs spread, arms crossed over his chest, and not an ounce of tenderness showing on his face. "Dad didn't know that the tepee had a special meaning. Duncan and your brothers did."

"I didn't come about the tepee."

The mist clung to his hair, making it even more unruly as she continued to walk toward him. His head tipped at an arrogant angle. "I meant what I said today in the arena. I'll be here when you need me. I've changed, Elspeth. I've found what I want with you. I'll be writing assignment stories, but I'm staying right here."

Fear ripped through her again, but she pushed it away, determined to let him know her mind...and her heart. "I love you, Alek Petrovna."

She gripped the shawl with aching fingers as he stared down at her, eyes narrowed. "Uh-huh."

"You're not going to make this easy, are you?" She should have known Alek wouldn't make anything easy for her. She tossed away the image of him running to her, kissing her wildly and bearing her off to the tepee. This was Alek, hard down to the core, nasty, tender, sweet, passionate—

"Hell no. You ripped the heart out of me today, riding as though your life didn't matter. It does matter.

To me. There you were, standing on that damn horse, that shawl flapping around your neck—''

She placed her hand on his, needing to anchor her tumbling world, share it with Alek. His fingers slowly wrapped around hers, and she sucked in air, just realizing that she'd been waiting for him to show that he hadn't stopped caring. "But my life does matter now, every color and every shred of it, since you've come into it. The weave has deepened, heated, come alive with you. I thought I was happy, living in Amen Flats with people I've known all my life. I thought I was happy when Duncan and Calum found their loves."

"Thought?" he shot at her, making her come all the way. Alek's fingers laced with hers, giving her support in a difficult passage. "And?"

Elspeth tossed away the need to shield emotions. She'd learn to share more easily with Alek in time. "And then you came, and I discovered that I needed more. I needed you."

"Did you?" The challenge was there, making her take that last step.

She moved close to him, so that he could see her face and know that she had no doubt about her love or her future with him. "Marry me, Alek. Give me your heart—I won't tear it. I'll be there when you wake up and when you go to sleep. I'll keep you warm in the hard, cold times and hold you when you ache. You ache, Alek. It rides just beneath the surface, what you've seen, what you'd like to change. I will help you—if you want to travel, I'll leave Amen Flats to be at your side. Give me your children—I'll love and tend them and then love you more."

"You love me," he repeated, his Texas drawl uneven. "Would you say that meant you were greedy for me? Really deep down, nasty greedy for me? Or just the innocent, temporary kind of greed?"

She'd hurt him, and his uncertainty had reared and his pride needed tending. She gave him that, because now it mattered; healing hearts wasn't easy, but was a blend of give and take. Elspeth placed her hand on his scars, smoothing them. "I'd say I'm on the high end of greed with you. You've walked into my life, turned it upside down, and I've lost most of my ability to see things clearly...no thanks to you. I used to sense things before they happened. Now I'm too busy with thoughts of you. Before you swaggered back into my life, I didn't let people too close to me, not even my family. Now I'm in a bog of people and loving every minute. I go a little lightheaded at the thought of you. I wonder how quickly I can corral you. Yes...I'd say I'm good and greedy for you."

She lifted on tiptoe to kiss his lips, to caress the smooth, hard feel of them until they softened to her touch. "There's no reason I should, of course. You're arrogant, demonstrative, and you scared me badly today. I didn't know what I'd do if anything happened to you a second time. I didn't want to care, Alek, but I do and you're the cause, the only cause...I love you."

"Say it again," he demanded, taking her hand to his lips and kissing her palm.

She leaned against him, this solid man who was a part of her life and a part of herself. "I love you, Alek Petrovna. I know we'll fight—I've grown to like a bit of spice in my life, thanks to you. You can set me off, and I'll set you off and then we'll make up. But there will be the quiet times, when I tell you what was in my heart back then, when we were struggling to stay together. I'll tell you what's in my heart for you.''

"Mmm. Sounds like a good story. I suppose I'll pay for that contract. You're getting good at pushing, if that horse-riding event was any indication.'' Alek placed his lips on hers, promising that the good times would be there, overshadowing life's hardships. He'd always be there for her, and she'd return the favor.

"Let's say that it will be useful to drag up when we argue. This time is for keeps, Alek. Isn't it?'' Elspeth couldn't help giving way to the last of her doubts.

"For keeps.'' He looked up to the big, round silver moon. It had filled the night sky that way so long ago in Scotland, when they'd first met. "Looks like a perfect night after a long, hard day.''

He wanted to know about the Marrying Moon, about what she'd said on that night long ago. But Elspeth wanted to give him that present at a moment of her own choosing....

She chose now and whispered, "See that moon? How big and bright it is, hovering over us? The legend says that 'when the Marrying Moon is high, a scarred warrior will rise from the mists to claim his lady huntress. He will wrap her in the shawl and carry her to the Bridal Tepee and his heart.'''

Alek placed his face in the shelter of her throat and shoulder, giving himself into her care, the gesture filling her with love for him. "Thank you, Elspeth.''

She kissed his damp, curling lashes, and he kissed away the tears flowing on her cheeks. Then, with a flourish, Alek wrapped the shawl around her. He stood looking at her in the moonlight for a moment.

Pleasure rode his expression, pleasing her in turn. "You're unpredictable, Petrovna."

"I'm in love for the last time, honey. Give me a moment to enjoy my treasure, one that I'll always cherish." Then he bent to lift her in his arms. "Tell me the rest of the legend. I can tell by your smirk that you're holding back."

"I do not smirk." She wouldn't be easy, not with Alek Petrovna, who enjoyed a good battle. Elspeth trailed her fingertip over his lips, traced the scar and kissed it. "Submit, Alek Petrovna. You're my love, my heart and dreams. Let me give you the best part of me, the part that's always been yours."

Later, after Alek had carried her to the Bridal Tepee, after they had pledged their love again and tenderly dined upon each other, unwrapping and sharing each other's hearts, they began again in a searing heat that made them one.

This time, Alek rose above her, straining to leash his body, his hands wound in her hair. "Tell me."

Elspeth fought the pleasure washing over her, strained to think—to give Alek what he needed—past the desires of their bodies ready to shatter in a heartbeat. "I love you, my heart, my love, my Alek."

His lips attacked hers, hungry for her, their bodies fused together as he took them over the edge.

"'Their song will last longer than the stars,'" she whispered later, wrapped in his arms as the Marrying Moon hovered in the sky.

Alek lifted her chin with the tip of his finger. "I love you, Elspeth-mine."

"Mmm." Elspeth gave herself to his kiss and dived into the images there of Alek, proud of his present, another Tallchief cradle. The baby would have Alek's

black, curling hair and the Tallchiefs gray eyes—
Una's inheritance. A girl this time, the baby would
look fragile in Alek's hands, devastating him with the
miracle of her birth. There would be a boy next, replacing another and astounding Alek, who would hold
his one-year-old daughter close against him in one arm
and his newborn son in the other arm. Tears would
shimmer in his black eyes as he looked at Elspeth, and
then he would tell her again that he loved her.

When the babies slept, Alek would come to Elspeth
in the Kostyas' renovated farmhouse bedroom.

They'd come full circle, and there would be more
circles, weaving their lives and love closer.

Alek smiled in the dim light. "Someday, you'll
have to tell me when the images come and share them
with me. From your expression, I'd say it was a good
one."

"A very good one."

She could have throttled Alek, a pushy man set on
a quick wedding. "What? You would ask me, a Petrovna, to wait months?"

She hadn't asked; she'd told him. So much for a
logical discussion in the Bridal Tepee the next morning. After a night of making love, dozing and making
love again, Elspeth had awakened to Alek packing his
gear. He'd bundled her off to the farmhouse and immediately started making telephone calls to arrange
their wedding.

No amount of arguing could stop him, but Elspeth
dived into the flaming arguments, delighting in them,
in the passion flaring in Alek's eyes when she did. Oh,
she'd meet him on a level he understood and not on
any nice, polite, shadowy, wishy-washy level, either.

She'd chosen to stand and fight, and Alek would have to reap what he had sown....

Now, a full week later—that was all the time he gave her to prepare everything for a horde of relatives and friends, including the Petrovnas' Texas relations—Elspeth rode Delight down Amen Flats's Main Street. Ribbons and flowers decked the horse, and she pranced, showing off. Leading the horse, Emily—Sybil's daughter—would one day find her love.

Her hair loose and flowing around her, Elspeth wore LaBelle's diamond stud earrings; Elizabeth's long, lacy veil, topped with a tiny braided coronet from Elizabeth's mother, fluttered in the fall air. Elspeth wore the garter her mother had given her years ago, decked with ribbons. On the lace high on her throat, Elspeth wore her mother's favorite cameo; as a judge, Pauline had sentenced Matthew to jail wearing that cameo. A long-legged, tough Tallchief, Matthew had burst into her courtroom and called her a hard-hearted, evil woman who made him love her. Pauline had him hauled off to jail when she ordered quiet and Matthew had continued "contempt of court." Later, in his jail cell, she'd admitted her love for him, and the cameo had always remained precious to her. Una's shawl fluttered from the saddle horn, a fiery blaze amid the yards of pristine bridal gown.

Elspeth smoothed the gown, remembering how Talia, Sybil, Mrs. Petrovna, Lacey and a revolving sea of loving hands had fashioned the gown.

At the end of the street, waiting with a crowd of people she loved, waited her husband-to-be, dressed in a Tallchief kilt.

She wasn't happy. Alek had pushed and shoved, and if she hadn't wanted the same so much and as soon,

she would have pushed back so hard she'd get that
swoon out of him yet.

Alek had insisted she wear a long bridal gown and
veil. She knew he still thought of how he'd taken her
years ago, and it was a small thing to concede. But
managing the whole affair on top of Delight's saddle
was another matter. Then, because Megan wanted to
ride the horse—Duncan was already making a horsewoman out of her—Elspeth held the toddler in her
arms, her wedding bouquet of roses tied to the saddle
horn with satin ribbons. She needed Megan's soft,
chubby body against her for support.

There Alek stood in the street, legs spread—he was
wearing proper hose and brogans, unlike her brothers,
who wore their western boots with their kilts. Of the
lot, there was nothing tamed in the men wearing kilts,
despite their ruffled shirts and tartans with broaches,
Alek's contribution. Into the broaches were tucked Mr.
Petrovna's orchids, looking extremely fragile against
the blue-and-green plaid.

Duncan stood next to him, then Calum with his new
daughter sleeping in his arms. Then Birk... *Ah, Birk,
love is coming to you sooner than you think,* Elspeth
thought, wishing that his road would be smooth. But
when he finally found love, it would be strong and
lasting.

Oh, she loved Alek Petrovna, Jr., more with each
heartbeat, though at times in the past week, she hadn't
liked him at all. If only he hadn't held her, rested his
face in the vulnerable part of her, her throat and shoulder and told her, "I want us to be married as soon as
possible. I'm dying for you, Elspeth."

She'd gone down too easily, loving him, letting him
have his way, because it was what she wanted. The

moment she'd agreed, he'd tossed her over his shoulder and strolled over to the Petrovnas next door, despite the names she'd called him. Alek had told his mother and father that Elspeth had agreed to marry him within the week, right while Elspeth was hanging upside down on his backside. She bit him, of course, on a place she hadn't nibbled before.

She could feast upon him now—a big, darkly tanned man with untamed black curls drifting in the September wind. Alek wore LaBelle's earring and looked as unyielding as Tallchief Mountain. Megan sat perfectly still, pacified, now that she was riding a horse with her aunt Elspeth. Elspeth bent to the toddler. "Isn't he pretty, Meggie? Isn't he just?"

The quickening stirred within her as Duncan took Megan and Birk helped her down from the saddle. Alek, dark and somber, didn't move, wouldn't touch her now. She caught the image of Alek, standing behind her in the mirror, his ruffled shirt opened at the throat. In the mirror, his hands trembled when he placed his grandmother's pearls around Elspeth's neck and then slowly, carefully began to undress her for their first night as man and wife.

The entire audience watched as Alek strode to the horse and worked free Una's shawl. He carried it to Elspeth and gently placed it around her.

Talia's soft sob carried through the silence, and Calum reached out a hand to draw her near. They stood there—Calum and Talia and baby Kira, Duncan and Sybil and Emily and Megan. Birk, the Petrovnas and Lacey stood on the other side.

Circles, thought Elspeth, her heart full where once shadows roamed. Love for each other had seen them through, and now Alek added another dimension to the Tallchiefs.

She caught the fire in his look, the promise of what he would do later to claim her as his wife. There was tenderness roaming his face, softening the scars, and hope and dreams coming true.

She slanted him a look that promised what she would do to him in return. Then she moved to his side, admiring him, this man she loved more desperately each day.

Epilogue

Elspeth knelt by the mountain heather, leaves killed by October's freezing descent. She dusted leaves from her parents' stone and placed her cheek against Alek's hand, resting on her shoulder.

Though they'd only been married a month, she didn't have to tell him the images moving through her; Alek knew. Her safe world had been torn apart by two bullets, taking her parents, and she'd struggled to tend her family. Now she had Alek, a part of her heart and soul, to share her life.

He'd come to her out of the darkness he felt, revenge in his heart. But love had grown and captured them, despite the wounding of another time.

She'd brought him here, her husband, to meet her parents.

"I think the heather will come back," he said,

drawing her to her feet. "If it doesn't, we'll plant more. They should have it in the summer."

Oh, honey, I'm so happy for you, Elspeth's mother seemed to say.

He'll cherish you all the days of his life, just like I did your mother, her father whispered in the wind.

Then Alek took Elspeth in his arms and kissed her, because he understood.

She clung to him and knew that she had crossed from one world to another. Their month of marriage had been sheer joy and promised more. The Marrying Moon was theirs to keep, a huge silver disk made for them alone.

The Bridal Tepee would be used again throughout their lives, as it had been the first week of their marriage.

Alek held her tightly, as though nothing could tear her away, and placed his rugged face within the hollow of her neck. "I like the name 'Heather Pauline,' do you?"

Elspeth held very still as Alek's lips drifted to her ear and nipped it. "Or Matthew. That's a good, solid name for a boy."

He cupped her face and drew it up to him. He grinned, the October wind sweeping through his curls. "Why, Elspeth-love. You're shocked. You actually have no idea, do you?"

She saw the images again, a black, curly-headed girl with gray eyes, a baby boy and Alek...Alek, forever her love.

"The legend of the shawl is true, Alek. How I love you...."

The wind slid through the pine boughs above them.

When the Marrying Moon is high, a scarred warrior will rise from the mists to claim his lady huntress. He will wrap her in the shawl and carry her to the Bridal Tepee and his heart. Their song will last longer than the stars....

"Aye," Elspeth murmured before she sought her true love's kiss.

*   *   *   *   *

Silhouette's newest series

YOURS TRULY

Love when you least expect it.

Where the written word plays a vital role in uniting couples—you're guaranteed a fun and exciting read every time!

Look for Marie Ferrarella's upcoming Yours Truly, *Traci on the Spot*, in March 1997.

Here's a special sneak preview....

1

——◆——

Morgan Brigham slowly set down his coffee cup on the kitchen table and stared at the comic strip in the center of his paper. It was nestled in among approximately twenty others that were spread out across two pages. But this was the only one he made a point of reading faithfully each morning at breakfast.

This was the only one that mirrored *her* life.

He read each panel twice, as if he couldn't trust his own eyes. But he could. It was there, in black and white.

Morgan folded the paper slowly, thoughtfully, his mind not on his task. So Traci was getting engaged.

The realization gnawed at the lining of his stomach. He hadn't a clue as to why.

He had even less of a clue why he did what he did next.

Abandoning his coffee, now cool, and the newspaper, and ignoring the fact that this was going to make him late for the office, Morgan went to get a sheet of stationery from the den.

He didn't have much time.

Traci Richardson stared at the last frame she had just drawn. Debating, she glanced at the creature sprawled out on the kitchen floor.

"What do you think, Jeremiah? Too blunt?"

The dog, part bloodhound, part mutt, idly looked up from his rawhide bone at the sound of his name. Jeremiah gave her a look she felt free to interpret as ambivalent.

"Fine help you are. What if Daniel actually reads this and puts two and two together?"

Not that there was all that much chance that the man who had proposed to her, the very prosperous and busy Dr. Daniel Thane, would actually see the comic strip she drew for a living. Not unless the strip was taped to a bicuspid he was examining. Lately Daniel had gotten so busy he'd stopped reading anything but the morning headlines of the *Times*.

Still, you never knew. "I don't want to hurt his feelings," Traci continued, using Jeremiah as a sounding board. "It's just that Traci is overwhelmed by Donald's proposal and, see, she thinks the ring is going to swallow her up." To prove her point, Traci held up the drawing for the dog to view.

This time, he didn't even bother to lift his head.

Traci stared moodily at the small velvet box on the kitchen counter. It had sat there since Daniel had asked her to marry him last Sunday. Even if Daniel never read her comic strip, he was going to suspect something eventually. The very fact that she hadn't grabbed the ring from his hand and slid it onto her finger should have told him that she had doubts about their union.

Traci sighed. Daniel was a catch by any definition. So what was her problem? She kept waiting to be struck by that sunny ray of happiness. Daniel said he wanted to take care of her, to fulfill her every wish. And he was even willing to let her think about it before she gave him her answer.

Guilt nibbled at her. She should be dancing up and down, not wavering like a weather vane in a gale.

Pronouncing the strip completed, she scribbled her signature in the corner of the last frame and then sighed. Another week's work put to bed. She glanced at the pile of mail on the counter. She'd been bringing it in steadily from the mailbox since Monday, but the stack had gotten no farther than her kitchen. Sorting letters seemed the least heinous of all the annoying chores that faced her.

Traci paused as she noted a long envelope. Morgan Brigham. Why would Morgan be writing to her?

Curious, she tore open the envelope and quickly scanned the short note inside.

Dear Traci,
I'm putting the summerhouse up for sale. Thought you might want to come up and see it one more time before it goes up on the block. Or make a bid for it yourself. If memory serves, you once said you wanted to buy it. Either way, let me know. My number's on the card.

Take care,
Morgan

P.S. Got a kick out of *Traci on the Spot* this week.

Traci folded the letter. He read her strip. She hadn't known that. A feeling of pride silently coaxed a smile to her lips. After a beat, though, the rest of his note seeped into her consciousness. He was selling the house.

The summerhouse. A faded white building with brick trim. Suddenly, memories flooded her mind. Long, lazy afternoons that felt as if they would never end.

Morgan.

She looked at the far wall in the family room. There was a large framed photograph of her and Morgan standing before the summerhouse. Traci and Morgan. Morgan and Traci. Back then, it seemed their lives had been permanently intertwined. A bittersweet feeling of loss passed over her.

Traci quickly pulled the telephone over to her on the counter and tapped out the number on the keypad.

* * * * *

Look for TRACI ON THE SPOT
by Marie Ferrarella, coming to
Silhouette YOURS TRULY
in March 1997.

MILLION DOLLAR SWEEPSTAKES
OFFICIAL RULES
NO PURCHASE NECESSARY TO ENTER

1. To enter, follow the directions published. Method of entry may vary. For eligibility, entries must be received no later than March 31, 1998. No liability is assumed for printing errors, lost, late, non-delivered or misdirected entries.

    To determine winners, the sweepstakes numbers assigned to submitted entries will be compared against a list of randomly, preselected prize winning numbers. In the event all prizes are not claimed via the return of prize winning numbers, random drawings will be held from among all other entries received to award unclaimed prizes.

2. Prize winners will be determined no later than June 30, 1998. Selection of winning numbers and random drawings are under the supervision of D. L. Blair, Inc., an independent judging organization whose decisions are final. Limit: one prize to a family or organization. No substitution will be made for any prize, except as offered. Taxes and duties on all prizes are the sole responsibility of winners. Winners will be notified by mail. Odds of winning are determined by the number of eligible entries distributed and received.

3. Sweepstakes open to residents of the U.S. (except Puerto Rico), Canada and Europe who are 18 years of age or older, except employees and immediate family members of Torstar Corp., D. L. Blair, Inc., their affiliates, subsidiaries, and all other agencies, entities, and persons connected with the use, marketing or conduct of this sweepstakes. All applicable laws and regulations apply. Sweepstakes offer void wherever prohibited by law. Any litigation within the province of Quebec respecting the conduct and awarding of a prize in this sweepstakes must be submitted to the Régie des alcools, des courses et des jeux. In order to win a prize, residents of Canada will be required to correctly answer a time-limited arithmetical skill-testing question to be administered by mail.

4. Winners of major prizes (Grand through Fourth) will be obligated to sign and return an Affidavit of Eligibility and Release of Liability within 30 days of notification. In the event of non-compliance within this time period or if a prize is returned as undeliverable, D. L. Blair, Inc. may at its sole discretion, award that prize to an alternate winner. By acceptance of their prize, winners consent to use of their names, photographs or other likeness for purposes of advertising, trade and promotion on behalf of Torstar Corp., its affiliates and subsidiaries, without further compensation unless prohibited by law. Torstar Corp. and D. L. Blair, Inc., their affiliates and subsidiaries are not responsible for errors in printing of sweepstakes and prize winning numbers. In the event a duplication of a prize winning number occurs, a random drawing will be held from among all entries received with that prize winning number to award that prize.

5. This sweepstakes is presented by Torstar Corp., its subsidiaries and affiliates in conjunction with book, merchandise and/or product offerings. The number of prizes to be awarded and their value are as follows: Grand Prize — $1,000,000 (payable at $33,333.33 a year for 30 years); First Prize — $50,000; Second Prize — $10,000; Third Prize — $5,000; 3 Fourth Prizes — $1,000 each; 10 Fifth Prizes — $250 each; 1,000 Sixth Prizes — $10 each. Values of all prizes are in U.S. currency. Prizes in each level will be presented in different creative executions, including various currencies, vehicles, merchandise and travel. Any presentation of a prize level in a currency other than U.S. currency represents an approximate equivalent to the U.S. currency prize for that level, at that time. Prize winners will have the opportunity of selecting any prize offered for that level; however, the actual non U.S. currency equivalent prize if offered and selected, shall be awarded at the exchange rate existing at 3:00 P.M. New York time on March 31, 1998. A travel prize option, if offered and selected by winner, must be completed within 12 months of selection and is subject to: traveling companion(s) completing and returning of a Release of Liability prior to travel; and hotel and flight accommodations availability. For a current list of all prize options offered within prize levels, send a self-addressed, stamped envelope (WA residents need not affix postage) to: MILLION DOLLAR SWEEPSTAKES Prize Options, P.O. Box 4456, Blair, NE 68009-4456, USA.

6. For a list of prize winners (available after July 31, 1998) send a separate, stamped, self-addressed envelope to: MILLION DOLLAR SWEEPSTAKES Winners, P.O. Box 4459, Blair, NE 68009-4459, USA.

In the tradition of
Anne Rice comes a
daring, darkly sensual
vampire novel by

MAGGIE SHAYNE

BORN IN TWILIGHT

Rendezvous hails bestselling Maggie Shayne's vampire
romance series, WINGS IN THE NIGHT, as
"powerful...riveting...unique...intensely romantic."

Don't miss it, this March, available
wherever Silhouette books are sold.

 Silhouette®

In April 1997
Bestselling Author

takes her Family Circle series to new heights with

In April 1997 Dallas Schulze brings readers a
brand-new, longer, out-of-series title featuring the
characters from her popular Family Circle miniseries.

When rancher Keefe Walker found Tessa Wyndham he
knew that she needed a man's protection—she was
pregnant, alone and on the run from a heartless past.
Keefe was also hiding from a dark past...but in one
overwhelming moment he and Tessa forged a family
bond that could never be broken.

Available in April wherever books are sold.

At last the wait is over...
In March
New York Times bestselling author

NORA ROBERTS

will bring us the latest from the Stanislaskis as
Natasha's now very grown-up stepdaughter,
Freddie, and Rachel's very sexy brother-in-law
Nick discover that love is worth waiting for in

WAITING FOR NICK

Silhouette Special Edition #1088

and in April
visit Natasha and Rachel again——or meet them
for the first time—in

The Stanislaski Sisters

**containing TAMING NATASHA
and FALLING FOR RACHEL**

Available wherever Silhouette books are sold.

Silhouette®

Look us up on-line at:http://www.romance.net

NRSS

You're About to Become a *Privileged Woman*

Reap the rewards of fabulous free gifts and benefits with proofs-of-purchase from Silhouette and Harlequin books

Pages & Privileges™

It's our way of thanking you for buying our books at your favorite retail stores.

PROOF OF PURCHASE

SPT-PP22

Offer expires March 31, 1997

Pages & Privileges ™

Harlequin and Silhouette—
the most privileged readers in the world!

For more information about Harlequin and Silhouette's PAGES & PRIVILEGES program call the Pages & Privileges Benefits Desk: 1-503-794-2499

™ *Silhouette*®

SPT-PP22

Harlequin and Silhouette celebrate
Black History Month with seven terrific titles,
featuring the all-new *Fever Rising*
by Maggie Ferguson
(Harlequin Intrigue #408) and
A Family Wedding by Angela Benson
(Silhouette Special Edition #1085)!

Also available are:
Looks Are Deceiving by Maggie Ferguson
Crime of Passion by Maggie Ferguson
Adam and Eva by Sandra Kitt
Unforgivable by Joyce McGill
Blood Sympathy by Reginald Hill

On sale in January at your favorite
Harlequin and Silhouette retail outlet.

HARLEQUIN®   V *Silhouette*®

Look us up on-line at: http://www.romance.net   BHM297